Unprecedented

by

C.D. Gill

To Charla, the forerunner

A friend in every season

Your joy and grace are a beautiful gift

Read more from C.D. Gill

The Freedom's Cry Series:

Read for FREE on Kindle Unlimited

Behind Lead Doors
On Wings of an Avalanche
The Apricot Underground

Against All Odds (Xander and Gia):

Prequel Novella: Perfectly Designed*
Undefeated
Unprecedented

*Free for newsletter subscribers. See cdgill.com

Ferra Empire:

In the Shadows

Chapter 1

It took great courage to move toward the dying.

For Gia Carter, love mixed with a small sense of lingering guilt drove her daily to Tia Carolena's sick bed at her home in New Orleans. Her second mom—the one who was there when Ma couldn't be—lay unmoving, covered in blankets. An IV tree towered above the hospital-grade bed with bags of fluids dangling as a life-sustaining force.

The nurse said Tia wasn't in any pain as the lymphoma shut her body down, which was good, because Gia's heart hurt enough for both of them.

To say goodbye forever to another person she loved so completely felt like performing surgery on herself without the benefit of anesthesia.

Each work day, she took a late lunch so others in the family could have the hours at Tia's bedside that they wanted. The last few weekends, Gia had spent her days off in the house just to be nearby. Most days, she couldn't speak through the tears as her *tia*'s frail body gave up on living, each rattling breath labored. Her skin coloring changed, and her skeleton became more prominent.

The grief came in waves, despite her best efforts to maintain her composure. The lost time, the milestones they would all miss sharing with Tia, the agony accompanying her body failing, and the discriminatory way death claimed the best far too soon overwhelmed even her best moods.

She'd stayed away for the last three years, believing it best to hide and atone for her part in Uncle Angelo's murder. Because of that, she'd needlessly missed out on so much. Joey had corrected her flawed thinking. Staying away had done more damage than good.

After the faux engagement party where Gia's ex-boyfriend Bronc and his business partner Grant were arrested, Tia Carolena's health took a sharp decline. Joey and his sister Cara spent every free moment by their mother's side, never leaving her to suffer alone. Tommy and Xander had overseen the final touches of the rebuild of Gia's burned bedroom, allowing her to stay in her parents' house and be by Tia Carolena's side where she should have been this whole time.

Xander managed to fly to New Orleans to see her a few times and combine the visits with meetings for setting up his businesses, but that pace couldn't last forever. The tension grew inside her. The longing to be with him without the urgency of their time ending was beyond her fingertips every time. He had been an anchor she didn't know she needed. And while phone calls were good, his strong arms and faint cologne scent settled her soul and gave her strength to keep moving.

A sigh welled up as her lunch break came to an end. Another day of goodbye, not knowing if today would be their last together. She brushed her hand across Tia Carolena's paper thin skin and kissed her cheek. The pain-masking medicine rendered Tia unable to stay conscious most of the time now.

"I'll see you tomorrow afternoon so we can visit some more. I want to tell you about this project I'm bidding for down in Brazil to build a school in the *favelas* near where Avó lives." A school Tia would never see in person. Gia's eyes pooled as her throat thickened. "Forgive me, Tia. I've been horribly selfish. You deserved much better. I love you so much."

Monitors beeped in the silence. She turned to leave.

"You don't have to ask her forgiveness every day, Gia," Joey said as he pushed off the door frame with his shoulder, his hands in his pockets. "She's told you over and over again that she forgives you, that she loves you. You can stop asking."

A sad smile accompanied his words. Dark rings under his eyes acutely contrasted his tan skin. His muscled frame had thinned under the stress of the last few months of watching his mama slowly dying. Cara hadn't faired any better. The burden was too great to bear.

Gia swallowed, trying to loosen the tightening in her throat. He didn't need her problems adding to his load, but he'd take them on because that's who he was. "I suppose I'm asking because I haven't forgiven myself entirely. My therapist says it's a process."

Joey collapsed in the chair and took Tia's hand in his. "Her color is better today. Not so gray."

Gia nodded. "She squeezed my hand a couple of times. She's listening."

"She always is. Hearing like a bat, this one. Couldn't ever mumble under my breath and get away with it. Eh, Mama?" Joey's grunt was the closest he'd come to a laugh in a long time. She'd take what she could get. His visible heartbreak made her want to wrap him in a hug so tight he couldn't breathe.

"You eat something today? I can make you a plate." She knew his answer before she asked. He had no appetite. Neither did she.

"I'm good." Joey rubbed his eyes. "See if you can get Cara to eat. Her protein powder and blender haven't been used in days."

Gia laid a hand on his shoulder. "Family comes in tonight. Don't forget the dinner at our house at seven."

Joey nodded. "We'll be there."

Their extended family flying in from Brazil affirmed again that this was goodbye. They would stay until just after the New

Year which gave them about three weeks in the States. Each family had a suite in a nearby Venha Hotel, courtesy of Ma and Daddy.

On her way down the stairs, Gia opened her texts to Xander. *Tia doesn't have much longer.*

His reply was instant. *I'll be on the first flight out. Just say the word.*

She smiled. He wasn't bluffing either. He'd proven that to her before. *Soon. Family comes in tonight. Wish I'd see them more often than at funerals.*

His answer came again. *Looking forward to meeting them. You okay?*

No, she wasn't. She missed him. She hurt. The constant sadness and grief drained her, leaving her exhausted and unmotivated. But if she said anything to the contrary, he would be at the door tonight. She couldn't do that to him when he had so many important things coming up this week. She needed his support for the funeral.

I'm ok. Missing you adds to the heartache.

She tucked her phone into her back pocket as she entered the sunroom where Cara had set up her sewing machine. She'd been working tirelessly to finish the quilt Tia Carolena had started before she couldn't muster the strength to get out of bed. Cara wanted to show it to her mama before she died.

"It's beautiful. Almost done."

Cara looked up from the machine. "A few more sections to add. Then, I finish the edges, and it's off to the auction."

"The Lymphoma Foundation is lucky to have it for the Christmas auction. If I'd been in charge of finishing it, they'd never have it. You're so good at this," Gia said as she ran her fingers across the soft fabric. The stitches were small and perfectly even.

Tia Carolena was an expert quilter with many prizes to her name. She'd taught Cara years ago as a fun summer project.

Selling off the quilt they'd made together had raised the money for Cara to take a school trip to Europe for a couple of weeks. Tia Carolena had also tried teaching Gia one summer, but Gia kept wandering over to where Uncle Angelo and Joey hunched over drawing boards talking architecture. Eventually, Tia Carolena gave up on Gia, but never scolded her for it.

"You eat recently?" Gia asked. Every day she asked the same thing.

Cara snorted. "You're as bad as Joey. I'll tell you, I've eaten more in the last two days than he has in the past two weeks. And he has the nerve to get on me about eating." She glanced up. "And you've lost weight, too."

Message received, loud and clear. "I'm headed back to the office. Don't forget dinner tonight at our house at seven. Plane lands around three."

Cara waved her on. The machine's whir drowned out her response. When that quilt was done, Cara would have nothing left to hide behind, and the emotions would hit full force.

By six that evening, Gia was in full hostess mode at her parents' house. Her outfit was a little looser on her than when she bought it, but it still looked stylish. Ma hadn't wasted any time in helping Gia replace her wardrobe when the insurance money came in to cover the smoke-damaged clothes back in Golden, Colorado.

When the cars pulled up, the whole Brazilian crew unloaded. Since the school term was over and it was almost Christmas, everyone had taken time off to come—Ma's sister Judita and her husband Mateus and their two sons, Ma's brother Roberto and his wife Neves and three kids, Ma's mother Avó Ana, and Uncle Ronaldo Cevere, Ma's cousin. Uncle Angelo and Tia Carolena had traveled to Brazil every summer as had Gia and her parents so they could stay connected to the family in Rio.

Family was everything in Brazilian culture. Tia Carolena's family was coming in from around the US and Brazil tomorrow to stay for a bit. Daddy had agreed to put them up in the Venha hotel, too, so Joey and Cara wouldn't have to host them in their house where Tia Carolena received hospice care.

Avó Ana was the first one to the door on Ronaldo's arm. "Giovanna Sophia, you grow more beautiful every time I see you." She clutched Gia's face in a surprisingly firm grip and kissed both cheeks. "You are a sight for these aging eyes. I've missed you. Will I be seeing this handsome young man of yours that I keep hearing about?"

Gia grinned. "I sure hope so." She glanced beside her to Uncle Ronaldo, Ma's cousin. "How's *futbol,* Uncle Ronaldo?"

He flashed her a bright smile. He'd once been one of the best players in the world and now was vice president of Brazil's Federal *Futbol* Committee. "Changing and hopefully going to get even better very soon. Keep an eye on those headlines." He winked as Avó Ana tugged him away to continue into the house.

Gia's face hurt from smiling as she greeted her cousins, *tias,* and uncles. Daddy pulled up last. He'd insisted on picking up Joey and Cara himself. Tia Carolena's nurse was there to keep her company.

She hugged Joey first. "Thanks for coming."

He smiled down at her. "Anything for family, but I also want it to be over with."

Gia felt his words settle deep inside her heart. They all wanted this to be over, didn't they? Not the dinner, but the goodbyes and endless nights of despair.

If they could just have more time with Tia Carolena and have her standing next to Ma as the hostess of their family. If they could hear her laugh and see her easy smile and the grace that lit her eyes. If they could laugh at her playful scolding of her husband acting like a child.

The "ifs" could fill a skyscraper and never buy more time. Wishes never became horses for desperate beggars to ride.

She looped her arm through Cara's and led them inside. As the night progressed, she lost her sadness in the love of their family that remained. The laughs, the memories, the catching up, the endless teasing.

Reminders of life and love.

Conversations shifted directions and languages as quickly as the wind with their huge family. A part of her heart chided her for not asking Xander to jump on the last plane out of Denver to be here in time for this circus.

As Uncle Roberto grilled Joey on work and his nonexistent love life, she could see Joey's eyes shift toward her in rapid succession. A sure sign he was about to dump the conversation in her lap and make her recent scandal the drama of the evening. It was bound to come up over their family meals in the next few weeks.

Not today, Joseph.

She jumped from her seat to take refuge in the kitchen until dessert. Tia Neves was already in there with Ma. Tia Judita came in behind Gia.

"Ah," Judita sighed. "I love our family being together, but it's way too loud out there."

Ma raised her glass and took a sip. "Next meal, we'll make a kids' table again."

"What's the age limit on that?" Gia asked, sneaking a chocolate truffle from the tray.

Judita snorted. "It's generational and voluntary since Ronaldo usually likes keeping up with what the kids are doing these days."

"How's fashion design, Judi?" Ma asked. "Hope you brought a suitcase of goodies for me."

Judita pressed her hand to her chest, offended. "Do you think I would dare come overseas and not bring my big sister—the hostess and brilliant businesswoman constantly in the public eye—a wide range of my very best work?" She leaned over to Gia and stage-whispered, "The younger girls are more fun to dress, so I'm hooking you and Cara up, too."

Neves smiled. "That and chocolate will make everyone feel better."

Judita stole a cookie from the tray. "I actually could use all of you for models for a project I'm working on."

"Me?" Neves said. "I'm just a music teacher. I have no modeling skills. In fact, I only do my makeup on Sundays for church."

"Neves, you are tall and beautiful and willowy. You just need to stand there and smile. We can even have you pose against a piano, if that makes you feel more comfortable," Judita said.

When Neves realized there was no way out, she muttered her agreement. Judita exchanged a grin with Ma when Neves turned her head. Their sister bond thrived on finding new ways to broaden Neves's modest horizons.

"Let's get the dessert out so people can feel free to leave the table," Ma said, picking up a pie. "Your flight has probably left you ready for bed."

Neves, Judita, and Gia each grabbed a dish and followed her into the dining room. Judita's son Silva was animatedly telling a story about a dental patient he'd treated in clinicals. The poor man had to be sedated to be treated and when he awoke, he apparently announced in front of his wife that he'd never loved another woman like he did the nurse who helped him through his procedure. The whole room burst into laughter.

Joey and Cara, too.

Their smiles lasted the rest of the evening as the cousins ditched the adults and went to play video games on the big screen in the basement. The eight of them were long-standing rivals on game nights.

Ze, Silva's brother, won the racing game since he was a video game designer. Cara won four rounds of Pictionary. Joey dominated Uno. And the girls beat the boys in the acting game.

As they packed up the game, Breno, Neves's son, flopped back on the couch. "I think it's time for Gia to spill the drama."

The chorus of agreement pinned her into a corner. Joey sat back with a smug smirk on his face.

"Well," Gia cleared her throat. "Once upon time, I made bad decisions. They caught up with me. The end."

A wall of pillows flew at her face along with loud boos and hisses. She laughed as she unburied herself.

The door to the basement banged open, freezing the moment.

Daddy's expression was tense. "Everyone to the cars. Tia Carolena needs us."

Joey and Cara raced out the door behind Daddy and they screeched out of the driveway as everyone else loaded into the other awaiting vehicles. The car caravan to Tia's house was almost comical so late at night. As they parked and filed in, the air was hushed and somber.

The ease of the last few hours disappeared, opening the floodgates of grief once more. Gia let the cascade of tears fall as she watched her family say goodbye to one of her favorite people in the world. It struck her that perhaps of all the people in her family, she had the hardest time letting go. Everyone took their turn at Tia Carolena's bedside. Joey and Cara begrudgingly gave them privacy.

When it came her time, Gia tiptoed into the room with a reverence. A gravid foreboding blanketed the room. Tia Carolena's wheezing breaths shredded her to her core. The remnants of her composure evaporated. She ran to kneel at her bedside, pressing her forehead to Tia's hand. "I know you forgive me." Her words came in hiccups. "And I promise you, I will learn to forgive myself. No more running." She swallowed hard. "You were kind, gracious, and loving. Everything I want to be." She took a shuddering breath. It didn't feel like enough. "I love you so much."

She kissed Tia Carolena's soft cheek. It felt impossible that she'd never see her again and yet there was a growing relief that Tia's horrible pain would be over. The fibromyalgia and lymphoma could take her body, but they'd never take the love and memories away.

"See you soon, Tia," Gia said. She steeled her mind, took one last look, and walked out the door.

As soon as the last person came out, everyone crowded in with Joey and Cara next to Tia on the bed. The large room felt small with all the family stuffed into it, exactly how Gia hoped the scene would be if she were in the bed instead of Tia Carolena.

They held hands and bowed their heads as Roberto then Daddy prayed. Neves led them in a quiet hymn accompanied by a chorus of sniffles. Tia was leaving a legacy of kindness and grace in her wake. If Gia could only be half as thoughtful and compassionate, she'd be happy.

A few hours later, Joey came downstairs to where everyone sat talking quietly. His presence silenced the group. Gia knew what he was going to say, but it didn't prevent the devastation she felt when he said, "She's gone."

Chapter 2

Xander Reinerman shoved his hands into his pocket, paced a few steps, and stopped. The upbeat Mexican music in the background strummed on his frayed nerves. Why had he suggested meeting over lunch again? It was a terrible idea. He couldn't possibly eat right now.

His fingers toyed with his car keys in his pocket. The nerves would be worth it. Good or bad, he was here for closure. Or as the therapist had said, "Starting the journey to emotional maturity by breaking trauma bonds."

What if she hated him?

His deep breaths didn't slow his racing heartbeat. He'd gained a lot of control over his anxiety and panic attacks in the last six months, but it wasn't gone. And when the stakes were high, as they were today, a panic attack rushed him like a three-hundred-pound linebacker.

He couldn't help but feel a trickle of fear over how life wouldn't likely give him another shot at reconnecting with Avri. She was his youngest sister, but that didn't mean her acceptance was limitless, regardless of how much he wanted it to be. Linc had given him her number and Xander had finally worked up the nerve to reach out to her. She'd agreed to lunch as it was her first day on Christmas vacation from physical therapist school.

Whatever the official term for that was. Did they go to medical school? He'd find out.

"Alex!"

He jumped out of his skin. There stood his petite, brown-headed little sister next to him. He'd not heard her coming, what with the borderline panic attack in his mind. She opened her arms awkwardly and gave him an unsure smile.

"Avri." He wrapped his arms around her, just as he had before his sentencing day. Her hair smelled just as flowery and her frame still felt so small. Always his little sister. "It's so good to see you."

"Do you hate me?" They both asked at the same time, then laughed.

"Never," Xander said. "I've missed you."

"I've missed you so much. Five years is an eternity," Avri said, gripping his arms. She exhaled hard. "I thought when all my letters came back, that you wanted nothing to do with me. I—"

"Wait. What letters?" Xander dropped onto the stone wall next to them, bringing her to sit beside him. "You sent me letters?"

Her mouth hung open a bit. She dug around in her extra-large, animal print purse and pulled out a bundle of letters bound in a rubber band. Return to Sender was scrawled in red. He took them from her. There had to be at least twenty.

Letters.

Addressed to him.

Letters that could have been a life raft while he treaded water in the ocean of despair.

Except they'd be rejected.

"Carlson State Penitentiary? I was only there until my trial. I got sent to White River Correctional after my sentencing," Xander said.

She gasped. "That's the address Dad gave me. I made sure to ask for your most current one. I'm so sorry, Alex."

Dad knew the difference between jail and prison. He'd even asked Quinn, Xander's lawyer, for the address after the sentencing. Anger heating to rage swelled inside Xander's chest. He stuffed it down.

Avri had done nothing wrong. She'd sent him letters. None of his other family members had done that.

She dabbed at her eyes. "I should have visited after those first few letters were rejected, but prison scared me—"

"Yeah, me too." He grunted out a half laugh.

"And I always talked myself out of it. I'm the worst sister." She threw her arms around his neck. "Please, forgive me."

"Av, of course I forgive you. I am relieved to have you back in my life. I didn't realize how much Dad had been sabotaging me and my sanity from out here." He ran his hand over his hair. He was going to have a hard time forgiving Dad for this one. "Can I keep the letters?"

She smiled and handed them over. "They're yours. From what I remember, they are mostly full of trivial day-to-day happenings or stuff I thought you'd think was interesting. Let's eat something, because I haven't been able to eat all morning. I was so nervous."

After eating their weight in chips and salsa, they split the fajitas and caught up on life. Avri had a pretty boy for a boyfriend. Chad.

But so long as there were more good times than bad, he'd keep his opinion to himself.

As they left the restaurant, Avri stopped. "You're joining us for Christmas this year, right?"

"Uh." Xander scratched his neck. "Actually, I might do Christmas Day with my girlfriend and her family."

Avri's eyes widened. "Girlfriend? Wow. You guys must be serious if you're spending Christmas with them."

Surer than he'd ever been about Macy whom his sisters adored. He pulled up a picture of Gia hugging his neck on his phone to show her. "As soon as I get my life in order, I'm going to propose."

"She is stunning." Avri scrunched up her nose. "Just put your life in semi-order. Don't wait too long to tie her down."

"I need to be making enough money to support myself, and hopefully both of us, so she can't write me off on her taxes as a dependent," Xander said.

Gia had done most of the heavy lifting herself and that grated on him in the worst way. She deserved a man who could give her the life she wanted and more. He wasn't close to that yet.

Avri hugged him goodbye and promised to meet him again for lunch soon. As Xander drove Gia's SUV back to Gia's office to work, he allowed himself a reprieve from fear, long enough to celebrate the really amazing lunch he'd had with Avri.

They were on great terms. His family minus Dad believed him. They were proud of him. They'd once been his biggest cheerleaders, the core of who he was. To lose them to a lie was unconscionable. Now, all he had left was to see Kelsey in person and work on Dad. Or maybe give up on him. What dad intentionally misdirected his daughter away from supporting her brother?

It wasn't right or loving of his family to bail on him, but he understood it in a small way. They'd been afraid and confused. Dad loudly passing judgment on Xander hadn't helped the situation.

Xander parked in the back of the office in Golden and texted Gia. The daily reminders of her made him miss her more than he'd anticipated. Logically, they hadn't been dating long enough for him to feel like he was missing his right arm, but surprisingly he did. Worse was that she was in deep pain about her aunt's health and was trying to be strong and brave about it all, but he was across the country and could only offer her his verbal support.

He trudged inside and checked his email. No orders. Still.

Reclaim That, his store of upcycled items, had a decent start, but sales had tapered off once the media circus from his launch and Coach Randall's admission had died down. Chances were good that sales might pick up again as soon as his wrongful imprisonment settlement hit the papers. His new lawyer figured it wouldn't be until the new year.

But the funds in his bank account weren't going to last much longer. Even though he felt like the world's biggest leech right now, he still spent his own money on groceries and business expenses. Gia was really sweet about it, saying that she'd be paying someone to house sit for her if he wasn't staying there, but he could not live on charity much longer. It made him crazy.

He spent the afternoon marketing on local garage sale pages and online listing sites. On social media, he had a message about commissioning a piece. He responded. The sale would pay for a few more groceries.

His phone chimed.

Colorado number: *They think you have something of mine. They're coming for you. Watch your back.*

Have what? Who was this? He hesitated a moment.

Wrong number, Xander sent back.

No response.

That was weird.

That evening, he walked out to his easel and giant sign on the sidewalk. Every Thursday at seven, he held a workshop for The Upcycled Life. He talked about the mission, his story, and then the rest of the time they each made an item that he would list on Reclaim That's page. At the end of the night, he would collect the creator's contact information, so he could give them the money when their product sold.

Gia's office was a block from the bus station so he had Lucy's permission to put a sign in front of Mother Hen directing riders toward him. She dropped by every Thursday with a box of baked goods to donate. Her tendency to linger made him think that she missed Gia more than she let on. Or maybe she was a self-appointed overseer of all that was Gia's to make sure Xander stayed in line.

He had, after all, spent five years in prison.

Inside, he restacked the resource pamphlets in even rows on the table. These weren't those unhelpful government trifolds that slapped a cartoon bandage on a gunshot wound. They were nonprofits offering their services to those in need. If someone wanted his help, that person probably could use other resources, too.

He'd been unbelievably fortunate to land in Golden and be given the hand up he needed most. Others didn't have that, but he planned to be a launching point for them if they'd let him.

Twenty till seven, Lucy breezed in the front door. A few stray strands of hair stuck out from her head. "Wow. What a day. Actually, more like 'what a month' but it's all a wash at this point."

She plopped the box down in the usual place and unpacked plates, napkins, forks, cups, and pitchers of drinks from her Mary Poppins bag. "Gia texted to say her aunt is failing quickly. Poor girl. She's absolutely beside herself."

Xander nodded. He didn't want to talk about Gia with Lucy, but he'd learned from experience that she'd keep going until he acknowledged her. "She's exhausted from what I hear."

Lucy turned with her hands on her hips. "I hope you don't mind if I stay tonight. I need to find someone to help in my store for a few hours a day and thought this might be the place to look."

He raised his eyebrows. Really, there was no way to calculate how disruptive she'd be, so he couldn't reasonably say no. "Okay, but please don't say crazy things and interrupt me while I'm talking, all right?"

She made a disgusted face at him, as if to say she'd never. But, oh, she would.

The door chime interrupted their talk. In walked three well-dressed women with their hair and makeup done, laughing. He greeted them.

"Hey, we're here for the upcycling workshop," the blonde one said with a firm grip on her Coach purse. Thanks to Gia for that education.

The brunette leaned in and winked. "We brought our own wine. Hope that's okay. We figured it might be like one of those *spirited* art classes."

The third laughed at the joke until she snorted.

They were definitely not sober. He smiled at them. "Actually, that's tomorrow night at seven. I hope you can make it."

They apologized dramatically and promised to come again tomorrow. It wasn't anywhere on his radar, but he could use the income and it wasn't a terrible idea. Girls' night had to be fairly lucrative. Xander made a note to add that to his business offerings. He needed to find a low-maintenance project for them that didn't require hammers.

"That sounds like fun. I'll come tomorrow night, too," Lucy said.

Why not? He could use a buffer.

An older woman walked in and glanced around. "Hi, I'm Edith. Hope it's okay that I'm here."

Xander shook her hand. "Anyone is welcome. Please, grab some snacks."

"Oh, I already had dinner. Thank you though, sweetie. I want to see if this is something I can do with my autistic granddaughter. She learns through working with her hands and—you know how expensive craft materials are these days—I just can't afford to keep buying those kits." Edith snagged three cookies with a napkin while she was talking and moved toward Lucy to keep talking about who made the cookies and how many eggs she used in her recipe.

Individualized children's craft kits. Xander made another note in his workbook. Possibly offered from his non-profit to autistic foundations as tools, but for his for-profit definitely marketed to bored children and desperate parents at craft and hobby stores. A couple of middle-aged guys came in next. Their long, greasy hair partially veiled their faces. He scanned their inked skin, looking for gang identification. A new skill he'd picked up in prison.

None that he could see.

He greeted them, offered them snacks which they loaded up on, and invited them to have a seat. They assessed the office, unsmiling. He looked around with them. The main room was sparse as far as decorations went. The exposed beams and brick walls had enough character to impress a newcomer. The interior office where Gia designed held her family pictures and ornately framed degrees. His degree lay in a box somewhere in his parents' shed still.

Assessment finished, they slumped into chairs with their smart phones in hand.

Something wasn't right.

He strode toward them to find out more, but his phone chimed in his pocket to tell him it was the top of the hour. When he walked to the front, they straightened in their chairs.

Controlled movements. No smiles under a scraggly beard. A few words said between them.

As he was about to get started, a black teenage boy slipped inside. Lucy met him and sent him to a chair with a full plate. He got settled and pulled a notebook out of his backpack.

Teenagers weren't usually attendees. Interesting.

"Thank you all for coming. My name is Xander, and I'm the founder of The Upcycled Life. My goal here tonight is to connect you with resources that you might need in order to start creating an income or supplementing your income by building products to sell. Rustic and upcycling are huge trends these days. Making new uses for old things speaks to us because we like the idea of being given a second chance."

Edith nodded at him encouragingly while the teenage boy in the back scribbled on his notepad with one hand and shoved food into his mouth with his other. Xander hadn't said anything worth noting yet. What was this kid doing?

"I've brought for you a sample of common discarded things that can be turned into something new. This egg carton can be used for planting starter seeds. This wine bottle can be turned into a candle or stuffed with a string of lights to become a decorative light. This pallet can become furniture or a play structure for kids or picture frames or anything that can be built with wood."

"Hey, man. Do you like dig through trash cans and stuff?" one of the long-haired guys asked him.

Xander hadn't noticed their pink eyes and puffy veins before. "Dumpster diving is all the rage. Lots of good stuff to be found at construction sites, but you don't have to do that in order to find things that can be upcycled."

The teenage boy raised his hand. "Is dumpster diving illegal?"

"In most places around here, it's legal. However, private property and no trespassing signs are pretty clear indicators that you don't belong there. A majority of stores have cameras around their buildings or signs posted near their dumpsters that are pretty explicit in what they allow."

The boy nodded, writing furiously.

"The internet has a lot of tutorials and ideas on things to use and how to use them. I even have detailed instructions on The Upcycled Life's website to help build some basic items. We're going to get started on some simple things here in a moment. You can choose whether you'd like to sell it on my website. When it sells, I contact you and give you the money and a free Reclaim That t-shirt." He clapped once. "All right. You are free to ask questions while we get set up. Please, grab some more goodies from Golden's very own Mother Hen Bakery."

For Edith, he grabbed the paper towel and toilet paper rolls and paint. For the men of questionable sobriety, he brought the bucket of wine corks. And for the teenage boy, he brought the coffee cans, paint, and ribbons to tie around them. With each one, he gave them a picture of what the finished product could look like and set them to work.

He made eye contact with Lucy and nodded toward Edith while he sat down next to the teenager.

"Hey, what's your name?"

The boy looked up and blinked. "Reggie."

Liar. He'd go with it for now. "Welcome to the workshop. What's your goal in learning upcycling?"

Reggie scrunched his eyebrows. "Income. Gotta pay the bills." He huffed out an awkward laugh.

"Your parents don't pay the bills for you?" He was that annoying adult that fished, but he couldn't help himself.

"No, they don't." Reggie dipped the brush into paint and lathered it over the coffee can.

"You eighteen?"

"Yep."

Xander snorted. "Dude, I got out of prison six months ago, but I'm not an idiot."

Reggie glanced up, his mouth open. "Prison. What'd you do? Kill someone?"

A sarcastic answer stopped at the tip of his tongue. Reggie's lies didn't merit drama from him. "I was set up to look like I was selling steroids to minors. Spent five years paying for a crime I didn't commit. When I got out, my family was nowhere to be seen, so I had to make my own way with some help from strangers. That's what I'm doing with these workshops. Trying to help strangers make their own way, too."

Reggie nodded but kept working as if there would be a grade at the end of the time. In a way, he wasn't wrong. If no one bought his work, he wouldn't make any money.

Xander stood to give him some space. "I'm going to check on the others. Be back in a minute."

The other guys weren't doing too badly with their cork vases. It was a little like Lincoln Logs from childhood. Edith and Lucy had a collage of small circles painted bright colors and glued together, ready to be put on a wall and filled with little trinkets.

Edith patted his arm. "You have been so helpful. This will be something great for my granddaughter to do with me. I'm going to go home and use the internet to look for more ideas."

He grinned as he handed her a contact form to fill out. That spark of joy carried him through each week. "When you get them finished, bring them to me and I'll list them on my website to sell."

She clasped her hands in front of her mouth. "Oh, that is a marvelous idea. I can't thank you enough, Xander. Thank you."

"Edith is going to come to my shop tomorrow to look into helping me part-time, too," Lucy said with a grin. So, she'd gotten what she came for.

"Tonight filled my soul. It was just what I needed. Thank you both," Edith said.

He handed the contact form to the guys to fill out and give back. When he got to Reggie, he offered one to him and a pen.

"Tell you what, man. Write down your number for me. I could use some help around here. How about you come here every afternoon say around…" What time did school get out these days? "Three thirty? Four? We'll see if we can't get you some more income."

Reggie's eyes grew wider as a smile spread across his face. "Yeah…yeah, I can do that. Cool, man. Thanks. See you tomorrow."

Xander gathered up the contact sheets and left the projects where they were to dry overnight. Reggie's coffee container planters were colorful and meticulously done. Add dirt and a bouquet of those succulents chicks loved and they'd sell first.

Sounded like Reggie needed some money.

He needed some income himself, so maybe this would work for both of them.

Chapter 3

"She didn't get to see it," Cara screamed through her sobs as she hurled the quilt at Joey. Ribbon wheels and thread bobbins skimmed his head and shoulders. The once organized sunroom lay destroyed by the tornado of Cara's grief.

He didn't catch the quilt. Instead, he stood with his hands in his pockets not saying or doing anything. Some projectiles bounced off him, rolling to a stop on the floor.

"I—I did this for her. And she didn't even live long enough to *touch* it. I told her she couldn't die until I was done. I told her, Joseph. But she didn't listen." Cara collapsed onto the nearby sofa with her face buried in her hands. "Why didn't she listen?"

Gia couldn't hear Joey's response as he folded Cara into his arms, his cheek pressed against her hair. It wasn't fair. Neither of them were thirty yet and here they were burying their last parent.

She was helpless. No words fixed the way the bottom had dropped out of the world. And they certainly didn't stop the freefall of despair.

It was two in the morning and the rest of the family had left to sleep for a few hours while Ma and Daddy worked out the details with hospice to get her moved to the funeral home.

She'd called Xander a few minutes ago to tell him the news, but she'd gotten his voicemail. Her ability to talk without crying was nonexistent, so she hung up. He'd find out in the morning when he woke up.

Cara stomped past her and up the stairs. Joey ambled in to where she sat in the living room on the sofa, snuggled with their Yorkie mix.

He sank onto the chair next to her and rubbed his eyes. "We shouldn't have gone to dinner. If we'd known—" His voice cracked. He cleared his throat. "I need some sleep."

As quickly as he'd sat, he left.

Gia stretched out on the couch.

Daddy shook her awake. "Gia, let's get home."

When she slipped in between her cool sheets, she sank into the dreamless unconsciousness that accompanied exhaustion and mourning.

By the time she awoke, the clock read two p.m. She hadn't slept like that in years. Her parents' bedroom door stood open. Their bed was made nicely, as usual. She dressed and made her way downstairs, feeling like a teenager about to face her parents' teasing for sleeping so long.

The house was silent and the kitchen empty. A note on the counter in Daddy's scrawl said they'd gone to finish the funeral preparation. He signed it, "Be a good hostess. Love you, D."

Hostess? No one was here, but her.

She grabbed the eggs and cheese, prepped scrambled eggs, and poured them into the heated pan. When she turned around, Xander stood with his hip leaning against the counter, looking devastatingly gorgeous.

"Did you make enough for two?"

Her hand slapped against her chest as she rushed into his arms. Her lips found his in a heated welcome. His gentle kiss deepened as his fingers worked into her hair. Oh, she'd missed this. He was her favorite kind of company.

He broke their kiss and murmured next to her lips. "Your scrambled eggs."

She grunted and turned around. "I'd have happily burned them to keep kissing you." She pouted slightly. The eggs were slightly overcooked but not terribly. "When did you get in?"

"Around noon. You were up late last night. I didn't want to wake you." He hugged her from behind, wrapping his arms around her waist. She leaned into him as she plated the eggs.

He held her hips. "I know it's supposed to be a taboo topic, but you've lost more weight since I've seen you last. You look beautiful. Always have. But that concerns me." She hummed as he kissed her neck. Lord, she loved this man's touch. "If it's because you missed me, that's sweet, but you need to eat more."

"I was spending my lunch hours with Tia Carolena." She led him to sit at the breakfast bar next to her with his hand on her leg. "I haven't had an appetite recently."

He nodded, quiet as she ate. When she'd finished, he took her plate to the sink. "Your dad said the funeral is tomorrow morning."

"Tia Carolena's family should be arriving today. Breaks my heart that they missed saying goodbye by a day." The tears hovering near the surface welled up and streamed down her cheeks.

Xander lifted her from her chair and set her on his lap. His arms enveloped her in his strength. She pressed her face into the soft skin of his neck, as the tears came unchecked. He said nothing as she sniffled.

He'd seen her in a lot of situations in the past few months and he'd been a rock through it all. Last time she'd cried was after the fire in her house. She'd tucked herself away in her closet so no one would see her tears. And then she'd run…again.

This time, he'd see the tears. And there would be no escaping to clear her head. If he couldn't bear her tears, better she knew now than when they were in too deep.

Who was she kidding? She was already in deeper than she'd ever been before. She knew it. He knew it. Her parents knew it. But no one sounded the alarm.

He swept her into his arms and carried her to the overstuffed chair where he sat and lowered her on top of him. With a kiss to her forehead, he brushed the pads of his thumbs across her cheeks. "You're even more beautiful when you cry. Tell me everything I've missed."

This was the time to tell him.

"First of all, I love you. Time is too short for me not to say it freely." She kissed his cheek as he stared at her a little bewildered-looking. No, she wasn't going to be embarrassed about it. It wasn't too soon. Everything about them being together was right. "Secondly, I have been thinking about our next steps a lot and I want to wait until we're married to consummate our relationship. Not because I don't want you like my next breath, but because I gave Bronc too much too quickly and I learned my lesson. Thirdly, I have a feeling my extended family is going to put you through your paces so be warned. We can be loud and insane—"

He kissed her so hard and fast she didn't see it coming. She shifted in his lap. Guess he didn't want to talk. She loved not talking with him. This boy set every inch of her on fire.

But then, he moved back a fraction so his lips grazed hers.

"I love you, Gia." He looked her straight in the eyes. There was no awkwardness or hesitation present. "I didn't want the moment to pass before I could express that, too. We both have experienced our share of devastation and catastrophic damage. We'd be fools to let these moments slip by without being honest with each other." His lips met hers again. "Love is patient. No one waited for me for anything while I was in prison. It'd be a joy to show you my love by waiting. Hard, but a joy."

His phone rang in his pocket. He shifted to ease it out, silence it, and set it on the side table. "As for your family, if they give me trouble it'll be because they love you deeply. I'd be disappointed with less. It beats tense dinner conversations where everyone walks on glass shards, like how things are with my family right now."

Her heart swelled in her chest, as she ran her fingers through his short hair. She'd forgotten how soft it was. "Tell me how things went with Avri yesterday."

He nibbled on his swollen lower lip as he shook his head. "She wrote me letters, a whole stack of them, but I never got them because Dad gave her the wrong address when he knew the right one."

Gia lifted her eyebrows. She tried to stay neutral about Xander's family, but had secretly already made up her mind about his dad based on his behavior. Who treated their son like that? "He intentionally sabotaged your relationship with your sister?"

"I read a few of them. They had funny moments, poetry, song lyrics we both liked, things she thought would cheer me up." He huffed and shook his head. "I haven't fully processed what I'm going to do about that kind of betrayal. Part of me insists that I be done and walk away. And yet there were all those times in prison that I vowed I would never turn my back on my family. I would never treat them like they treated me. Here I am six months out and ready to give up on my dad after being so persuaded that family didn't do that to each other. Ever."

"You're adults now which hopefully means Avri sees his attempted control for what it is. You can't make someone love you, so be there for the ones who want you there. Not that I'm an expert on that, but I'm trying." Strange how easy offering advice was, but following it felt like climbing a mountain in sandals.

He squeezed her thigh. "And you're doing well. You've been here for months. After tomorrow, you can come home and put more bids in for international projects. And you and I can go on normal dates and see each other every day."

She groaned. "Things have been crazy since we met. I swear my life was semi-normal before," she waved her hands around, "all this happened. I am looking forward to normal life with you."

Her phone beeped in the kitchen. She slid off his lap to get it. Joey had texted her, asking her to come over whenever she woke up. "Joey needs us."

They grabbed their things and drove to Joey's house. When they walked in the front door, Uncle Roberto and Aunt Judita sat in the front room. She stopped to make introductions with Xander. Uncle Roberto shook Xander's hand and began to ask questions. She made eye contact with Aunt Judita and grinned. "Have you seen Joey this morning?"

"I think he's in his room still." The set of her chin made Gia think that they'd expected as much.

She squeezed Xander's hand and gave him a questioning look. He nodded. He could hold his own. As she left the room, Uncle Roberto called Breno in to talk *futbol* with Xander. Her family would embrace Xander and his *futbol* passion wholeheartedly.

Upstairs, everything was quiet. She knocked on Joey's door on the left.

"Come in," came the response.

The room looked similar to how the sunroom had looked last night. Clothes, shoes, and bags cluttered the floor. An almost-full suitcase lay on his bed.

Her jaw fell slack. "Are you just now unpacking from when you were at my place?"

Joey's swollen face was a mix of desperation and misery. "I'm leaving after Mama's funeral tomorrow."

Leaving. Her heart lurched. "Well, you need a vacation. You work too hard and never take time off."

He pinned her with a stare that was hard to read. "I took time off to be at your place." He turned his back and added more items to his suitcase. "This is different. I'm going to be gone for a while."

Her mouth opened and shut with the questions of why, with whom, and how long. Instead, she said, "Where are you going first?"

"My flight leaves for Lisbon tomorrow night." Turning around, he sat on his bed facing her full-on for the first time. "I need you to do me two big favors."

"Anything, Joey." And she meant it.

"I've been working on the design for the Rio Venha Resort, and it needs to be done by the end of the year. Preferably before Christmas. Your dad insisted on keeping the design in the family instead of me putting one of my best architects on it. So, since I can't do it, can you finish it for me? You can have the money, the credit, whatever. I don't care. Take it all. It's the last thing on my plate for me to be free and clear for the foreseeable future. My other architects are sharing the rest of my workload."

A resort? She hadn't done anything that big in a while. Resorts were really visible. She could not afford to mess that up. "Of course. I'd be happy to."

"Good. All the details are in your email." He gave her a sheepish look. "I counted on you saying yes or me begging until you did."

Biting her lip, she tried not to ask him to stay. "Is Cara going with you?"

"Just me. I've been trying to keep my family, my business, and Mama's health together for the last three years and I never properly grieved Dad's murder. Now that we know the murderer and Mama's gone, too, it's long overdue that I get some space to get my head on straight." He pursed his lips as the tears welled in his eyes. "I can't stay here."

Down to her very soul, she understood. If she hadn't already committed to staying, she'd go with him. But someone had to stay behind, as Joey had done when she'd left.

She hugged him tightly. "You be safe out there. And check in as you go, so we know you're still alive."

Designing a resort thrilled her a little. She'd been doing smaller scale designs for most of her career. It was good to have a challenge every once in a while.

Saturday morning dawned sunny and mild for a December day. The funeral was scheduled to be held in the local Presbyterian church Tia Carolena was a member of. Their music staff were performing the ceremony with a piano, a violin, and a harp. Tia Carolena had loved the whimsical sound of the harp.

Outside on the sidewalk, a small group of protesters circled with their signs bobbing.

"It's sick," hissed Cara.

"So disrespectful," Gia said as she waited to turn into the parking lot. A twenty-something protester made eye contact with her and booed at them. Did they think about what they'd feel like if someone they loved deeply was protested the day of their funeral? "They have nothing better to do with their lives on a Saturday than show the world how awful they are?"

"They need to get over it. It's not like Dad cleared the forest where they put the conference center he designed. They should be protesting at Microchasm's headquarters. Mama had nothing to do with it."

"They want others to be just as miserable as they are," Xander said from the passenger seat. "I had a huge group of people protesting me at my sentencing date. Fools who believed everything they heard. They feed off hate."

"They'll get their reward in this life or the next," Cara murmured.

Gia parked around the side of the church. They'd drive to the cemetery for the burial and come back for a lunch provided by the church for the family. Joey and Cara kept their heads down as they walked in the side entrance. Gia grabbed Xander's hand and squeezed. The last time she walked into a funeral, she came in ashamed, alone, and inconsolable.

The guilt ate her alive.

But now, Tia Carolena's forgiveness had set the stage for her to take back her life. To move forward with Xander and her dreams with her architecture.

She'd never take for granted the change love made inside her, the healing blanketing her soul. The words Tia whispered to her fiercely as they embraced over Uncle Angelo's coffin stayed with her— "Love never gives up. It never looks back and it continues to the end."

That thought that once heaped guilt, now felt like ice on a burn. As she stood in line accepting condolences from people she didn't know, the truth that Tia lived came alive to her. Love always looked for the best.

Xander found a spot in the back where he could watch her to see if she needed anything and talk to Uncle Ronaldo. Likely *futbol* again.

During the ceremony, he tucked her into his side, pressing her tightly against him as if he could lend her his strength through his touch. He'd wedged a small tissue box between him and Ma so he could hand out tissues easily. Gia's eyes were raw from the constant wiping and dabbing, as they listened to a song about seeing her again.

Joey and Cara sat next on her other side and didn't fare any better. By the end of the service, the graveside service, and the lunch, they had drained every last emotion. Joey and Cara's faces reflected their exhaustion. Xander tilted his head toward them.

She nodded and whispered to Joey, "Let's get you back for a nap before you leave."

They went without a backward glance.

Four hours later, she and Cara hugged Joey one last time as he rolled his carry-on behind him, looking slightly less haggard but determined. There was a hint of excitement in the way he carried himself through airport security. As they waved before he disappeared, she breathed a prayer that it wasn't the last time she'd see him alive.

Chapter 4

While Gia took Joey to the airport, Xander sat staring at the flames in the stone fireplace. Overhead, the space heaters kept him warm enough to be without his jacket. Nearby on the back patio, Burley and Ronaldo drank a nightcap and talked politics and business strategy. On one wall, a huge flat-screen television showed a golf tournament on a channel entirely dedicated to golf. No doubt supported by insomniacs looking for a non-medicinal cure. A few feet away there was a square of turf as a tee box for launching golf balls into the yard.

No wonder Gia had grown up loving golf.

He'd visited here a few times and could never get over the fact that Gia grew up here as an only child. He would have killed for this kind of space from his three siblings. Their childhood homes were very different from each other as were their families and their lifestyles.

This however-many-million-dollar home was sheer luxury. The patio was the size of his last apartment or bigger. The outdoor furniture alone was more comfortable than any piece of furniture he'd ever owned. In addition to the recessed lighting and ceiling fans, strings of exposed bulbs were draped between raw wooden beams. On the opposite side of the patio from the golf set up was a built-in grill, a smoker, and an outdoor kitchen. A huge table with a bench on one side and chairs on the other took up the space in the middle.

It was all similar color tones and patterns—something he wouldn't have noticed before listening to Gia talk through her bedroom design decisions with him.

"How are sales, Xander?" Burley asked when there was a lull in the conversation.

Burley could sniff out lies like a hound dog, especially when it came to business. But nothing inside him seemed to think it was a good idea to tell Gia's dad the whole truth about how slow things had been recently. If he wanted permission to marry her someday, then he needed to stay in Burley's good books.

"I'm hoping to see an uptick over the next couple weeks as we head toward Christmas. I've got a few new ideas I want to implement when I get back that could help revenue streams." Thanks to three women who had girls' night with Lucy last night. She'd collected thirty dollars each for him and they'd brought two additional friends Lucy said.

"When are you going to get back into *futbol*? I'm sure selling stuff is good for paying the bills, but *futbol* feeds your passion and a man cannot live a full life without that," Ronaldo said with a smirk.

Xander rubbed his neck. "I thought I'd get back into it after my wrongful conviction suit is settled, so I don't have a black smear across my name legally anymore."

Ronaldo shook his head. "You said the coach confessed on video. People want to see you win now. Everyone loves an underdog. Find a team looking for a good comeback story and forget about waiting."

That was exactly what he wanted, but didn't know if he could have.

Burley chuckled. "Might be more complicated than that, Ronaldo, depending on the legal system." His words deflated Xander's hope a bit. Burley turned to him. "That said, I agree you should get back into coaching soccer. Ease yourself into it. You might have some PTSD to try to conquer as you go."

"I certainly won't be touching any food or drinks the team gets," Xander said. The men laughed.

"Talk to Gia about locations of where you want to live and work long term, but I have a C-level contact in the US National Team's office thanks to Invicto and Invicta being their apparel partner. I'm sure there's a U-19 or U-20 club around that could use an experienced coach, unless you're planning to get back in at the college level."

Locations? As in Gia wanted to move from Colorado? She hadn't mentioned anything. Somehow, he'd envisioned them in Colorado together. The thought stunned him briefly. In his cautious dreaming of the future, he hadn't included them moving, but it didn't really matter where they lived as long as it was the right thing for both of them.

He shifted in his seat to extract his phone from his pocket. She'd been here for months with her family. Maybe she was considering moving back. He glanced at his phone as if she'd have texted him about it, then made a note to mention it to her when the time was right.

"You could spend some time at the Coaching Education Center in Kansas City. They have a decent set up that could get you back on the sidelines," Ronaldo said. "We've sent some coaches there for an international exchange program of sorts."

Xander shook his head. "That's time and money I don't have yet. I need to expand and add some employees so I'm not the only one running everything. I want to offer girls' night upcycling workshops and I can't be at evening practices if I have to be leading craft night."

"Once you get them happening regularly, put out an ad for a part-time manager. I saw Gia's office space. Maybe you could turn the front area into a shop for your stuff. Have you considered some pop-up workshops in different locations? Here, for example?" Burley asked.

It was brilliant. "That's a fantastic idea. I'll gather some materials tomorrow and send out a press release Monday. One for The Upcycled Life and one for a girls' night. Maybe Sophia could send out the information to some ladies who want to craft and drink beverages of their choosing." If he could tap into the Carters' contacts here in New Orleans, he might have a chance at making this a profitable idea that could expand nationally.

Burley laughed. "Flip and Sip."

Ronaldo and Xander made eye contact and raised their eyebrows. Ronaldo chuckled and raised his glass. "Beats Craft and Draft."

Xander smiled. "Too bad I can't just call it 'Hammered: BYOB to craft time.'"

Burley and Ronaldo doubled over laughing.

"I can't decide if it's a terrible idea or genius," Burley said, standing up. "I'm going to get Sophia out here so she can give you girls' night ideas. I'm no expert in that industry, but I can see people loving the idea." He laughed his way inside, giving Xander a pat on the shoulder as he went.

When Burley closed the door behind him, Ronaldo smiled. "You and Gia make a really good team." His words dangled in the air between them.

"Permanently, I hope."

"Is that so? Soon?"

"I've only been out of prison for half a year. I have goals emotionally, financially, and with our businesses on where I'd like to be when I ask her to marry me so she'll know she'll be taken care of by me. I don't want to be depending on her family in those ways when we should be standing on our own feet." He gave a quick smile as an offering of no offense.

Ronaldo nodded his understanding. "Just make sure she's clued in on where the goalposts are set. Burley almost lost Sophia because he thought she'd love him more if he had more to offer. She about gave up on him, because he couldn't see that he was enough. When he finally realized it, he married her and they built their empire together way better than if he'd done it without her." With a short laugh, he shook his head. "Those two are a force. And you and Gia are, too. That's what you want your lifelong partnership to be."

His words touched a part of Xander deep inside, a worry he hadn't named. They were good together and she made him a better man. They'd need to have that chat soon, depending on her desire to move.

"Hey, I've got some *futbol* duties I decided to work into my leisure schedule while I'm here." Ronaldo shifted in his chair, his fingers grazing his trimmed goatee. "If you're interested, I'd like you to join me, Xander. I am researching how others are running their kids' leagues that feed into their U-clubs and then into the national teams. Our Brazilian *futbol* infrastructure is haphazard."

"I can tell you how it all fits together. I spent a lot of time studying how I could place myself strategically when I was applying for coaching positions." Back when he had all the confidence in the world that he was going places. And he was…to places he never wanted to go.

Ronaldo sat back with a satisfied smile. "Perfect. Next week, I have a visit to make. Maybe you'd like to meet my former teammate? He lives with his family not far from here."

"Sure, if he's willing to entertain a third-wheel. Anyone I would know?"

He shrugged. "Cruz Mora thinks he's well-known, but is anyone really as big of a deal as they think they are?"

Xander's jaw dropped a bit. "The Cruz Mora? I didn't know he lived in the States."

Ronaldo shook his head. "He's only here on a visa. His daughter needed some specialized surgery to treat a rare genetic disorder she has. But he's doing a lot of work on the side with para-Olympic sports coaching, specifically vision-impaired *futbol*. They've made some progress with it. Cruz is incredibly talented and doesn't waste it with money and fame. He's out to do some good. You and he have a lot in common."

Blind *futbol* was a discussion for another time. Ronaldo thought he was talented? "I appreciate the vote of confidence. I'll be honest, upcycling has gotten me mostly on my feet, but it's a bridge until someone finds me employable again in the coaching realm."

If.

This case had to clear his name or he'd be stuck indefinitely.

"You can always come to Brazil. I know a guy." Ronaldo winked. They laughed as Burley came back out with Sophia and Gia behind him.

Xander uncrossed his legs as he snagged Gia's hand and pulled her into his lap. "I didn't know you'd returned." His lips found the soft skin under her ear.

She leaned in, a sure sign she liked that. "We just pulled in. Tell you more later."

That caught his attention except Sophia settled into the chair opposite him and pronounced herself ready to talk shop.

They talked out some of the finer points of his workshop ideas like reservation only and a waiting list for the next workshop so he'd know when he had enough interest to host another one.

"I'll book the country club and invite the neighborhood ladies. They were all growing tired of the same boring ladies' nights anyway." She grinned. "If you don't mind, I'll send out a picture of you with your flier. Young, attractive men always draw a crowd."

Burley snorted.

"Ew, Ma." Gia covered Xander's eyes loosely. "Xander is mine. Keep your cougar friends away."

Xander gathered her in his arms and stood. "On that note, I'm going to excuse us as Gia promised to beat me handily on Mario Cart. I think I just saw the cousins swarming into the kitchen for a late-night snack, so the gaming console should be open."

"Put her in her place, Xander," Burley called as Xander walked in with Gia in his arms.

"You have to stop carrying me places." She giggled as he banged her feet on the door jamb. "I'm capable of walking."

Xander grunted. "But would that make you feel loved and cherished?" With a heave, he tossed her on the couch and pretended to do a WWE move so she scrunched into a ball. When she looked up, he was sitting calmly next to her holding out a controller. He smirked. "Get ready to be beaten."

She was two laps ahead of him when he asked her how the airport run went. "Cara was quiet the whole way home. Said she was tired, but I think she's sinking into a place she might not come back from. We all agreed Joey needed time away. And she'd never keep him from doing what he needs to do, but she's going to be lost staying in that house all by herself after all these years living with family. I'm worried about her."

Talking had broken Gia's concentration and he caught up with her. "Are you thinking of moving in with her?"

"That's not a bad idea. I've committed to staying here until the New Year, so I can finish the design on the Venha Resort for Joey." She crashed into a barrier and hissed as he passed her to cross the finish line first.

"Best out of three," she said pressing the button to restart.

He paused it and moved her legs so she faced him. "Are you planning to stay here in New Orleans after the New Year?"

Her playful smile faded. Her eyes searched his. "I don't know. I built a new life in Golden that I enjoyed, but I've missed my family and I want to be here for Cara if she needs me. And my parents, too. It's a huge decision. I've been avoiding it, because you're in Colorado and having a long-distance relationship is…" She sighed.

"Maddening. Lonely. Not exciting."

She peered up at him with a sad smile. "And more. I want a relationship with you, and moving here would send you the wrong message."

"As soon as my settlement is over, Gia, I can move anywhere. Your parents have a network here that we could really benefit from with our businesses."

She grabbed his hand. "But that's not fair to you. You're just getting your family back."

"Family shows up no matter where you live." He shook his head. It was amazing that he still believed that after years in prison without his family. "Well, should. Long distance is easier with family. You and I are my priority." He kissed her. "I'm going to see if your dad can connect me with a soccer coaching opportunity in the area."

"Really?" Her eyes lit with excitement. He nodded. She squeaked and threw her arms around his neck, peppering his face and lips with kisses.

Making her happy gave him this unbelievable feeling. It should probably terrify him, but it didn't on any level.

"Get a room," muttered Silva as he plopped down on the couch near them with a bowl full of popcorn in his hands.

They laughed as the other cousins came in one by one to watch a movie. The day's grief had certainly taken its toll.

By Monday, they had finished five different sci-fi and fantasy movie series. Xander's mind was mush. He hadn't watched that much television in over a decade. He was more than ready to head out with Ronaldo to see Cruz Mora while Gia went to work.

As he kissed her on her way out the door, he could feel the tension in her body. She was distant and short. The pressure was on with such a visible project, not to mention all the codes that had to be fulfilled for another country.

He walked her to the garage and captured her face in his hands. "Please, let me know how I can support you best. You have a lot going on right now, and you do not have to carry it all alone."

She sagged against him and mumbled how much she loved him. "Once I see what I'm up against with the resort design, I'll have a better idea of what life is going to look like. I'm worried about Cara and Joey. And sometimes when I think about Tia Carolena, I can't breathe." Her shoulders sank. "Thanks for being here, babe."

"I wouldn't want to be anywhere else." He tightened his hug and kissed her once more, relishing the feel of her under his fingertips. "I'll see you for dinner tonight."

Inside, he plopped on the couch and texted Reggie again that he wouldn't be back in town for a few days. He'd sent him to Lucy's bakery Friday and Saturday. She'd let him at the pallets behind her building with a saw, a hammer, and some nails.

By Saturday evening, Lucy sent him a picture of Reggie's pallet bookshelf with Reggie holding it up, beaming. He planned to sand and paint it today. Then, Xander would post it for sale.

He'd dropped his office key by Lucy's before he left so she could grab him more equipment if he needed it. There was something about this kid that made him sit up and take notice.

He had the build of an athlete and the drive of a grown man. He'd searched Reggie's name on the internet in hopes of coming across social media profiles, but didn't find any. More confirmation that Reggie wasn't the kid's real name. Hopefully, he'd come to trust Xander enough to tell him his story. Making money was okay, but did the kid have a place to sleep? Or support through the tough times?

His gut said no.

Ronaldo's car showed up right on time. They sat in the back while the driver took them where they needed to go. It felt pretentious but necessary so he could walk Ronaldo through the soccer league system while Ronaldo took notes. When the car pulled in, they were at a field of sorts.

People milled about. News anchors and cameras set up for the perfect frame. There were short sections of stands and field lights looming above.

Ronaldo got out and shrugged on his suit coat. Xander was in the collared button down and dress pants he'd worn for the funeral, but he hadn't expected this atmosphere.

"What's going on here?" he asked, lengthening his stride to match Ronaldo's.

"The grand opening of the blind *futbol* pitch. First of its kind here in United States and Cruz is giving the opening speech. Prepare to be amazed at their skills."

A lady with a clipboard greeted them with a handshake and gave them both lanyards with VIP Pass written on it. Ronaldo walked him over to the field. The sides were bordered with kickboard.

"It's five-on-five. All the players are blindfolded. The ball jingles and the coach stands behind the goal post and taps on the poles so the player can know where to put the ball," Ronaldo explained, tapping on a post so it rang.

Xander couldn't really imagine that working.

"Ronaldo!" A voice spoke in rapid Portuguese behind him, something Xander couldn't understand.

Ronaldo laughed. "Watch your language, Cruz. There are children everywhere."

Cruz waved him off. "None of them speak Portuguese, and if they did, they'd know I spoke the truth anyway."

"Cruz Mora, this is Xander Reinerman, a university men's *futbol* coach." Ronaldo motioned to Cruz. "This is Cruz Mora, former captain of the famed 'yellow canaries', now a handsome relic."

Xander shook Cruz's hand, pushing aside the star-struck feeling threatening to capture his tongue. "As a kid, I watched you and Ronaldo dance around opponents on the field in international matches. It's an honor to meet you."

Cruz smirked. "Ronaldo danced. I was too busy carrying the team on my shoulders." He brushed off his suit coat clad shoulders and faked an injury at Ronaldo's punch.

"You did well here, Cruz. This place is first class," Ronaldo said.

"It's a start. Wait until you see these players in motion. They're stunning. Sighted players should train with these guys to tune their senses. There will be a match after lunch," Cruz said.

"Mister Mora, a photograph?" a voice called behind them.

Cruz turned, his dazzling smile in place. He stepped between Ronaldo and Xander with his hands on their shoulders. They smiled automatically.

The photographer sidled up with his notepad out. "Who are your companions, Mister Mora?"

"Ronaldo Cevere, former midfielder of Brazil's Men's National *Futbol* Team and now vice president of Brazil's Federal *Futbol* Committee. And Xander Reinerman, a university *futbol* coach."

The word "former" stuck in his throat as the journalist backed away with thanks. It wouldn't take the journalist long to do an internet search on Xander's name and get the scoop on a good story.

"Ronaldo, I'm not sure I should be in the public eye with you guys. It might tarnish your reputations," Xander said into Ronaldo's ear.

"Your past is no threat to our present. Our careers speak for themselves, Xander. A newspaper's opinion in America does not change our expertise and what our platforms stand for. But your career is still in the making. When people go digging for dirt on you, they'll find some from the past. What you need now is to make sure they find enough gold of the present to ignore the dirt of the past. If you've moved on, eventually they'll look bad for holding on to the past," Ronaldo said.

How often did the media let past failures disappear in favor of present-day good? From this side of the scandal, it seemed redemption would always be just out of reach. Ronaldo had a point though. If he held his head high, perhaps others would start believing in his innocence.

Chapter 5

Gia's stomach lurched as she opened the file Joey had sent over to her and three dozen documents appeared.

Her pounding pulse and tension headache were normal, right? She always had new project jitters.

Except this one felt very different.

She was psyching herself out. Abbott would tell her to come back to her place of control before teeing up the drive.

But golf was her comfort zone.

Luxury resorts were not.

In fact, this was the first time she could ever recall being scared to take on a project. Even in college, she'd designed from a place of security and confidence, knowing she'd have a job after school whether she graduated with honors or not. Her portfolio was her showpiece, not a way to prove herself. She'd taken that for granted.

She wouldn't have called herself spoiled, because she worked hard. Her parents made sure of that. Nevertheless, Uncle Angelo coached and mentored her. His unwavering support freed her to learn, take risks, and try new things. When she chose to join the non-profit side of his architecture firm, he'd celebrated it.

"Choose where you believe you can design with your whole heart and soul," he'd said.

The choice was easy.

Now, years removed from that decision, she found herself cannonballing into the shark-infested waters of a luxury resort. Nothing about this felt safe. If she failed, she'd disappoint her family once again.

Small steps.

By lunch, she'd immersed herself so far into the requirements that she couldn't break away and lose her momentum, so she plunged on. She'd eat later. Joey had only a portion of the design done. The magnitude of what was left to finish bowled into her. Why had he done this to her?

No, she wasn't going to think like that. He always put his family as priority and that made him a superhero in her book.

She pulled out her phone and texted him. They'd heard he arrived in Portugal safely, but not much else. Hopefully, he was grieving, resting, studying the ancient architecture how he'd always wanted to, and being very safe. If she lost him too, her heart might never recover.

A picture of him, Uncle Angelo, Tia Carolena, and Cara sat in a frame on his desk. Rio de Janeiro made the perfect backdrop for their smiling family hug on Copacabana Beach. They rarely went to Copacabana when they visited since Avó had a place on the water further south, but Cara had wanted to silence a few of the jealous haters at school who didn't believe she had traveled to Brazil, much less spent her summers there.

They'd taken a full album of pictures with recognizable landmarks in the background that trip. Uncle Angelo didn't put any stock in the naysayers, but he'd done everything he could to help Cara feel comfortable in her own skin. If she remembered right, the album silenced the haters and elevated Cara's social status for the rest of high school.

Gia had no idea those were some of the happiest times they would ever have together.

She sighed. One of Joey's other architects would probably love to have this resort. They did these huge projects regularly. But when she looked at the consulting list of engineers, interior designers, and landscape architects, they were all Brazilian and required a Portuguese-speaking correspondent.

Trading was out of the question.

She typed out a quick email introducing herself and letting the contractors know she was taking over the project and why. The rest of the afternoon fell into an easy flow of doing the preliminary work so tomorrow she could get down to the design.

At six-thirty, her phone chimed. Ma was asking when she thought she'd be home for dinner. She closed out her files and locked her computer. How was this her life again?

It was incredibly easy to fit back into the routine of having someone else provide dinner and worry about the groceries in the house. Her swan-dive into adulthood had been a bit of a shock after someone had cleaned the house, repaired the cars, tended the yards, and did the cooking for her since birth.

She packed up her bags and made a quick visit to the bathroom. The office was quiet and empty. Everyone else had been smart enough to get home at a decent hour. When she got back, she leaned over to pick up her things and snagged her arm on the edge of a cracked-open drawer.

How long had that been like that? She pushed it shut. Had she used that drawer today?

An eerie feeling crawled over her skin. What if someone had been in her space? She swallowed and checked the drawer. Nothing seemed out of the ordinary, but she didn't have the contents memorized. She'd used Joey's office today, since he had paper files in there she'd needed for reference.

It had to be nothing.

She pushed the drawer closed and locked it. Then she swung her bags over her shoulders and clicked the lock into place on Joey's office door behind her. The office space required an access badge to get in. No one would be able to fake that. It was leftover paranoia from her bad patch with Bronc and Grant earlier in the year.

Nodding goodnight to the building's security guard, she strode to her car, checked the backseat was clear, and shut herself in.

A drawer. She was panicking because of a drawer that wasn't completely closed. The stress was getting to her more than she thought.

When she drove up to the house, a body lay on the other side of the driveway. She popped out of her car and jogged over, fumbling with her phone to get the flashlight on.

A beam flickered across Xander's face a second before he yanked her into his arms. She yelped as she fell on top of him.

"You've lost your ever-loving mind, Alexander Reinerman." She slapped his coat-clad shoulder half-heartedly. The heat from his skin warmed her as she snuggled next to him on the concrete, looking up at the sky. This was the kind of thing none of her other boyfriends had done with her.

The lights from the front of the house didn't quite reach out this far so their view of the stars was stunning. They stayed in silence for a few moments, two tiny specks in a vast universe.

"I considered astronomy as a major when I was in high school," Xander said, his voice a low rumble. "But I lost faith in the astronomy community when they downgraded Pluto in '06."

Gia laughed. "As good a reason as any to become a soccer coach."

"That and high school physics absolutely sucked the joy right out of it for me." He pushed to his feet and extended a hand to Gia. "Your family went ahead with dinner. The 'grown-ups' have a Christmas event to attend tonight."

She gasped and walked faster toward the house. "They had better not be going to see Nutcracker or the Vienna Boys' Choir without me. I told them I wanted to go."

They were Christmas traditions she'd missed out on the past few years, but not this year.

Xander laughed. "Whoa there." He pulled back on her hand to slow her down. "They said it was a work party they needed to make an appearance at to shake hands and kiss babies before they went out on the town."

"Oh." She slowed her gait. "Then that means my cousins are planning something, too."

And they were.

The ChristmasFest—complete with ice skating, rides, lights, and Santa.

They laughed their way through the majority of the festival, taking pictures with Santa like the mature new adults they were, stopping to dance under the lights of the giant tree in the center, and sampling the overpriced snacks from the vendors as if they hadn't already eaten dinner.

Happily, they saved ice skating for last. She was functional on ice skates, because her parents made sure she was well-rounded.

But Xander…

Xander skated like he had always lived with blades attached to his shoes. He laughed when he saw her standing with her hands on her hips watching him.

He twirled in circles around her. "You can't possibly be surprised. I lived in Colorado my whole life and Linc is a professional hockey player. How do you think he got so good?"

She scrunched up her face. "Lessons, practice, games—like everyone else."

Xander nodded. "Practice and games with me when he wasn't on a team. I played hockey, too, for a while. I just loved soccer more."

"It's *futbol*," Breno shouted as he skated by.

Xander sprinted over to him and semi-checked him into the wall. Breno wobbled frantically, laughing his fool head off. Boys never did grow up, did they?

Gia laughed at the way girls turned to watch when Xander skated by, his thousand-kilowatt smile on full beam. A surge of pride swelled in her chest. He was hers. Tall—or medium height in her cousins' cases—dark hair and tan skin drew lots of attention. It certainly did for her with Xander.

She was so lucky. Her cousins were the siblings she never had. And watching Xander play and laugh with them gave her joy she had not expected. He served them, listened to them, and teased them as if he'd known them for years instead of days.

Antia and Sara shuffled on the ice, clinging to the wall and insisting everyone skate on without them. Silva, ever the gentleman, skated next to them to help them. Truth be told, he couldn't afford to injure his dentist hands in an ice-skating accident, so he had volunteered to stick close to the wall holders. Cara had opted to stay home. Ze stayed to keep her company since he needed to log on to the video games system and get some work done.

A part of her worried that Cara would be upset that they weren't staying home to grieve. As if they'd moved on already because they were going out. If Cara hadn't thought that, going out still felt a little wrong, yet Tia Carolena would have pushed them out the door to celebrate life because she always had. She made a mental note to talk to Cara about it some night and tell her that they wouldn't simply forget.

As she skated slowly around the rink dodging the kids, she found herself looking for Joey to make a comment about his recklessness on skates as a kid. Joey was the hurricane force that was missing. Her heart ached. She missed him so much. He'd always been the life of the party.

Xander swung back around and grabbed her hand in his. He glanced over his shoulder and then flipped so he skated backwards in front of her. "Don't look now, but Breno's looking for payback. He bumped a kid into the sideboard, because he was going for me and I got out of the way but he couldn't stop."

Gia gasped and craned her neck. Sure enough, Breno was holding on to the wall, helping a kid stand to his feet while the mom stood on the other side with a scary look on her face.

"Should we go help him smooth things over?"

Xander shook his head with a grin. "Breno's a big boy and responsible for himself on the ice. You are the daughter of a very well-known couple and do not need someone recognizing you and concocting a lawsuit because they know who your family is."

Gia rolled her eyes and yanked him closer. "Let's go get a warm drink. You can tell me about your day."

Xander's expression softened into a smile with a glint in his eye. Digging his skates in, he swung Gia around so she glided directly at the exit. He skated next to her as they went. He hopped off the ice and extended his hand to her to help her off. She barely stopped before hitting the wall.

She pinned him with a look she'd seen Ma give Daddy ten thousand times that she didn't appreciate his actions. His sheepish smile said the message was received. In line, he hugged her back to his front and kissed her neck. She smiled, tightening her grip on his fingers laced between hers. The settled feeling of belonging washed over her.

She ordered a mulled drink and Xander got a hot chocolate, because it was absolutely unthinkable to ice skate without hot chocolate.

He, the ice-skating aficionado, would know.

As they laughed and joked together, she could feel her body relaxing. She should have gone to the driving range tonight to work off some of her stress, but this was better. Her family needed her with them.

Xander brought her drink and sat next to her where they could see the whole rink.

"You should have seen these blind soccer players. They were graceful and stunningly accurate in their passes. I've never seen anything like it in my life. I thought it was going to be a lot of ball chasing like how little kids play soccer, but it was precise and measured. Infinitely more challenging than actually using your eyes. They click so their teammates know where they are and shout when they are going for the ball."

She could watch his animated expressions all day, and soccer was one of the only things he got animated about. "Uncle Ronaldo probably loved seeing your surprise."

Xander laughed. "He and Cruz Mora spent more time laughing at my shock than actually watching the game. They introduced me to every person they spoke to. Said I was a university coach that had been short-listed for the national team coaching staff. The New Orleans Jesters' coach said he'd call to set up an interview soon, based solely on Cruz's recommendation." Xander crossed his ankle over his knee and took her hand.

"Jesters' are major league?" When she had time, she needed to study soccer.

"Semi-pro. Minor league."

She raised her drink. "Cheers. You deserve it, babe. To chasing that dream job again."

"Cheers." He grinned, tapping his hot chocolate against her cup. "Speaking of dream job, how's the resort looking?"

She opened her mouth to say everything was fine, but the words didn't come. "Joey got a decent bit done on it—all things considered." She shook her head. It wasn't his fault. "But it's going to take a miracle for me to finish this before the end of the year." She sighed as she rubbed her neck.

Xander brushed his thumb across the back of her hand. "Can't you ask your parents for an extension?"

The knot sank further into her stomach. "The opening of the resort is supposed to coincide with the international beach volleyball championship that Invicto and Invicta sponsor. Really big names will be there. Any delay on my end wouldn't give enough leeway for the construction teams. Brazil isn't known for their punctuality."

"Not exactly the way you wanted to end a tough year."

He stared off at the rink, his mood pensive. This man was gorgeous, smiling or not.

It wasn't remotely how she'd envisioned winding down the year. "My extended family rarely comes here and we haven't had this much time off together ever. I want to be with them and show my cousins around, but I'm going to either have to disappoint them or Joey and my parents if this project is going to get done."

Four days since she promised Tia Carolena that she'd be what her family needed and already she was failing, stuck between two impossibilities. She needed to accept that she wasn't going to be able to keep her promise. She couldn't magically change who she was overnight.

Xander stood and offered her his hand. "Let's make the most of your last night of freedom then."

If she wasn't mistaken, a shadow of sadness passed over his features before he sent his charming smile her way. He'd heard what she said without her saying it. She shoved the guilt aside. Xander was the most supportive person she knew. If they could get through this, she'd make it up to him.

Chapter 6

The next morning, sunlight streamed into his room when he awoke. The sinking feeling in his chest said that he'd missed Gia entirely. He pinched the bridge of his nose and checked the clock.

Nine.

He'd slept through his alarm to wake up early, make her breakfast, and chat with her before the stress of the day hit.

They stayed up too late last night to enjoy cousin-bonding time and Gia endured it all with a smile and her usual grace. If he was tired this morning, she had to be exhausted.

His work day might start later, but it'd end later tonight. His to-do list dragged on in a way that made him think he probably shouldn't have gone out to the opening with Ronaldo yesterday. He called a car from GetThere and stopped at the store for her favorite flavored, caffeinated sparkling water.

While he was on his way to Gia's office, his phone rang. "Hey, Maddox! Got some good news for me?"

His lawyer chuckled on the other end of the line. "Some of the best news I could give you in the current scenario. All that press from yesterday has renewed the media's interest in your situation. University of Colorado is talking about potentially settling to get this out of the public eye."

Shaking hands with internationally known Brazilian soccer players might have spurred the university into action. He laughed out loud. After Coach Randall's confession, he'd found a lawyer to go after Coach Randall (and thus the University of Colorado from whom he got his pension) for wrongful conviction. His lawyer said if it went to court, the case could draw out for up to ten years.

Maddox told him to stay tuned, because they might want to move quickly now that they were considering settling. The state of Colorado gave a regulated allowance of $50,000 for each year he was in prison, but the university had deeper pockets which could mean a bigger payout in addition to that stipend from the state.

Two hundred and fifty thousand would be enough to give him some savings and take the edge off his money stress for a bit. He couldn't get his hopes up yet that the university was finally taking him seriously.

Just how intentional had Ronaldo been about getting him into the spotlight yesterday? He'd ask next time he saw him. The man was a genius and knew how to work the system.

Arms full of water and snacks, he jogged up the stairs to Joey's corporate office, but he got stopped at the reception desk. Gia had asked for calls and visits to be held unless it was an absolute emergency. He wanted to insist that her love life and her need to be awake in order to work was an emergency, but this wasn't a trivial deadline to her. So he left the six-pack, snacks, and a note so she'd get it when she surfaced.

Tonight was the ladies' night at the country club. Sophia had insisted on writing him a signed note of permission so property managers would allow him to raid all their business dumpsters for things to upcycle. The ladies were bringing drinks of their choice, so the project needed to be something simple but pretty.

Women wanted to go home with a pretty decoration that they could brag about or regift without embarrassment.

The pressure for tonight to go well felt astronomically high since everyone coming knew Sophia which by default meant they knew Gia. If they knew he was her boyfriend, they'd be assessing his potential as a husband all night long.

A husband, fresh out of jail that went dumpster diving and polished up trash for a living.

He already wanted to call tonight off, but that would be more humiliating than actually pulling off a fun night for some women who just wanted something new and fun to do.

Trendsetters, Sophia had called them. Always the first to try something new and brag about it if they loved it. They could make or break his idea.

By the time seven forty-five rolled around, he had everything in place at the country club for ten women to flip and sip, including cheap aprons he'd found at the craft store while he was buying cheap paint brushes and glue.

The entire day had passed without a word from Gia. She had warned him. Nevertheless, he'd hoped for a laughing emoji or funny gif to the joking texts he'd sent her as he collected trash.

As the women started to trickle in, he stuffed his phone in his pocket and turned on the charm. Sophia came in second, donned an apron with a wink, and insisted on doing the introduction.

By eight o'clock, nine well-dressed women with black aprons tied around their waist sat in their seats with a drink in hand.

"Girls, welcome," Sophia said above the chattering and loud laughter. They quieted down quickly. "How long have we been talking about doing another girls' night? Thanks for coming. I know how much you all love being on the front-end of trends and this is one. We are upcycling ordinary items to make them as fabulous as we are." The group laughed. There wasn't a frown in the crowd. They were eating this up. "We have Founder and CEO of Reclaim That with us tonight to teach us how. Let me introduce our talented and charming host, Xander Reinerman."

Everyone clapped as he stood and walked to the front. "Good evening, ladies. Thank you for coming out tonight. Keep those glasses full for our Flip and Sip. We are going to work our magic and make the extraordinary out of the ordinary."

Inside his pocket, his phone vibrated briefly. Here's hoping it was Gia texting him back finally.

"Four lucky women will be turning these coffee cans into chic planters." He held up the picture of what the end result could look like, and the women began to buzz. "Three of you will be turning these boring plastic bins into pretty vases." Again, he held up a picture. "One will be turning this small mirror into a sunburst mirror with these paint stirrers. And the final two will be turning two paint cans into fancy ice buckets."

At this point, he expected a group revolution when they clearly had the money to buy much nicer items at the store. Instead, their faces beamed with sheer delight. It was a miracle.

"I assured Sophia that no ages would be revealed tonight. So, all you twenty-nine-year-olds, check your apron pocket for a slip of paper with a number on it. And since bigger numbers always get a bad rap, we're going to let number ten come choose her preferred project first."

One of the ladies squealed and danced her way to the front while the others laughed. The other nine didn't waste any time forming a line behind her in their number order. He handed out pictures and supplies and reassured each of them that he'd stop by to help.

While they got settled, he pulled out his phone and checked the screen.

The random Colorado number from before had texted him again. *You'll be getting a gift soon.*

He deleted the text and blocked the number. Probably someone's grandma who got a digit wrong.

Another text sat unread in his inbox. *Mm you look good tonight. You fit right in at this country club.*

Gia was here. Smiling, he pushed his phone into his pocket and headed for the first table of women who already had questions. As he helped them, he glanced around the room. She wasn't standing in the wings or in the hall that he could see.

When the sunburst mirror lady finally stopped talking, he excused himself to check on the others. As he turned, he caught a glimpse of someone walking out the door that looked a lot like Gia. He maneuvered through the tables and out the door. She turned down the hallway to the right. He snagged her arm and backed her into a dark alcove as she giggled.

Her kisses washed away his anxiety of the evening. Her love burned his fear to ashes.

Gia pulled away far too soon. "You have a bunch of cougars eagerly awaiting your return."

He moved back in with a grunt. "The only woman I'm worried about is the hard-working, fun-loving spitfire in front of me." Nevertheless, he stopped kissing her and slid his arms around her in a tight hug, as her head rested against his chest. "Busy day, huh?"

She groaned. "Your gift was a lifesaver. I had to drink three to jumpstart me." With a sigh, she moved him into the hall. "I need to go before I fall asleep standing up. I'm headed to bed. Good night. I love you."

"Hate to see you go, but I love to watch you leave." He winked.

Her nose scrunched. "Work on your lines, cowboy."

They laughed as she waved goodbye and sashayed out the front doors. No one had seemed to miss him in the room. Many of them were almost finished with the painting. The quick-dry paint took a mere fifteen minutes to set, so they would have plenty of time left to decorate their projects.

A few minutes, he stepped to the front of the room again. "Ladies, while we wait for the paint to cure for a few minutes, I've got a quick video for you to watch on my non-profit project called The Upcycled Life." He dimmed the lights above the screen—another perk of the country club meeting space. While they watched, he refilled drinks, removed painting materials, and cleaned up spaces.

When they finished, the ladies gathered their projects, thanking him profusely for his time and promising to tell their friends about how much fun it was. His video must have left an impression, too, because on their way out quite a few dropped donations into his Upcycled Life donation bucket that was—of course—upcycled.

Sophia walked past with a friend. "I'll drive you home. Meet you at the car?"

He nodded. The clean-up was easy. The drop cloths balled up into bags. The plastic table coverings went in the trash. And the rest of his resources went back with him. He'd need to find a place to store everything if he planned to move and do this more often.

With everything packed up, he stopped by the bathroom which was tucked away in a nook so the members didn't have to see the doors. When he came back out, he had lifted the bags when he heard hushed giggles nearby.

"She said Gia is dating him seriously. Can you believe that?"

"The man is gorgeous and smart, but I'd never let my daughter date an ex-convict no matter how innocent he claimed to be."

Xander's stomach plummeted to his feet. His chest hurt from holding his breath.

"Gia's always been a bit of a wild card with men. You heard about that last boyfriend who got arrested—"

"My son was at the party and saw the whole thing go down." She laughed. "She likes her bad boys to be really bad."

Their laughter faded out as they walked out the front door. His jaw ticked as he struggled to keep his temper in check. A string of colorful words slipped from his mouth.

Their opinion didn't matter.

They had no bearing on his life. Their words could reflect everyone's thoughts of him tonight, and it still didn't change the decisions he made.

In the parking lot, Sophia stood talking to her friend. She unlocked her SUV and popped the trunk open for him. The contrast hit him in the chest as he slid the supplies into the back.

What if Gia's parents merely tolerated him and this embarrassed them?

Sophia waved goodbye and ducked into the driver's seat by the time Xander got in. She beamed at him. "Well, tonight was a hit. Congratulations."

Was it though? "Your friends liked it okay?"

Sophia laughed. "Oh, those aren't my friends. Those were NOLA's top female influencers that you hosted tonight. They are catty sharks who thrive on drama. Businesses have skyrocketed or been nuked by their opinions." She waved her hand. "I would never actually affirm that to their faces, because if they knew their power, they'd run away with it. Right now, they just suspect it."

His temples ached from the tension in his clenched jaw. Her genius was admittedly astounding. What better way to test his new business idea than launch it into the stratosphere or pronounce it dead on arrival. No need to waste time. "Well, that explains it."

"Uh oh. What happened?" Sophia glanced at him, the street lights reflecting the worry in her expression.

"A couple of them seemed to think Gia has a thing for jailbirds which reflects poorly on you and Burley in society. It doesn't help that I'm digging through trash for a living."

A soft snort took Xander by surprise. "That's rich coming from them. They're all talk. Sadly, half of their husbands should be in prison from scams they've pulled or insider trading, but they've bought their way out of trouble. Sooner or later, someone will blow the whistle and the things they've done in secret will strip them of everything." Her hands were in full-blown Brazilian sass mode as she spoke. "Yeah, so you dumpster-dive for a living. It's almost non-existent overhead. The real difference between you and them is that you have integrity which is an extremely rare commodity."

Sophia let the silence rest between them for a second. "You and Gia make a really solid couple. Not to scare you away, but I think you are exactly what she needs. Burley and I both do."

Done with delicacy, he pushed forward with brutal honesty. "I've only been out of prison for half a year. I have goals. When I ask her to marry me, I want her to know without a doubt that she'll be taken care of by me. Call me old-fashioned, but I don't want to be depending on you guys."

"That's as it should be. You need to be self-sufficient for the good of your relationship and your general wellbeing. Just make sure Gia knows your goals. I almost walked away from Burley because of his stubbornness. When we were dating, he was a poor businessman taking risks and trying to make an idea stick. He couldn't see that I loved him with or without money. When he finally realized it, it changed his view of love that someone would want to be with him at his poorest."

"So, your daughter marrying an ex-convict wouldn't destroy your reputations with a scandal?"

Sophia recoiled. "Scandal? Burley and my wedding was a scandal. Interracial marriages were not approved of back when we met. We know all about creating a scene. Know this. You are not a harm to our reputation in any way. You can make peace with that fear right now. We support you. We believe in you. But what matters most is that Gia does."

Her words soothed the ache in his chest, but he still wanted to prove he was worthy of her, to be the guy who had it together. When that day came, he'd propose.

Chapter 7

Gia didn't want anything but to soak in her tub after a hot dinner and go to bed. And yet, when she opened her mouth to tell Judita she couldn't model tonight because she was tired and mentally drained, it came out as "be there in a minute." No one was more surprised than she was.

Putting her desires aside was part of being there for her family.

She pasted on a smile, took the fruit-laden drink offered to her, and joined the party in the living room. The furniture hugged the walls to make an open space in the center, bordered by racks of hanging clothes. How had Judita fit this stuff in her suitcases? Judita stood in the middle with her glasses perched low on her nose, pins clenched between her teeth, and a measuring tape dangling around her neck.

"Gia, *anjo*. This rack is for you. Grab an outfit and get changed," Judita said, waving toward a rack nearby but focusing on the shirt in her hands.

Gia set her drink down to sort through the clothes. A pair of trousers caught her eye. She laid them over her arm as the whole room went up in squeals for Tia Neves's entrance. A strong pair of arms wrapped around her from behind, lifting her off her feet. Her squeak didn't register amongst the others' fawning over

Neves. She didn't get put down until they'd reached the kitchen where a full plate of food sat on the kitchen island. Her whole body sagged in relief.

Dinner.

Xander pulled back her chair. "Sit, *anjo*. Eat." He winked.

A marriage proposal almost escaped her lips. What had she done to deserve this man? "Oh, bilingual now."

He nipped her neck on his way to get her water. "Long day?"

The noise that came from her throat that was supposed to be a laugh sounded like a strangled cry. "A non-profit client moved their deadline forward two weeks because the board meeting had to move, so the time window I had to do this resort became much narrower. Then, some files I needed disappeared off my computer. Thankfully, Joey is part old-school and likes to have paper copies on hand. Angelo's influence. I have been carrying them with me so that they can't disappear, too."

"Did you check with IT?" His hand ran the length of her back, easing some of the tension. "Maybe they could restore them. There's no way that Joey runs a business with such vital documents on every computer and doesn't have a virtual backup system for it. He was neurotic about making several copies of my press release with the Coach Randall thing."

She looked at Xander as he spoke. Really looked at him. His short hair was a bit longer. His skin was tanned and flawless. Slight crows' feet had creased next to his eyes. The beginnings of a beard had sprouted. Her fingertips reached out to touch it. He stopped talking about Joey's storage system and leaned into her hand. His smile wasn't quite as ready as usual.

"You seem sad," she whispered as her fingers brushed over his jaw.

His response was to kiss her. "My lawyer called again and said Monday morning we're going to start the preliminaries of discussing a settlement with University of Colorado, so I bought my return ticket for Sunday night."

Another goodbye. Her heart sank as the corner of her mouth tipped upward. "I wish you could stay, but that's great news that they are entertaining settling, instead of drawing this out in court."

Xander snorted. "The evidence is pretty clear cut. The university would be fools to try to deny it. Tommy and Joey could be investigative reporters if they ever need fallback jobs."

"Giovanna Sophia. You'd better not be hiding from the camera," Judita called. "Bring that *ardente* boyfriend of yours if he's with you. I have many things for him to model that my boys are too short for."

Xander's eyes widened. "Don't tell her I'm available. I've been hiding. She's scary." He glanced over his shoulder and whispered. "She wanted to put me in these shiny leather pants with an elastic waistband and crocodile-skin loafers." He shivered. "It was horrible. Can you imagine if I fell and broke a leg and, God forbid, had to go out in public like that?"

Gia laughed into her food. She needed that to be in photo evidence. "Baby, she is a world-famous designer. People pay thousands to get her clothes. And she clearly thinks you'll fit the stuff she brought. Maybe you should put them on and then tell her how you feel." It was bad advice from top to bottom. No one told Judita they didn't like her designs and escaped without a tongue-lashing, but Gia absolutely needed to see Xander in the crazy things Judita cooked up.

She set her dishes in the dishwasher and grabbed Xander's hand to pull him into the fray. He hid behind the door frame as soon as she let go, so she strode over to the rack and picked out a flowy, short melon dress. Pressing it to her body, she twirled so Xander could see it. His eyebrows raised.

She pointed to him and to his clothes rack, then to her and her dress. His shoulders sagged. He read her loud and clear. He'd only get to see her in the dress if he put something on from his rack. Huffing, he trudged over and made pained faces as he looked through the clothes.

"There's nothing gray in here," he said loud enough for Judita to hear. "I thought rich people loved wearing neutrals."

"No, just tech giant CEOs," Judita said. "And they don't shop with me."

Gia changed in the bathroom, stopping to tame a stray curl. When was the last time she'd gotten her hair cut? She'd treat herself after the resort was finished. Every spare moment she wasn't working on the plans left her with lingering guilt. What if she couldn't finish on time?

Her entrance coincided with Xander's as he debuted a navy polka dotted shirt and slim-fitting yellow trousers. He looked straight out of a men's magazine.

She blinked again.

Xander sauntered over to her, clearly enjoying the attention. "Like what you see, *anjo*? *Me beija.*"

Couldn't turn down a request like that. Pulling him to her, her lips collided with his in an emotional upheaval. Her sadness, exhaustion, happiness, and love mingled there. His hands skimmed her back where the dress had an oval opening. His fingertips sent chills skittering across her skin. He moved his lips a fraction out of reach, so she could see the heat in his eyes.

"Can I keep this outfit, Judita? I think Gia likes it," he murmured. "Also, Gia would like to keep her dress."

"Her dress is dry clean only. Do not get your drool on it. Come into the light, so I can see you better," Judita said.

Trance broken, they held hands into the family room.

"Arms up." Judita immediately went to work on Xander, tucking the shirt further into the waistband and pinning the waist so his lean abdomen was accented. Xander watched her, mouth open, as Judita fluttered around him stabbing pins here and there. Finally, she stood back. "Good. Head into the photographer. Oh, Gia. I love this color on you. Your skin tone is perfect. Forget architecture. Come live in Rio and model for me full-time. Most of the models for my upcoming show are going to be your skin tone or darker." Her eyes sparkled. "We're going to annihilate the fashion world's norms by having a largely black and biracial lineup of models. It's divine."

A few more pins and Judita nodded her off to the photographer. As she walked through the front hall, a faint orange light glimmered through the decorative front door windows. The white light from the photographer exploded again and again, snagging her attention. The poor photographer shouted directions at Xander which might have been second nature to models, but was probably infuriating him. She grinned, peeking around the corner.

A huge light setup swallowed the formal living room whole. It almost never got used, so this was as good of a use as any. The white backdrop draped from a black stand. His case with cameras and accessories sat on Ma's expensive glass coffee table where coffee mugs were hardly allowed.

Instead of going into the front room, she tiptoed over to the dark library across the hall to look through the telescope at the stars. It'd been a really long time since she'd stared at the skies through it.

Except the library wasn't dark.

A bright orange light danced over the furniture.

Fire.

She ran to the window. The front lawn was on fire.

Sprinting to the door, she slid into the hall. "Fire in the front yard. Call 911. Fire."

Flashbacks to her bedroom going up in flames shot a spike of terror through her heart. Was Bronc seeking revenge from behind bars? She wouldn't put it past him.

Family emerged from everywhere, rushing past her to the open door where Xander stood with his phone against his ear. Ma and Daddy pushed out the front door. Xander hung up the phone and announced the fire department and police were on their way. His gaze locked onto hers.

She made her way to his side, gripped his hand, and followed her parents outside. Everyone stayed on the front steps. The grass wasn't on fire as she'd originally thought. Four large piles of rock sat on the lawn. Something lay atop each one, burning. The stench was ominous. What was that?

When the police pulled in, Daddy met them on the driveway. They talked with gestures and hands on hips. As Daddy walked back to the house, the officers unrolled crime scene tape around the area.

He shooed everyone toward the door. "Inside. Police are going to investigate the area. No one's allowed in the grass until they're done."

He had that look in his eye—the deadly serious one that meant something major was happening and he was trying not to alarm everyone about it. And when he cast a worried look her way, she lost it. As soon as they stepped inside, she pulled him into the library. Xander came in right behind them.

"Is it Bronc? Is this him trying to get back at us?" she whispered. Her stomach rushed toward her throat. She was going to be sick. This on top of everything else was far too much for her to handle.

Daddy took her arm. "It's not Bronc or Grant. They are securely put away and monitored." He scratched his neck. "Baby girl, you know Ma and I have gotten a lot of threats in our lifetime. People who don't even know us hate our marriage. They hate my skin color or Ma's Brazilian upbringing. They hate our business. They hate our success. They hate that they don't have what we have." He moistened his lips. He was nervous. "We've tried to shield you from a lot of that, especially since most were baseless claims. What Joey didn't tell you before he left was that he'd been the target of a variety of attacks and threats recently."

"Like the picketing at Tia's funeral." Xander shifted closer as she spoke, but didn't interrupt.

Daddy nodded slowly. "Someone is very upset about the new resort in Rio that you're designing, saying it's flattening a vital part of Rio's ecosystem and endangering the species that live there. I don't know for sure the display outside has anything to do with it, but if it does, then you need to know that you are now the target."

She crossed her arms over her chest. "Why does no one tell me these things until I'm in serious danger?"

"My head of security, Amos, and I hoped the threats might go away when Joey left town. We have kept it under lock and key that you transitioned to lead, but of course there is only so much privacy when you're contacting the other team members to get the project done."

Her teeth snagged the inside of her cheek. Daddy had never put her in danger nor worried her without reason. If he kept things quiet, there was a good reason. That truth deflated the annoyance rising up inside her.

"Let me talk to Amos when the police get done investigating and we'll see what needs to happen. Your safety is my first priority, baby girl." Daddy kissed her forehead and walked out of the room with his phone in hand. "Amos…"

The door closed behind him. Xander leaned against the back of the couch, his intense gaze leaving her shifting uncomfortably.

"More drama," she said with a small laugh. "My life was not this chaotic before…"

Xander tilted his head.

She groaned, letting the fatigue wash over her. "Okay, my life is endless chaos."

"I'm going to call Maddox and let him know I'm not coming back Sunday. He's going to have to proceed without me." Xander crossed his arms over his chest.

Her heart twinged, but she couldn't tell if it was panic or adoration. "Babe, I love you for suggesting that, but you can't do that. This settlement is too huge. It's potentially the start of a brand-new life for you, not to mention clearing your name."

His shoulders shrugged. "What is a new start if you're not around to enjoy it with me?"

She met him in the middle and wrapped her arms around his torso, her head laid against his heart. "Please. For me, will you go back and settle this once and for all? Daddy can afford trained security. Amos recruits the best."

"Listen. You don't need some washed-out military has-been protecting you. I learned a lot in prison. I can be what—"

She pressed her finger to his lips. "You are what I need as my boyfriend. Let someone else have the anxiety and pressure of watching my back, okay?"

A low grunt reverberated through his chest.

"Gia?" Judita's voice called from the hallway.

She was still wearing Judita's dress. With a lingering kiss, Gia attempted to project her confidence in Amos and his guys. Her fake smile and glower at the camera masked the questions running through her head.

That night, she slept hard through the exhaustion, but not without bad dreams.

The next morning, Xander met her in the kitchen. He looked like he'd been up for a while. In his hand was a steaming cup of something in a mug. Probably that heavy metal cleansing drink that Ma made every morning—cilantro and lemon. She scrunched her nose.

The edge of his eyes crinkled in a smile just for her. He tilted his head toward the front door. She nodded and followed him out. Might as well get this over with. She'd thought of nothing else.

The crime scene tape sagged under the morning dew. The grass laid trampled under lots of feet. The investigators would likely be back soon to look at it in the light of day to see what they missed.

Four piles of rocks sat parallel to each other. One pile had a sign with GREED written on it. On top lay branches that didn't completely burn. The second pile was labeled SELFISHNESS. On top were dolls with burned middles. Gia inched closer. A doll's head hung off one side of the pile and the feet off the other.

"Human sacrifices?" Xander said.

The third pile was labeled FAME with animals on top. And the fourth was more like a pyre with a doll that looked remarkably like her. The sign read: STOP THE DESTRUCTION OR THIS WILL BE YOUR FATE.

Was it a scare tactic? Or did someone truly believe they'd burn her alive on a stake? All this for designing a building that she had no control over what land it sat on or who entered its doors? Someone must have seen her as a more vulnerable target than the leadership team of Venha Hotel and Resorts who had put the project in motion.

"Gia." Daddy's call snapped her from her thoughts. She twisted to see him in the front door. "I'm glad you're still here. Amos will be here in a minute." He motioned her inside.

Xander accompanied her. "It might have been my imagination, but one of those dolls looked like it had been wearing a soccer jersey."

Did that mean someone would target Xander? Uncle Ronaldo? Breno? It was the detectives' jobs to uncover intention or coincidence. Worrying about it wouldn't change anything.

She pulled a breakfast smoothie from the refrigerator and sat in the library as Amos walked in. Xander finished speaking with Daddy in low tones and touched her cheek on his way past to the door. He hadn't smiled or winked, a sure sign of his deep concern.

"Good morning, Gia, Burley." Amos unpacked a document from his briefcase and handed it to Daddy. His kind gaze met hers. "You have to get to work, so let me make this quick. Our front lawn decorator flexed a bit last night. Security has been a tad more difficult than usual since family is in and out so much right now. We will be upping the staff with eyes on the grounds so nothing goes unseen. We'll be talking to family and making sure they have identification on them in case they get stopped. It's inconvenient, but for everyone's safety. We also have wristbands with tracking and health checks wired into them. They look like fitness tracking watches so they can be inconspicuous."

Daddy nodded.

"Burley, we can go over more detail in a minute, but Gia, I wanted to introduce you to your new bodyguard, Andivo. He's former military with extensive security training. Not only will he be monitoring your watch personally, but he will also be physically within reach any time you are outside of the house."

Andivo strode from behind them where she hadn't even known he'd been and stood next to Amos. He was tall, toned, medium build, black, and had a warm smile. He looked safe.

"Thanks for taking this on, Andy," Daddy said from behind his desk. "You come with outstanding recommendations. We're taking all precautions until we can catch whoever is sabotaging things."

Gia sat forward. "Daddy, is a bodyguard really necessary? I'm slammed at work. Does Andy need to be sitting at the office for hours every day watching my door?"

No one moved a hair. Daddy just smiled. "Yes, we're confident this is the right call."

"Whoever it is has access to the office." Well, that did not make her feel any better.

"Andy is and will remain fully briefed on possible suspects. Rest assured, he will not be staring at your door all day, bored. You can go about your life as usual and forget he's around until he needs to check something. We'll be introducing him as your new personal assistant."

How long would it take before the rumor mill assigned her a boyfriend and a side piece?

She sighed. The people who mattered would know the truth. Xander would understand.

Chapter 8

Of course, Xander understood Burley's decision to assign a full-time professional bodyguard to Gia, but it ruffled his feathers more than he would have liked. In prison, Jerry had taught him a lot about how criminal minds worked. And the thought of losing Gia to a psycho who watched her every move and planned his accordingly like a twisted dance of fate made Xander furious and—most importantly—helpless.

He'd had years of experience with the target painted on his back. Now, the best he could offer the girl he loved was long-distance moral support. The words from the horrible woman at his New Orleans's workshop echoed in his mind. Was he good enough for Gia? Or a placeholder until she found someone more put-together?

How put-together was Andy?

Private security paid pretty big bucks. Xander slapped his expense receipts into a folder in his Golden office. More money than a startup with trash. Overhead costs were low, but sales were lower. He needed a fresh angle to get a handle on this.

After the hearing though.

With his keys stuffed in his pockets, he closed up the office for lunch and headed to Lucy's to collect his mail. A line curled around the inside of her shop. Lucy and her new-hire Edith weaved around each other as if they'd been working together for years. Mother Hen featured a new full coffee shop setup with all the syrups and whistling machines and the display case had every tray full.

He'd been gone a little over a week. It felt like months, because everyone's life had picked up its pace or reached a new level of success while he floundered in frustration.

"Xander, come on back." Lucy waved him behind the counter. Edith nodded and smiled as she dished up baked goods with both hands. He wanted to ask about her granddaughter, but he'd have to wait for rush hour to be over.

On the prep tables, balls of dough on tin pans waited to be shoved into the oven. Pastries and sweet breads filled the cooling racks. It wasn't the same mess he'd seen in the past. Edith's influence, perhaps.

"You look swamped, Luce. Business is really going well for you."

"Don't jinx me, you fool." Yet she beamed at him. "Things couldn't be better right now. Tucker is around the most he's ever been and we're really happy." Her expression softened into something more vulnerable. "This doesn't make up for all the junk that's happened in my life, but it's a start."

Xander nodded. Gia hadn't gone into much detail as to what difficulties Lucy had endured, but her flouncy flirty side wasn't all there was to see.

"Your place seemed really quiet." She unburied a plastic bag and handed it over. Propping her hands on the table, she leveled a look at him. "Now, tell me in detail how Gia is."

His murmured thanks bought him a few seconds to think over what he should say. "She's as strong as ever."

Lucy's eyebrows shot up, unamused.

"Her grief has been set aside in order to care for her family and finish out her work for the year." And now to also avoid an outside threat of a stalker.

"Of course, she's putting herself aside." Lucy thumped the table with a fist. "That's who Gia is at her core. I knew she would."

A fact that Gia would likely dispute, because she didn't see herself like that.

"She's underwater at work trying to help Joey out, so if you don't hear back from her right away, don't panic." Lucy was the queen of panicking on a dime. With current events, he was going to be in the same boat as her. "And you can remind me of the same thing." He continued before Lucy got a question in. "I need to get going to my meeting. Mind if I grab a sandwich on the way out?"

She nodded. "See you on Thursday. Last workshop of the year, right?"

He hadn't thought that far ahead this morning. Nevertheless, he offered her a salute, grabbed a couple sandwiches on the way out, and stuffed a few bills in the tip jar to pay. After the meeting this afternoon, he'd hit the planning hard.

At a stop light on his way to the mediator's office, he leafed through the mail. Bills, ads, mail for Gia, a coupon booklet for services he'd never use, and a plain white envelope with his name handwritten on it.

A car honked behind him. No time for that now. He focused on the road and swung into the parking lot a couple of minutes before the hearing started. His heart raced at the sight of the brick building. Five years ago, he said if he never saw a law office again it'd be too soon, yet here he was voluntarily pursuing a settlement in hopes of avoiding a lawsuit. He stuffed the envelope into his bag, in case he had a second to look at it.

As he walked to the building, he shrugged on his suit coat. The moment he stepped inside someone ushered him to the conference room where his lawyer and the mediator waited for him. The middle-aged man shook Xander's hand. Maddox introduced him as Chris Hudson.

All those years ago, he'd imagined being on the offensive came with a hurricane of more confidence in the outcome than he felt right now. While his entire life's direction didn't dangle on the sharp cliff of this mediator, the weight of desperation pressed in on his sternum. His reputation, his exoneration, his exhumation relied on a rescue mission to move the mountain off of him.

Even if this case didn't clear him, he'd never stop trying to move the mountain himself.

They settled into the well-depressed leather chairs.

Mr. Hudson leafed through the papers in his thick folder. "Mr. Reinerman, I've reviewed the details of your case and former conviction. Since this is the first meeting in this settlement case, I would appreciate it if you told me in your own words what has brought us to this point. Feel free to include the mention of any evidence you have submitted or may submit."

Maddox nodded his permission. Xander wiped his sweaty palms on his trouser legs as he recapped his life and the jobs he'd had and lost, then moved on to the player and staff interviews Tommy and Joey had done on his behalf after his release. Finally, he addressed Coach Randall's interview and confession.

"Yes, I've seen both the complete video interview as well as read the transcript to make sure I didn't miss anything. Our third-party tech professional did verify the video was unedited or retouched, so that will remain as strong evidence in this unusual case," Mr. Hudson said.

A small thrill ran through him that the biggest piece of evidence he had had been validated. One hurdle cleared in a long line of boobytrapped hurdles awaiting him. Maddox had given the mediator the interviews with the other players as evidence as well as affidavits from the players to use their testimonies in the case. None of that carried the weight Randall's interview did, but not surprisingly they had no signed affidavit from him.

Mr. Hudson turned to Maddox. "Mr. Callahan, in conclusion would you please state for the record what you are seeking from the defendant?"

Maddox straightened in the chair. "Yes, my client survived five years in prison, multiple months spent in solitary due to death threats, having his character slandered, his job and potential jobs on an international level made void, and his savings depleted, leaving him on the streets with mere dollars to his name to start over. We are seeking ten million dollars in damages and losses. Additionally, we'd ask that Colorado University take appropriate steps to restore Mr. Reinerman's good reputation and see that former Coach Randall be aptly and publicly disciplined and disowned for his actions."

Xander almost choked. They'd spoken about setting the bar high to show the severity of the case. Ten million was way higher than he'd expected. He couldn't fathom the university cared about getting rid of him that much. But Maddox was a veteran at these kinds of cases, as hard-hitting as they came, according to the testimonies of other lawyers and clients. Xander trusted him.

Mr. Hudson nodded as he scribbled in his notebook, seemingly unfazed. "I'll contact you with our next meeting date once I have met with the defendant. I hope we can settle this quickly."

Xander thanked him for his time and walked out of the room with his mind spinning. And dare he admit to a shred of hope that something like this might work out for him?

Maddox had stayed back to chat with the mediator but caught up to him before Xander reached his car. "Xander, great job in there. That went as smoothly as we could have hoped. I'll be in touch with the next meeting date. Mr. Hudson is hoping to get this settled before the New Year so stay close to base. We may be seeing an end to this sooner than you think."

Xander consented and watched Maddox leave in his shiny, perfectly clean luxury sedan. No doubt he'd won many cases with a ten-million-dollar-plus settlement attached to it in order to afford driving that kind of wealth on Colorado's pinball-esque winter roads. For a second, he allowed himself to imagine what kind of vehicle he'd buy when he could afford it. A beefed-up pickup truck. A Land Rover. A convertible sports car to weave through those mountain roads on a summer's day. Maybe a hatchback with all the bells and whistles so he'd have enough room to carry sports equipment like Gia's golf bag and a bag of soccer balls and cones, or his old snowboarding gear, aging untouched in the shed.

Whatever it was, it'd be sensible and not obscenely priced—just based on principle.

No, he couldn't go there yet. There were countless ways this could all go sideways at a moment's notice landing him in a long, drawn-out court battle where his culpability would be determined by skeptical strangers again.

At 3:45 PM, a knock came at his office door, yanking him from the intense study of his online ad performance metrics. Reggie stood at the door with his hands in his pockets.

"Reggie, come on in. Good to see you," Xander said.

Amidst the stress of the day, he'd forgotten Reggie was coming this afternoon. He led him upstairs to his workshop where the raw materials and tools lay untouched since before he had left.

"This is all I have. If you want more materials, we'll have to go find it." Xander checked his watch. "I have a few things to finish up on the computer, so you have a couple of hours to create what you will."

Reggie nodded as he set his backpack on the floor next to the work bench. As Xander left, Reggie pulled a notebook from his bag and opened it. The kid had come armed with ideas. That impressed the suspicion out of Xander.

At 6:20, Reggie marched down the stairs and stopped at the door. "Uh. I left my notebook on the bench. Hope that's okay."

Xander smiled. "Does it hold all your design secrets?"

Reggie's furrowed brow eased as the teasing hit its mark. "Yeah. Yeah, it does. Don't show anybody. I'll see you tomorrow, Xander."

At 6:30, Xander locked the front door and headed upstairs to see what kind of state the work room was in. The room appeared untouched except for the rectangular box on table. The pieces fit together like a puzzle, requiring no nails or glue to hold them together. On the side, a wooden piece slid off and on as an opening. On the top panel of the box, pencil markings showed where there would be shapes carved out.

A wooden shape-sorter with no hardware fastenings.

It was genius and intricate. How had he managed that in the last two-ish hours? Xander leafed through Reggie's notebook. Tomorrow, he'd be in the workshop next to Reggie. This kid had lots to teach him.

Tuesday when Reggie knocked on the door, Xander wasted no time in getting to work with him. As they moved around the work bench getting tools set out, he admitted his nosiness.

"That shape sorter design is brilliant, man. How'd you come up with it?"

"The internet."

Xander blinked. Of course. The internet had an answer for everything these days. "You have someone in mind for that?"

Reggie picked it up and twisted it in his hands. "Nah, it just seems like people pay more for kids' stuff."

He was right. Kids and special occasion items made way more than the average product off the shelf.

"Product design research. Market research. Is there anything you don't do?" Xander laughed.

Reggie didn't look at him. "Make enough money to survive on my own, but I'm hoping to change that."

"Right there with you, man." And he was. Strangely enough, this kid with his secrets and half-truths had Xander desperate to see him succeed. He knew from experience an ally could make all the difference with survival.

He let Reggie take the lead with the conversation as they worked on their separate projects. Reggie's influence had given him a boost of hope and entrepreneurial energy he hadn't tasted for a few months.

By Wednesday, two items had sold off his website, Reclaim That. His Christmas advertising was working. One item was a wooden kids' shelf and the other was the set of cork vases that the set of long-haired guys from his last workshop had made. He called the phone number they left on file and left a message that he'd have their check and t-shirts at his office any time during business hours.

Gia had been able to video call the last two days and fill him in on her day of work and how irritating it was being followed by Andy. Her annoyance gave him a small hint of reassurance that she might keep Andy at arms' length. She hadn't been told about any definite leads on the stalker, but Burley would keep information like that very close to his tailored vest.

Thursday morning, he went fishing for a power cord in his work bag and came out with a letter. The handwritten note he'd forgotten about on Monday. The "Alexander Reinerman" scrawl on the outside looked even but unfamiliar. He tore it open.

You're being scouted when you least expect it. Keep everyone under suspicion. The scope is on you from afar, but the crosshairs never leave center mass. Do not let them get you alone.

The first letter was easy to shrug off, but this letter was much more unsettling, more direct. Considering he now spent the majority of his days alone, the chances of someone cornering him were pretty high. Everyone under suspicion? Physical harm? Assault on his businesses? Death? What if this were a code of some kind?

The more pressing and probable answer was that this was related to Gia's situation. Burley had insisted Xander save every possible contact point of Amos's. Did he really want Burley knowing about another threat? Not when he'd put his bid in to be her protector and got denied.

He'd handle this on his own.

He logged into Gia's video security feed, scrolling back to the Thursday night he'd closed up after the Upcycled Life workshop. She'd upgraded her package to retain a month's worth of video feed, so he should have access to see whoever slipped the envelope into the mail slot on the front door. At first, he watched at one and a half speed. Once he got into the groove, he sped the video up much faster. Only Lucy and the mail man approached the front door. No one passing by spared a glance.

But then, a male figure with a backpack stopped and knocked at the door. A few seconds later, he turned toward the camera. Reggie. The time stamp said Monday 3:43 PM. In addition to Lucy and the mailman, Reggie stopped by every day, stayed for a minute, and then left. Saturday Lucy met him so he could work for the day.

Xander really couldn't blame him for stopping by though. Reggie barely knew Xander and had no real reason to trust him. He'd made it only part of the way through the week's worth of video when two knocks at the door were followed by it cracking open. His body went on alert.

Reggie gave him a chin jerk without stopping, headed for the stairs.

"Hold up. Quick question for you, man. Do you recognize this handwriting?" Xander held the envelope toward Reggie at his chest level. He wanted to see Reggie's eyes when he looked at the writing.

Reggie scrunched his nose. "No, sorry. Can't say I recognize anyone's handwriting except maybe from my teachers."

The truth was there in his face, plain as day.

Another dead end.

"Thanks. Got this in the mail and no one signed it." His explanation fell into the space where Reggie had been. His pounding footsteps echoed in the stairwell. The kid was driven and hopefully not looking for any trouble.

Instead of joining Reggie for another build session, Xander trudged back to the video feed. There were no suspects by the time his phone alarm went off to remind him to set up for the final workshop of the year. Stomping up the stairs, he attempted to mentally yank himself from his frustration.

Seemed clear enough that he was a target, but for whom?

Reggie worked under the blisteringly bright shop light Xander had for those intricate pieces he needed to see perfectly. Just outside the blinding pool of light sat the wooden shape sorter with a handful of chevron-painted pieces drying on wax paper next to it. Xander blinked. The project would have easily been finished by now if he'd slapped some paint on each block and been done, as Xander would have when he was a teen. But Reggie was going for detailed.

He gathered a handful of general tools. What was he going to set out for this evening's workshop? The tools in his hands went back to the hooks above his bench. Newcomers in a one-off workshop wouldn't be able to handle Reggie's interlocking design. He gathered the wood scraps and some rope. They could do trays or wooden boxes for a table centerpiece. It was basic, perhaps too plain to sell online.

He'd tell them to paint designs.

His mental funk was clearing as Lucy stormed into the space that he had just gotten set up.

"I'm testing out a new cupcake flavor on the crowd tonight," Lucy said. "I love the taste of them, but they were my grandma's recipe so I may be partial. And I can't tell if Edith is being honest with me or saying what I want to hear so she can stay employed."

She loaded the plates, stood the signs up next to each item, and backed up to survey her work. If she'd said which one was new, he'd missed it. He snagged a coconut butter pecan cupcake and took a large bite. Unexpectedly magnificent.

Lucy's wide eyes stared at him. "And?"

"It's incredible," Xander muttered around a mouthful of cake.

Her ponytail slapped her cheeks as she bounced happily. "Hopefully, others will agree."

When he leaned to ditch the cupcake paper in his trash, the envelope caught his eye. "Hey, Luce. Do you recognize this handwriting?"

Again, he held the envelope up.

She glanced over and barely took a second, her nose scrunched. "Yeah, that was the envelope that was sitting in the middle of my floor when I opened one morning. I stepped on it and almost slipped and died."

Xander froze. "The middle of your storefront floor? Or your backroom floor?"

"Storefront."

His nerves tingled. "Do you have a mail slot in your door?"

"No, but the seal at the bottom of the door gaps if you get close enough to see it. It wouldn't be hard to shove that under the door." Lucy shrugged as if it were old news.

His head spun. Someone had analyzed his life enough to know that Lucy was collecting his mail or close to him and Gia. Gia hadn't been back in months for her protester-stalker person to connect her with Lucy.

Whatever it was couldn't be involving Gia. The timeline didn't fit.

But who else was targeting him? And why?

Chapter 9

Having a body guard was turning out to be a good-mood killer. It's not that she resented having someone protecting her. It's that she feared what he represented—someone who wanted to hurt her for their ridiculous notions. Not to mention, reporting her every move to Andy reminded her a lot of her days of dating Bronc and the abusive power he wielded. As she had then, after two days she minimized her daily movements to what was absolutely necessary. To stay safe, she needed to do only what was required.

Her stress-relieving runs now happened on the treadmill in the early morning in the basement—not at all the fresh air therapy she craved. She didn't have time for the golf course, and she missed it more than anything.

When her movements were leashed, her mouth found renewed liberty to say whatever she wanted. Her sass got the better of her in her normal conversations now more than ever. Thankfully, Xander enjoyed her attitude, because Ma did not and reminded her of that in every language she spoke. Daddy just smirked and kissed her forehead.

Gia hung up from her call with Xander as she pulled into the driveway. Another night of nothing exciting to report—work and home and work again. But Xander's huge news had her clutching her steering wheel with a gasp. The lawyer sought ten million for the settlement.

Money like that would flip his world upside.

If there was anyone who deserved to have their life back with interest, it was Xander. Half that would allow him the ability to comfortably hire a solid team to run his new businesses while he pursued coaching again. She could hear the longing in his voice.

At dinner, she sat next to Antia. "What'd you guys find to do today?"

It pained her greatly to ask because they told her, tag-team, about the fun day they'd had touring historic buildings and eating gumbo. Sometimes, depending on the cousin, they'd try to downplay it to keep her from feeling like she was missing out. Antia did try. Of course, that was the biggest farce because she knew, they knew, everyone knew what she was missing and that she pretended to not miss it.

With every twinge of guilt of her absence with her Brazilian family, the mental reminder came barreling in behind. This was for Joey, to grant him time to grieve properly—wherever he was. Another part of it felt like penance to her parents for not stepping into the gap during her time in Colorado. Who knew how many "family projects" she'd missed out on because of her insistence on paving her own way after escaping Bronc's abuse.

After dinner, she found Cara alone in the front room. She sat by herself a lot, staring at her phone or disappearing to run errands, unable to stay with the family for longer than politeness required. Gia couldn't shake the feeling that something dark had stolen in. Since Tia's death, Cara's schedule which should have been empty had become jam-packed.

Gia plopped down beside her on the couch, tucking her feet under her. "How was your day?"

"The same." Her voice was monotone as she brought her phone a little closer to her face.

How had they gone from sisters to strangers in a week? "I didn't get to say bye last night. You left really quickly. Everything okay?"

"Yeah. I just didn't feel well."

Gia already knew thanks to Antia that Cara had excused herself from another day of cousin fun. "Did you sleep it off today?"

Cara's hand flapped limply. "Yeah, yeah. I'm much better."

She let the silence lapse, then sighed. "I miss Joey and Tia so much—"

In a blink, Cara stood staring down at Gia, her phone at her side. "No, I can't do this. Not with you."

Gia's mouth hung open as she frantically searched for what to say to make things better. "I'm sorry?"

"I can't, okay Gia?" Cara whirled around so fast, Gia almost missed her saying, "I have things I need to do."

What things were those?

Cara had given up her job to care for Tia Carolena. Ma and Daddy were in charge of settling the estate, so if anything needed tending to there, they'd do it. What exactly was she doing with her time?

Wednesday at noon, she sidled up to Andy's desk outside of her office with her bag of celery in hand, ready to badger him into helping her. Crunching celery loudly could be very useful in getting what she wanted in a timely manner, but the silence of the cubicles around them quickly dissuaded her. Anyone could have been listening in.

"Andivo, good sir. Can I see you in my office for a moment?" She shuffled back into Joey's office and leaned against the edge of the desk while Andy's lanky form filled the doorway. He shut the door silently, looking at her with his hands shoved in his pockets.

A smirk toyed with his lips. "What can I do for you, Miss Carter?"

His low voice reminded her far too much of the authoritative males in her life. He was her employee, technically.

"You seem like a man who has great taste and discernment in life. Would you say that of yourself?"

His expression didn't change, but he nodded slightly. "I would use synonyms of those terms, yes."

"Would you also say that you do your homework on the people you are assigned to? Knowing them in and out. Their schedules, routines, wants, needs, innermost loves…passions."

The corner of his left eye twitched. That was all that moved, as if unaffected. Collected and calm under fire. A worthy opponent. She almost growled in frustration. She'd wanted him squirming in discomfort.

He took a step toward her. "It's what makes me an expert at what I do and keeps people and myself alive."

"And you've studied everyone around me to ensure my day-to-day safety."

A dark eyebrow arched. "Is there someone you've noticed acting suspicious?"

She feigned a look of what she hoped appeared to be slight fear. "Yes, but if I tell you their name, I'd like your promise that you will report to only me on your findings."

His back stiffened as he cleared his throat. "I can't do that, Miss Carter. I report any findings to Amos directly. We're a team here."

With her head cocked, she took a step toward him, willing him to feel intimidated.

"Unless…" he dragged out.

She waited.

"Unless you aren't talking about suspicions directly related to who might be targeting you."

Bingo.

"And if I were?"

"Then you'd be sending me chasing a red herring while anyone could be ready to pick you off. It'd be signing your own death certificate." His voice raised a fraction.

When he put it like that, it did sound ridiculous to send him after Cara to find out what she had gotten herself into recently. There had to be another way.

What turned Cara into an over sharer usually? Being super caffeinated. Enjoying really delicious food. Holding baby animals.

"Okay then. Unfortunately, I'm going to have to ask you to accompany me on a girls' night out some time in the near future. Be prepared." She flipped her hair and sat back in her chair. This would require advanced planning if she wanted to get on Cara's calendar these days.

"I've been on more than you know." Andy laughed. "Oh, the secrets I could tell you."

Now he had her full attention.

"But I won't." He winked. Tease. "I'll be a fly on the wall, not even listening to your inappropriate stories and disrespectful girl talk."

Sure, he wouldn't. She hmphed, as he walked toward the door but stopped.

"If I may, Miss Carter," his voice softened. "I know it's a huge drag to have me knowing your whereabouts constantly, but please don't let it stop you from living your life."

She lowered her chin to look at him. "And what makes you think I have more of a life than what you've seen this week?"

It was idiotic to ask. He probably had pages of reports on her normal comings and goings. Daddy wouldn't have held back and Amos knew a fair bit.

Andy shrugged. "I've seen fear crush the life out of my former clients, stealing from them what no stalker should ever be able to take. And I would hate for that to happen to you."

As he left, she called, "You're getting bored with my schedule, huh?" When the door closed behind him, she muttered. "Yeah, me too."

Living her life would have to wait until after she got feedback at Friday's blueprints and design check-in with the engineer team. With two-and-a-half weeks until the end of the year, the pressure sat on her like a two-ton boulder. She had made amazing progress. Things were going much smoother than she'd anticipated, but still the performance anxiety set her senses on fire.

The whole space needed to have the open flow that allowed claustrophobic guests to see the ocean on one side and exit out the other to a majestic view of the mountains nearby. Shade from the heat, but plenty of exposure for the sun seekers. She'd planned for infinity pools on every side of the U-shaped building with a few luxury cottages down closer to the water's edge with private beach access.

Joey was a pro at these things, but he was no romantic. She, on the other hand, had envisioned her honeymoon at this place with the potential to take her future children back and still have them enjoy it. One side of the resort boasted green space with nooks to tuck into for privacy while other sections of the resort had clean fields of vision with low greenery and wide-open spaces for families to be near each other without being on top of each other.

The family space featured a kid friendly food hut with shorter table tops and lots of colorful animals and fairly easy access to the beach. The other food shacks boasted a variety of colors, food options, and TVs for those who didn't want to miss the games. The romance side had no such distractions. Instead, it offered intimate dining spots, adjustable lighting, and acoustic ambiance. The amenities offered babysitting services for when parents wanted to steal away for a dinner alone.

A dream vacation.

She stared at the renderings, imagining herself newly married walking along the quiet pathways hand-in-hand with Xander. No work pressures or endless survival demands. Waking up with the sun and dozing in the shade of the trees. Calling room service late at night to their romantic hut with a dessert tray or local seasonal fruit. Just the two of them chasing their passion wherever it led them.

It'd been far too long since she'd been back to Rio. Next year, she'd make it a priority.

The clock on the desk—once Uncle Angelo's—unobtrusively passed the time with a quiet clicking. She wasn't happy with her design. Something was off. Saving her project to three different places, she then printed off the mock-ups to take home and run by her family.

Someone would see what she couldn't.

The blue water taunted her. A peace out of reach.

Restless, she packed her bag to leave for the evening. How much would a flight to Denver cost her if she booked one for this evening? But Andy would still follow her. This past year was agonizing proof that trouble would find her there as easily as here.

The sigh started in her lower abdomen.

Joey was probably having the time of his life. No, she wasn't going to think like that. He was her brother overcome with grief, not a college friend taking a gap year to see the world on his parents' yacht. Nothing about this situation deserved her envy. In pure disgust, she marched out of her office, waited a few seconds for Andy to scramble to get his things together, and drove straight to the driving range. She didn't stop to see if Andy ambled around the shop and checked for exit points or queued up next to her, driving that little white ball to the back fence.

Why had Cara rejected her so bluntly? Suddenly, they weren't allowed to talk about this tsunami of grief they were both drowning in? They couldn't share the pain of Joey's unexpected absence?

With a solid whack, the ball flew into the air, but the wind cut it right. Flighty. Cara was almost jumpy. Gia adjusted her stance and brought her driver down hard. Had she been like this after Uncle Angelo died? Joey had never mentioned it. The ball's path stayed true bouncing and rolling near the flag.

Maybe she needed a puppy or kitten to care for. Somewhere to direct her love.

Gia yanked out her mobile and shot off a few texts to Cara's friends she'd hung out with a few times. They might know where Cara disappeared to.

A few more balls disappeared onto the range before she switched clubs and worked her irons. She pinned a frustration to every little white missile.

One for the intense pressure of this resort project.

One for the underlying fear that Joey wasn't okay.

One for Cara cutting her out.

One for the stupid stalker.

One for the hole that distance left in her relationship with Xander.

One for the dream of wishing she could figure out how to be what her family needed for once.

And the rest for the endless need to run away from her growing problems.

Her bucket of balls had run out when a server approached her with a drink. "Excuse me, this is for you from Mr. Mallington. Says you're the best with irons that he's seen in years."

The server placed a fruity looking drink on a table near her bag. Mr. Mallington was the flirty, old golf pro shop cashier who worked there to keep busy in retirement. He regularly asked her to marry him. She laughed.

No one had ever bought her a drink here before. "Thanks to you and Mr. Mallington."

She polished her irons and dropped them into place in her bag. It'd be nice to sit here, sipping a cold beverage versus running home. There was a coconut scent to it. She brought the glass to her lips, but a pair of arms wrapped around her middle as the force of a body hit her from behind. A warmth pressed against her neck. The liquid sloshed over the rim, spilling near her clean golf shoes.

A squeal of annoyance came unchecked. "Excuse me."

The hands gripped her waist, steadying her. Her heart lurched. The cologne was not Xander's. A low mumbling filled her ears as Andy twisted her toward him.

"Hey, baby!" he said in a too loud voice. "Oh, your drink. Sorry, sorry." He had napkins, patting at her hands, feet, the ground. In an almost whisper, he said, "But I *know* you were not about to drink without any hesitation something a virtual stranger bought for you." His glance up at her was a scolding in itself. "Please, tell me you were putting on a show."

Plopping the glass onto the table, the heat burned in her cheeks. A hundred retorts whizzed through her mind. Normal Gia would go for gracious restraint. Today that girl was nowhere to be found.

"You know what? Yes, I was." She propped her hands on her cocked hips. "I forgot myself for a minute, that I'm not the girl who is allowed to accept a kind deed from a sweet, old man. In my thirst, I almost ingested a cold beverage from an unknown source. What a fool." When Andy stood, his face was inches from hers, so she had to do no more than hiss. "I spent the last hour trying to forget and instead feel something that wasn't guilt or confusion or grief or pain. I guess it worked." She looked him up and down. "At least enough to scare the likes of you into reminding me of who I am with a body check."

Sliding her golf shoes off her feet, she stuffed them in her bag. What was she doing here messing around? The glass of cool liquid sat on the table sloshed, but untouched otherwise. An embarrassing reminder of what happened when she tried to free herself from her present restraints.

"Thanks for that," she said to Andy as she shouldered her bag.

The shaky exhale came in the car. Such carelessness amidst the feeling of…peace. When she drove past the driving range on her way out of the parking lot, the glass had disappeared from the table. This was exactly why she'd not gone anywhere for the last three days. Where would she be if Andy hadn't been there? If Xander wasn't there to help her keep her mind on straight? If someone wasn't always keeping her between the lines?

Dead.

Or worse, married to the biggest abuser east of the Mississippi.

At home, she cut straight to her bedroom's en suite to wash off the day. By the time she came down, dinner had been cleared and the family had dispersed to their nightly entertainments. She raided the refrigerator for cooling leftovers. As she sat down to eat them, Avó Ana shuffled over to the sink that was piled high with dishes. Ma left yellow plastic gloves out for her to protect Avó's frail skin. After years of persuading, Ma had finally convinced Avó to only work on the big dishes that couldn't easily fit in the dishwasher.

Although she was an eighty-three-year-old guest in her daughter's home, Avó still refused to let the dishes sit unwashed for any length of time. Ma said it stemmed back to her childhood in Brazil when flies and ants would swarm into the house to get what was available if traces of food and drink were left out. Avó didn't like to talk about her childhood much because she said it was very difficult. If anyone asked, she'd clam up tight.

If anyone knew hardship, it was Avó.

Gia finished her dinner and grabbed a rag to dry what was on the rack. With the family eating here every night, the dishwasher ran overtime, but the nice serving platters and pans couldn't go in.

"How did you do it after Vovô died?" Gia asked her in Portuguese. "How did you raise two kids by yourself away from your family?"

Avó said nothing for a bit, except for the quiet clicking of her tongue as she thought. Her careful words pulled no punches. Gia admired how much weight her words carried—positive or negative.

After two more dishes, Avó hung the gloves to dry. There were still dishes to be washed, but Avó didn't seem to notice. "That's enough for tonight. Let's sit on the patio."

Avó grabbed a tonic and lime to pour in her glass and followed Gia outside. They sat under the heaters as the night came to life around them. Warm and comfortable, Gia felt the drowsiness hit her square in the chest.

"For years when the kids were small, I struggled to keep us alive. Bento felt that trusting others would force us to be dependent on them and then they'd pull the rug from under our feet when we weren't watching. In those days, women dare not speak against her husband's leadership. We were married so young that I had become accustomed to living that way. And others had let us down time after time. So when he died, I continued to feed that lie in my mind, justified when someone took a misstep. I was so sure if I was to be a real adult that I needed to be independent, stand on my own two feet. There were countless times I wanted to drop the kids off on a church's steps and start a new life alone. My independence suffocated me."

Avó took a long pull of her tonic drink. Gia had heard about Ma's birth father, Bento, a handful of times, but he'd died when Ma and Uncle Angelo were very little so their memories were restricted to the few things Avó had told them. After a few years, Avó remarried Grandpa Ignatius and had Roberto and Judith.

Avó Ana coughed. "See, it's a lie we're conditioned to believe—that we don't need community to stay alive, physically and mentally. Self-sufficiency is as much a poison as co-dependency, but wounded hearts struggle to believe that. When I stopped thinking of my needs as a weakness and an inconvenience, that is when we started to thrive. I met Ignatius through that community I'd held at arms' length, and I can say I know what true love is because I stopped blinding myself."

Gia swallowed the lump in her throat. Was it a lie she'd been believing? Listening to Avó's story brought up the ugly reality that Bronc and Grant had really messed with her ability to trust people.

But could she afford to stop shouldering all these burdens alone? Could she afford not to? There would be pain either way.

Chapter 10

"He found what?" Xander growled into the phone.

"Boy, you need to listen better. Ar-se-nic," Gia stated it again so calmly that he wanted to reach through the phone and shake her, or hug her and never let go. He couldn't decide. "Andy took the drink with him when we left the driving range and had it tested for any possible traces of a contaminant."

"How did the person get it into the drink without the bartender seeing?"

"Bartender was working alone since it wasn't a peak hour. One of the waiters tripped on the way to deliver drinks to high-profile clients, so the bartender prioritized their beers, giving whomever it was time to drop enough liquid arsenic in the glass to shrivel my organs in minutes." Her voice wavered, but she paused and cleared her throat.

She was crying. He'd put money on it. Pulling the phone from his ear, he let out a shaky exhale. "Andy did his job and might have even earned a small Christmas bonus."

Gia's small laugh lightened his mood. He ran his hand through his hair. This attack accentuated his envelope issue. They might not need to get him alone if they could get to his food or car.

Andy, Andy, Andy. He was a hero. Xander might even send him a personalized thank-you note, too, but the admiration in her tone made him unreasonably jealous. It was proof that five plus years without a mature, adult relationship had him fighting the same immaturity he thought he left behind in his early twenties. Gia wasn't like other girls, falling for the shiny armor nearest her.

"How did the last workshop go tonight?"

"Oh, aside from Reggie, there were two others who had come before." It was a low attendance night, but that was okay because his mind had been elsewhere. However, the video feed was no longer relevant since the envelope had come under Lucy's door.

Lucy's door. He shot off a quick text to Lucy asking about seeing her video feed.

"Uh, well. I need to go. I have a big design meeting tomorrow. I sent the plans to the engineers today. Tomorrow, they'll let me know how much they don't like and what I need to redo." She huffed out a laugh.

They said goodbye. Lucy responded to his text as he hung up. Perfect timing.

Probably can't. Security feeds were on and off last week, due to a reno project at the antique shop next door. Why they need to update anything is beyond me. They're supposed to look old.

Of course, they were. How convenient. Someone was spending a lot of time doing the footwork to keep secretly informing him of other people covertly watching him. Like playing poker, everyone watching each other watching other people.

The thought kept him awake for a while as he turned over the possibilities regardless of how ridiculous they seemed. It was no comfort that whoever was watching him would come out of hiding eventually.

The next morning, he dragged himself into work. He'd wasted time on the security cameras yesterday, but today was his day for profitability. Tomorrow, he and Reggie were scheduled to go out dumpster diving to get whatever they could get their hands on. There were at least a half-a-dozen new housing developments to explore within a thirty-minute radius.

He compiled lists of the supplies he'd need to collect in order to put together these children's kits he wanted to put out to stores and nonprofits. Following Reggie's lead, he searched the idea online. People posted anything and everything online if you knew what to look for.

His notebook had pages filled with ideas of children's kits to make. Competing companies sold similar kits for twenty-five or thirty dollars. Maybe he could make this business profitable next year after all.

Not until early afternoon did Xander surface from his productivity to check his email. Both of Reggie's items sold. The sales number gave him a shot of adrenaline. He tucked the cash payment into an envelope.

Buried in the middle of seventy-seven new emails was an email titled "Invitation to Interview." Those job search websites never gave up. His mouse hovered over the delete button.

But he opened it instead.

The letter started off with "Dear Mr. Reinerman,", introductions, saying he'd seen him with Cruz and Ronaldo, surprising but likely untrue flatteries about his coaching skills that escalated into an offer for an interview to be a U-19 men's coach in Denver. The season started January 4, like usual. Would he be available for an interview December twenty-second?

Xander sat back against his chair hard.

It wasn't semi-pro like the Jesters, but coaches from feeder teams for the Major League Soccer teams often recruited from the nineteen-year-old's league. The job would give him a national platform. His heart raced. This could be the breakthrough he needed to get back into the coaching world.

He paced around the room, his hands on his head. How mad would Gia be about him considering this? She had been so excited about him looking for positions in New Orleans. The thought made his stomach turn.

But this could be his one chance. What if he missed it? Surely, she'd understand the year-long commitment as a stepping stone to get him where he wanted to be in New Orleans or traveling with the men's international team. She loved Colorado, and it'd take her time to wrap up everything she had going in there to move to New Orleans anyway.

Once she finished with Joey's project, she'd be free to come back so they weren't doing long distance anymore. Not to mention, he wasn't going anywhere until his settlement closed out, or God forbid, went to court.

The more he rationalized it in his head, the more positive he was that Gia would see their very near future needed to be in Golden. Together.

He clicked Reply and wrote out an email accepting the interview. If they offered the job, he wouldn't have to take it, but this would buy him time to talk to Gia to about their future. However, after today's high-stress meeting was not the time.

He opened a text to her. *Thinking of you. How did your meeting go?* He sent the text as fast as possible so he didn't have time to wonder further if he should tease his big news.

Instead, he buried himself in creating a campaign for launching a regular craft night, Flip and Sip. If he got the coaching job, he'd be able to hire someone to run the nights without him since he'd have games and practices. He couldn't stop thinking about how much he wanted this coaching position.

A knock on the door followed by its opening pulled him out of it. Twisting in his seat, he faced Reggie who stood with his hands stuffed in his pockets, shuffling his feet.

"Hey, uh, Xander." Reggie licked his lips. What had this kid so worked up? "Would you be able to write a letter as proof of employment for me, stating my hours I work and what I'm doing?"

Well, that was unexpected. Xander kicked a rolling chair in Reggie's direction. "How about you level with me first?"

Reggie dropped into the chair, his shoulders slumped.

"How old are you actually?" Xander asked, arms crossed. Reggie perked up. "Don't tell me eighteen again. IDs can be faked as easily as the names you give out. I want to help you, so give me the respect of your real information."

He sighed. "Fifteen."

"Your real name?"

"Bernard Reginald Harrison."

Yeah, he'd go with Reggie, too. "Who's asking for the letter?"

Reggie rubbed his face hard. "My foster parents think I'm out doing drugs or part of a gang. I told them I have a job making stuff. They said no one would hire a fifteen-year-old. I said I'd prove I was working after school. Look, these people are the first pair that haven't abused me in some way in the last few years. They aren't great, but I need to make it work there for as long as I can. Last night, they threatened to call social services."

"What happens if they do that?"

"I get sent to a group home for kids." Reggie shook his head. "I'm not looking to be in a gang or stuck in juvie. I want a legitimate start to life when I turn eighteen. That means working now. Please?"

His words took Xander's breath away. This was the very reason he'd started The Upcycled Life, yet he couldn't push the anonymous warning from his mind. "Are you telling me the absolute truth?"

Reggie pulled out his wallet and shoved a handful of cards at Xander. His ID, his social worker's information, his school ID, and a picture of him standing with his arm around a little boy. It didn't seem to be a con from whoever was out to get him. If it was, it was genius to use a kid to get close.

"Okay, I'll write your letter," Xander said. "On one condition."

Reggie spread his hands. "Anything."

"I drive you home tonight and meet your foster parents in person. A letter, certified or not, can be faked. I'll take everything I need with me to show them who I am and what I do."

The smile that spread across Reggie's face was pure excitement. "That'd be perfect. Thanks, man. They'll believe me then. Write the letter to Regina and Carl Destarny." He grabbed his bag and headed for the stairs.

"Wait a second, Reggie," Xander said, extending the envelope with the cash in it. "Here's your payout. You wear a medium or large shirt?"

"Medium."

Xander strode over to his box of shirts and yanked an M from the pile. "Congrats on your first sales. You do really good work. It's no surprise your stuff sold already. Keep it up."

Reggie took the shirt, still grinning. He pulled a dorky teenage dance move, then he jogged up the stairs to the workroom. Xander laughed. As much as he wanted to suspect Reggie, his gut trusted him, but not enough to go to Reggie's "house" alone tonight.

He needed a plan.

Who could he call that wouldn't require lots of explanation, but would back him up?

The phone told him his call was connecting as he lifted it to his ear. He closed himself into Gia's inner office. Already his mental defenses were up, assuming it'd be a no.

"Hey, bro," Linc answered.

"Linc, hey. You busy tonight? Because I have a favor to ask."

"It's Friday night, so I'd planned to go out around eight which you're welcome to join. But I'm not busy until then. What's up?"

Xander had no great way to phrase this. "I have a high-school kid who has been coming to my office every day and making really nice products to sell on my website. He wants help convincing his foster parents that he has a job and isn't into drugs. I'm taking him home around six and want to convince the parents in person, but if they look into me at all, it might throw more shade on this poor kid."

Linc snorted. "I'm a great wingman and have a very honest face. I'll be there at 5:30 to introduce myself to the guy first."

A cooling sensation ran across his chest. Since walking out of his parents' house on Father's Day, Linc had taken every effort to make their relationship better and be there for him—the way things used to be. "Thanks, Linc. And can you bring your personal protection just in case this guy diverts us to somewhere we don't want to be?"

"Sure thing. As a thank you, you'll join me and the guys for a night out, right?"

No doubt, "the guys" would be Linc's hockey teammates—rowdy, immature, and eager to waste their money on a morning hangover and curdled stomach. The decline sat on the tip of his tongue, but he'd been out of prison for six months now and had a mere handful of friends to show for it. Xander blinked. It beat sitting alone trying to find something on TV or feeling like he should be working. "Yeah, I'll join you. Thanks for the invite."

When he hung up, a text buzzed through from Gia. *Survived the meeting. 6 days to get the revisions done if I want to relax on Christmas Eve. Call you tonight.*

His smile faded as he processed the situation. She could be finished with this project by Christmas, but Maddox hadn't sent any word on when his next settlement meeting was. There wasn't much of a chance that she'd ditch New Orleans for Colorado with her family there.

One problem at a time.

He typed up a quick note to Regina and Carl and printed it on his company letterhead. It sounded plenty official for what Reggie had asked for. His long legs easily took the stairs two at a time to his workshop. They had an hour before Linc showed up.

If he didn't do something with his hands, his anxiety would get the better of him in a heartbeat.

In the workshop, he waved the paper toward Reggie. "Here's the signed document." Reggie's bag sat open, so he tucked it inside.

"Thanks, Xander. I really appreciate it," Reggie said. His phone sat on the workbench beside him playing songs Xander thought he might recognize as pop.

Those window flower boxes weren't going to sand themselves. Xander set to work on them with the sandpaper instead of the electric sander.

"We still on for material collecting tomorrow at nine, assuming all goes well with Carl and Regina tonight?"

Reggie nodded. "I made a list of what I want to look for." He hummed along with the song.

"I respect your plan. You seem like you know what you want from life, and knowing how to get there is half the battle. Staying out of one of those group homes sounds like priority number one."

The humming stopped. "Took one of my foster brothers getting killed on the street during a drug deal to wake me up. Until then, I didn't care that I had one strike left. Screw the system. But now I see the best way to stick it to the system is to succeed, to do the best for myself despite them."

"I feel that," Xander murmured. There it was. His life ambition laid out by a fifteen-year-old.

No time at all passed until Xander got a text from Linc. *Here.*

"I'm going out tonight with my brother after we drop you off so he's going to ride along, if that's all right," Xander said as he walked to the door.

"Cool."

Xander opened the front door to Linc, then locked it behind him. Linc's casual glance around could not have been more obvious.

"On a scale of one to ten, how concerned are we about personal safety with this kid?" Linc whispered.

"My gut says zero, but my mistrust of human beings in general puts it around a 4," Xander said, walking to the stairs. "Hey, Reggie. You ready to go?"

"One minute," Reggie called.

"I've got my reloadable taser in my pocket in case."

At one point, Linc had told him it was frowned upon for athletes of their status to go out without personal protection of some sort. They weren't the pros, so it was hard to imagine who was going to recognize them and pick a fight, but he was grateful for the backup all the same.

"Your hockey meatheads meeting us out tonight?" Xander asked as he closed up shop.

Linc laughed. "Yeah, but we've got practice at the crack of dawn, so they'll go easy tonight."

From Linc's stories, his teammates didn't know how to "go easy" doing anything. It was face mask to the plexiglass one hundred percent of the time. Xander could already feel the headache forming.

Reggie trotted into the room and followed them out to the SUV. Xander drove, Reggie got the front, and Linc tucked into the back. As they went, Linc introduced himself and asked a few questions.

"I'm not far." Reggie directed him down one street, a left, a mile or so down, then right and into a subdivision.

The knot of tension in Xander's shoulders eased. The homes were mid-sized for families with kids' gear in the yards.

"Second house on the right."

Xander pulled in. Looked like the fight would be for his dignity, not his life. Linc followed them to the front door and Reggie let them in. The house smelled amazing. Homey decorations and family photos graced the walls in collages.

Reggie motioned them toward the front room. "Stay here. I'll go get Regina."

A minute later, Reggie walked in. "Regina, this is Xander from Reclaim That and his brother Linc."

Xander extended his hand first to the short, dark-haired woman in front of him. She might have been Asian, but he knew better than to guess. "Regina, nice to meet you."

Her grip was firm and her smile seemed sincere. "Reggie just showed me the document you drew up for him. That was nice of you."

She greeted Linc as well.

"I don't mean to intrude this evening, but I wanted to reassure you in person that Reggie is not getting into any trouble between 3:45 and when he comes home. He's the hardest working kid I've met in a really long time and he's great at the designs he does." Xander scanned Regina's face, waiting for the cynicism and doubt to come.

"He's very good with his hands," Regina said, patting Reggie on the shoulder. "Thank you for your reassurances. Maybe after Christmas, Carl and I can peek in on your workshop and see exactly what it is you do."

Xander nodded. "Stop by any time. In fact, next year I'm offering custom creation classes for ladies' nights out if you and a few of your friends want to upcycle something for fun."

Her smile didn't quite reach her eyes. "Thank you. We'll keep that in mind."

And that was his cue to go. "We should get going, but it was a pleasure to meet you, Regina."

As she walked them to the door, Xander glanced over his shoulder at Reggie standing in the entryway. Reggie's thumbs up gave him permission to breathe easier as they ducked into the car to drive to dinner. He had a good feeling he'd see Reggie tomorrow morning at nine am.

They stopped by the office to pick up Linc's car and drove to a place called George's that boasted *Live Music, Gourmet Deserts, 8 PM Fri Nites*. By the look of it, there hadn't been anything gourmet in there in decades, much less the desserts they'd probably accurately called deserts.

Inside, the energy exploded. TVs showed sports, and overhead music played loudly enough that they had to yell. Linc motioned to a high-top near the pool tables. The menu was sticky with a film on it and the table surface wasn't much better.

Why had he agreed to come out again?

"Because you missed this part of humanity for the last few years," Linc shouted as a new song started up.

Guess he'd asked that out loud. Xander laughed. "Dirty spaces and crappy food, we had plenty of. You were the missing link."

Grinning, Linc slow-clapped at his play on words. They ordered drinks and an appetizer from the very young-looking waitress and claimed a pool table to wait for the others.

At 7:15, the guys showed up. The music started at 8. And by 9 PM, Xander was tapped out on the loud, obnoxious incessant competing of Linc's teammates who were several drinks up on the "going easy" promise.

"Hey, buddy. I'm headed out," Xander shouted into Linc's ear. Linc said something but Xander couldn't hear it, so he waved. He paid his bill and walked into the freezing night air.

Partway to his car, his feet went out from under him. His face landed hard against the gravel parking lot. A heavy weight pressed into his back, squeezing the rest of the air from his lungs. His shoulders screamed in pain as his arms twisted behind his back.

"Been waiting a long time to get you alone, pet." A low voice growled in his ear. The stench of sour whiskey on his breath made Xander's nose burn. "Where did he hide it?"

Even if Xander knew what he was talking about, his lungs still weren't getting enough oxygen to stop the gasping and black spots in his vision.

"We know he told you where it was. Now, play nice and tell me before I snap your arms off."

Fighting the adrenaline, Xander relaxed his whole body, creating a bit of room. The knee moved off him as he flipped onto his back. Cold metal pressed against his forehead.

The last thing this beast of a tattooed muscleman wanted to hear was that Xander didn't know. "I—I," he gasped. His mind blanked in a panic. He'd die in a gravel parking lot of a dive bar and his dad wouldn't be surprised.

Chapter 11

The international video call with the engineers had, in a weird way, energized her. Sure, they'd picked her work apart as if they were her college professors grading her college project. But now she had the steps to take to finish the project and enjoy her Christmas.

It was a welcomed distraction from yesterday's upheaval. When Gia made it home on Thursday evening, Daddy, Ma, Amos, and Andy waited for her in the library like an intervention gathering pulled straight from a sit-com. She asked them to wait for a quick minute while she dashed up the stairs to change into a sweatshirt and leggings. If she was going to get bad news, she needed it to be while she was comfortable.

When she returned hidden away behind her layers of protection, she gave them her bravest smile and braced herself for the worst.

Andy started. "I drove the drink directly to my contact at our nearby lab and they graciously agreed to expedite processing it." He paused, rustling his papers.

"I'm guessing there was something in it, or this meeting would have been an email." Gia's words earned her an arched eyebrow from Ma and a half-smirk from Daddy.

"Condensed fertilizer, enough to poison you in minutes or worse."

Gia nodded, but her mind dropped in a freefall. Careless. Foolish. The words scrolled across her mind in a string. Her fingers massaged her temples where the pounding took residence. What had she been thinking to almost drink that?

Amos finished the meeting with how they were trying to track down the people the bartender had seen at the bar. Mr. Mallington was as innocent as he was a flirt. Someone had told the bartender Mallington had asked to send it to Gia. Amos said they'd seen plenty of hate spouted online about how the resort would poison the area and the environment. Apparently, it was fairly common for this level of antagonism to accompany a new build with international recognition.

That didn't make her feel any better.

Then when she relayed it all to Xander, she felt even worse. Although understandably livid, he had seemed distracted during their conversation. She'd been hoping for solidarity of some sort. His distance hurt.

She pushed his attitude aside in order to focus on the corrections meeting. She and Xander had plenty of tiffs in the last six months, enough to know that distance greatly exaggerated issues. When they could video call, they'd work through everything.

She hoped.

A tiny thought had sprung in the back of her mind. Did they need to take a break until she could work through her current life messes? Not because she didn't love him, but because her overloaded plate weighed heavy on her and something needed to get the pause.

For right now, her relationship concerns moved to the bottom of the priority list in favor of hitting her Christmas deadline. One stress at a time.

A knock came at her door. No one had knocked on her office door since Andy had been assigned to watch it. Andy opened it and poked his head in.

"Uh, Gia. Save your work and bring your files with you. We have to get out of the office now and won't be back today." He glanced over his shoulder.

Loud voices filled the hallways that were usually quiet, even on a Friday. A shriek echoed off the walls. Fear punched her in the gut.

"What is it?" She saved her document and stuffed her paper copies into her work bag. To be safe, she added a few more folders to the stack.

"Rodents are loose in the office," Andy said, looking both ways as she followed him into the hall. "Also, three dead opossums with mutilated corpses were delivered with the daily mail. Pictures of employees with graphic, threatening messages also showed up. Looks like we're going to need to vacate the office for a while."

They jogged down the back stairs to the parking garage. Her paranoia got the better of her. She glanced around, clutching her bag to her side as Andy did his routine car checks on her vehicle. The garage seemed emptier than usual. He started her car with her keys and walked around the outside of the car to open the passenger door.

His deep brown eyes caught her wide stare. He motioned her toward the seat. The man thought he was going to drive her somewhere. She was perfectly capable of driving herself home.

This was his job. Her protest died as a sigh on her lips.

Andy's head never stopped its swivel as they drove through the parking garage. Her heart raced. What kind of threat was he expecting? She was afraid to ask.

By the entrance, Andy slowed. He reached into his bag and pulled out a hat and sunglasses. "Put these on and keep your head down."

They crept past the gate into the sunlight where a huge line of picketers pushed signs into the air in time with their chants. Gia slouched in her seat. The picketers stared at her car while shouting as they passed.

Andy turned up some pulsing music as someone stepped right up to peer into her window. He pulled her torso across the armrest, brushed his lips across her cheek, and laughed with a deep rumble as if she'd said something funny. She laid her hand on his chest, keeping her head tucked into his shoulder. With his arm around her, he pulled into traffic.

Two turns later, Andy exhaled hard, retracting his arm back to his side. "We're in the clear. That was tense. I thought that guy was going to try to open your door or break your window."

Gia sunk further into her seat, her hand on his arm which rested on the console between them. "Andy, I can't thank you enough for keeping me safe this past week. It's been…"

"Eventful?" He asked.

"A nightmare I never saw coming." Gia groaned. "I'm going to beat Joey up so hard when he gets back here, leaving me in this mess."

Andy chuckled, his warm laugh a balm to the constricting in her chest. "You should have seen Malorie standing on her desk in her flowery skirt and white socks with tennis shoes when those rats went by."

She shouldn't laugh, but the absurdity of it struck her hard.

"And you know how Jim is always subtly flexing around the office? He was chucking chairs at the wall completely missing the rats and then he went sprinting out the office door. And I'm ninety-eight percent sure I saw a rat chasing him."

Andy and Gia laughed together until they couldn't breathe. In a week at Joey's office, Andy had picked up what Gia had observed in the last six months. With her own office in Golden, she didn't miss the awkward smiles in the kitchen or the random pop-ins from people who wanted to waste time chatting, but she did miss the consistent comfort of knowing someone was always around if she needed them.

"Such a shame that I missed this while on the phone today. My headphones block sound out really well, I guess."

Andy turned into the driveway. "I tried not to bother you until I saw the Do Not Disturb light go off your desk phone." He swiped at his nose. "Those carcasses were starting to stink up the room. We shoved them in an office for the police to investigate when they arrived, but that smell filled up the whole place."

Gia met Andy's dark gaze. "Thank you for getting me out of there safely. This rescue thing is becoming a little too frequent for my liking. Whoever this is needs to stop."

Andy cleared his throat and glanced out the driver's window. "I'm afraid it's going to get worse in the next few days."

He reached between the seats to his bag, his chest brushing her arm. His cologne was subtle, but nice. What was wrong with her? She had a boyfriend whom she missed so much. She rubbed her neck. Six months of short visits messed with her head. Once Xander's settlement was over, he could move down here permanently and they could really give their relationship a fighting chance.

Andy sat back up and handed her a rolled magazine. There on the front cover was a grainy and unflattering picture of Daddy and Ma walking together, their expressions unsmiling. The headline read, "American multi-millionaires in hot water for destroying cherished green zone in Brazil". Gossip magazines never did bother picking a decent picture if they were upset about something, which was always.

The heat rose in Gia's chest. Garbage. She tossed the magazine onto Andy's lap. "Every so often the gossip rags cycle through the usual misinformation. Guess it was our turn again." She opened her car door, but stopped part of the way out. "Are you sticking around?"

Andy nodded. "I'll be meeting the team here in about an hour. We have new location procedures to talk over."

Gia caught her breath. Now that she had been flushed from the cover of her office, that made their house the next prime target…again. "Let's eat lunch and you can tell me about your insane life experiences that make this," she waved her hand around, "seem like high school drama."

He snorted as he followed her into the house. It was quiet which meant her extended family had found more fun to get into without her. She smiled. They deserved the best. And she couldn't help but be grateful no one was around to question what was happening at the offices and worry over the situation. They'd find out tonight at dinner.

"Nothing about private security is any less severe than the military operations I've engaged in. The enemy is usually unknown, the timing is a surprise, and life of some kind is always on the line, but on a smaller scale."

"Didn't you want to be done with the never-ending stress of your life always being in danger?" She'd trade the stress of unwanted surprises in a heartbeat. It seemed like a no-brainer to her, but she didn't want to insult him.

"They say when you find something you're good at to stick with it, so I did." He shrugged and joined her at the counter to make himself a sandwich.

"And your family doesn't worry?"

"They understand I do what I need to do in order to keep my life on track."

Huh. That was an interesting way to phrase that. How was putting your life in danger for strangers a way of keeping "life on track"? "Of the far-flung places you have no doubt traveled to in your career, what was your favorite?"

Andy plopped a slice of cheese on top of the pile of lunch meat. "An island unavailable to tourists in the French Polynesian archipelago called Mai'ao. They are deeply suspicious of foreigners and very few outsiders are ever invited. When anyone pops up, the whole island knows instantly and tosses them out. One of the easiest security trips I ever took, because everyone on the island was doing my job for me."

That kind of life was another world away. Gia pressed her sandwich together, then took her plate to the table. Bet they didn't eat cold cuts there. World travel was on her bucket list. She and her parents had mainly spent their vacations in Brazil, apart from the odd cruise here and there. Since neither of them preferred cold climates, they'd never spent any time in the snow and ice.

That had been part of the appeal of Denver. It was so opposite to New Orleans. Everything about her life in Colorado was meant to be a diversion, a life separate from what she'd known and became entrenched in. Xander wasn't that, was he?

She shoved the thought from her mind. The distance was messing with her again.

"And in the military, did you get stationed internationally?"

He swallowed his bite and shook his head. "I did a tour abroad, but mostly stayed stateside. My squad was based in North Carolina while I was active."

"You were one of the elites then. It's hard to have extensive military experience if you are always here." He was a puzzle. His vague answers did nothing to satisfy her curiosity of him. He'd endeared himself to her at the driving range and confused the mess out of her with his display in the car. It had been him acting, she was sure. She wanted to know more. "Give me something, Andivo. It's okay to let people get to know you, isn't it?

Andy studied her. "Yes, I was on an elite squad which is why I'm very good at what I do. I have a special skill set in intelligence and I'm lucky that I've found a place for it outside the military. My job is to assess risk and avoid it or stop it. If I do my job right, it's not supposed to be dangerous. Lives are only in danger if I trust or assume too much."

She understood his meaning. They wouldn't be discussing his personal life anymore. "In your professional assessment, how long do you think this is going to go on?"

He sat back. His broad frame making the chair look small. "Your deadline is soon. Then, the fight heads overseas. Whoever this person is has no reason to continue the personal attacks since the job is finished and out of your hands."

The relief felt good. "The sooner I'm done, the better."

His head cocked slightly. "Theoretically."

And the dread came back with force. "Someone might have it out for me or Joey indefinitely."

"People are very passionate about green space and nature. Also, you're the daughter of a very visible power couple." He set his hand gently on her arm and leaned forward. "I don't know that you'll be able to fly under the radar in your lifetime."

The words came like an elbow to her chest. Her parents had told her that in veiled terms, but hearing it from an outsider who made it his life work to analyze this kind of thing really drove it home. He was right. And she'd tried so hard to live as if she could have a low-key life.

What a fool she'd been. Embarrassment heated her cheeks. How was she edging up on thirty and just now realizing the truth about her life? He probably thought her some spoiled naive rich girl. What if they all did? The whole world could be laughing at her.

Her stomach churned violently. She tried to nonchalantly excuse herself from lunch to get started on work. She opened her laptop and typed her name into the internet search bar, something she'd trained herself not to do. The headlines touted the latest on the office getting picketed. But one article stood out.

An architectural defense site laid out the mud they'd seen slung around about the project. Then went into great detail about the laws, preservation code, and so on that resorts had to follow to even get approved to build.

Finally, someone who was knowledgeable.

The author finished up by saying Venha had a history of deeply respecting the area they moved into and hoped with this new project in Rio that they would continue to show the cultural insight they'd been known for.

Wow. Did Joey know about such high praise? She copied the link and emailed it to him with a quick note asking how he was. She abandoned her usual attempt to shield him from her emotions and told him she missed him so much.

Inspired, she pulled the paper plans from her bag and laid them on the drafting table. The light above shown like a spotlight on the page. She'd felt for a while that something was missing.

Something was.

In her fear of getting it wrong and messing up the resort, she'd stuck to what she knew of other resorts and how they did things. But that wasn't what Venha was known for. That wasn't what Rio needed.

It needed an oasis that preserved as much nature and cultural history as possible. The resort shouldn't be a hub of western culture with a hint of Brazil. It should be all Brazil with enough conveniences to make visitors from around the world comfortable. She ripped off a fresh piece of paper and smoothed it onto the board. After a moment of acknowledging the excitement of a blank page, she hunched over the board to bring a new concept to life. When she was done, no one would be able to complain that Rio's culture had been abandoned. Time to let her creativity run wild.

Chapter 12

Finally, he regained his mental capacity and ability to breathe. His prison training kicked in. "Everyone wants to know where it is. If I hand it over, what do I get out of it?"

The pressure of the gun eased a fraction. "To live."

Xander clicked. "But if I die, the information dies with me and that wouldn't work in your favor."

"Just tell me where the hard drive is and the boss will give you three percent of the cut."

A hard drive. Okay, now they were getting somewhere. "Ten."

A loud whack was followed by the big guy dropping to the ground. Above him stood a panting Linc holding his hockey boot bag.

Linc's eyes were wild, his chest heaving. "You forgot your phone on the table. Gia called."

Xander shot to his fcct. "Linc, you're a lifesaver. Thanks for not using the taser." He leaned over the unconscious guy and snapped a few photos of his face and tattoos. Then he fished in his pockets and grabbed his wallet, ID, cash, credit cards. The phone wouldn't be of much use since it was locked with a number code, so he smashed it into the gravel.

When he looked up, Linc stared at him open-mouthed. "I have so many questions."

Xander glanced around. "I don't know that I have any answers, but we need to get out of here in case this guy has a buddy nearby."

A few more questions might have gotten him the answers he needed, but he had more information than he started with. The idiot had gotten impatient and made the mistake of jumping him in public. Seemed too amateurish for a hit.

Whose hard drive would he have known about? "He told me?"

It didn't make sense, but these guys would be back for him. And he'd better have an answer the next time or they might actually kill him for being useless.

The night out ended with Linc following him to his house to make sure there weren't any other nasty surprises awaiting him. Xander gave him the all-clear and sent him home with strict instructions to stay in touch regularly in case whoever was after Xander went after Linc by association. Alone, his anxiety got the better of him and sent him into a full-blown attack like he hadn't seen in months. No number of exercises or other mental tricks stopped its onslaught.

When he could breathe again, he scrambled for his notebooks. Someone thought he had information from prison. His therapist had him writing memories and triggers from his stay in prison to help him cope with his anxiety. The only person he'd really formed a relationship with had been his first cellmate, Jerry Sorentino.

Abandoning the notebooks, he searched Jerry on the internet. Jerry had been dead for three and a half years. There wasn't much information on him. He might as well have been a ghost. It had to be someone else.

Xander spent the rest of the dark hours searching every name of the criminals he'd met in prison and their backgrounds. None of them did he know well enough for an outsider to assume they'd tell him about a hard drive.

And with what on it? And why come after him now?

When dawn came, he changed his t-shirt and drove to the office. The exhaustion would strike hard, but he had things to do. His work email had a response from one of the long-haired guys who had taken his workshop earlier in December. He wanted to stop by this morning.

Xander texted him to say he'd meet him at Mother Hen's at 8:30 AM. At 8 AM, he got a text saying he would be there. The meet-up went quickly and the guy was gone with the money and two shirts in minutes. Xander grabbed a couple muffins for Reggie on his way out the door. The longer he stayed, the more likely Lucy was to engage him in conversation. She'd already asked him why he looked so bad.

Reggie showed up ten minutes early, talkative and ready to dumpster dive. Carl and Regina had agreed to let him continue working so long as he stayed out of trouble and his grades didn't fall. They visited four different work sites and had the back of the vehicle packed full by lunch time.

They dropped all the supplies off at the office and—on a whim—went back out to two more dumpsters so they'd be well supplied for a couple of weeks, at least.

By the time they reached the office a second time, Xander couldn't clear the fog from his brain. He sent Reggie home instead of accepting his offer to build the kids' kits together.

The intense relief that washed over him as Reggie left was quickly curbed by the presence of two uniformed officers hiking their heavy belts up over their paunches outside the cruiser in the front. They glanced down the sidewalk but back up at his office door.

Now was not the time for this. He muttered an expletive. They could be here for any number of reasons. He could slip out back and claim to have not seen them.

The knock at the door came too soon. Criminals ran. He had nothing to be ashamed of. He hoped. Swinging the door open, he greeted them.

"Good afternoon, officers. Can I help you?"

One nodded. "You Alexander Reinerman, owner of Reclaim That?"

"Yes, sir." He motioned for them to come in.

"I'm Officer Barley and this is Officer Calfi. Someone broke into and vandalized the Newmans Men's Mission over in Lakewood last night," Officer Barley said.

"I'm sorry to hear that," Xander murmured. It had nothing to do with his current issues.

Officer Calfi stuck a picture out. "You happen to recognize anyone in this picture?"

The photo was a pixelated shot of the tops of two heads covered in knit caps. Their clothes were dark except for the very clear Reclaim That long-sleeved t-shirts they both wore. Portions of their face and neck exposed dark skin.

Xander shook his head. "I did a few workshops at the mission with my non-profit The Upcycled Life over the past three months. I have lists of the attendees, but that might not provide you any insight. T-shirts are easy to pass along. The only help I can give you is that I only give those shirts out to people who have sold something on my Reclaim That website. I have a list of those people and their contact information if that might help you."

Officer Barley leveled a squinted stare at him. "Criminals can be thoughtless, but their matching t-shirts being the only identifying article of clothing seems deliberate. Can you think of anyone who would be trying to send you a message, Mr. Reinerman?"

He swallowed. "Like an actual message?" He had about point two seconds to decide if he was going to involve the police.

Officer Barley widened his stance. "You could say that."

Officer Calfi pushed another photo toward him. The spray-painted message said, "Give us what the doctor ordered."

The doctor? Now he really didn't know who they meant. And he, for sure, would end up dead in their territory.

"Want to tell us why these guys who we suspect are members of a Denver gang are trying to get in touch with you?" Officer Barley asked.

"Over the past few weeks, I've been receiving anonymous messages saying that I'm a target for someone and to not let them get me alone. I disregarded them at first as pranks, but then last night a man tackled me in the parking lot of George's, held a gun to my head, and told me to tell him where the hard drive was. He was so sure I knew." Xander scrubbed his eyes that burned with a lack of sleep.

Officer Calfi folded his arms. "And you didn't report this, why?"

"This seemed very obviously about something that happened in prison. There wasn't an actual crime. Just a threat about something they thought I knew from my time in prison. What are the cops going to do about it?"

Officer Barley grunted. "Well, there's a crime involving this homeless shelter and it seems someone else wants to know what you know, so the police are involved whether we can do anything or not."

"Now you can make sure I don't turn up dead for something I don't have any clue about." He was needling these cops, but he also did want them to look out for him if they were going to mess around in his business.

Calfi raised his eyebrows. "Give us all your contact information and we'll be in touch. We'll need for you to stay in the area, so we can call you into the station for more questions when they come up."

Reassuring.

They turned to leave his office.

A niggling thought wormed its way to the surface. "Hey, do you guys have any information on Jerry Sorentino? It'd be really helpful in keeping me alive a little longer."

Barley jotted the name down. "We don't, but we'll look into it. Thanks for the lead."

As they ducked into their cruiser casually, Xander bent over his knees. All the air in the room had gone out with them. More than one group of what looked like gangs was after him. An explanatory note from his anonymous overseer would be nice right about now—a clue of some sort to keep him from reliving the hell he experienced in prison of trying not to get killed for no good reason.

He regained control and locked up the office. By the time he set the door alarm at the house, he had just enough energy to stuff some food in his mouth and fall into his bed. In his dreams, wave after wave of criminals came after him. He narrowly escaped.

In a panicked sweat, he woke up. "Give us what the doctor ordered." His thoughts raced. He hadn't seen any doctor but Ed, his mom's psychologist, which had been highly coincidental. The one time he visited a therapist for himself in the past few months hadn't been anything to speak of, a favor to Gia who went regularly. The prison infirmary had checked on him once or twice the whole time he'd been there. It couldn't have been that.

Except when he'd been sliced open from armpit to hip about to be gutted like an animal.

One minute he was in the prison yard enjoying the fresh air, back to the fence as far away from the staked-out groupings of the prison gangs as he could be. Then something outside the fence drew his attention away from carefully watching the orchestrated dance. Suddenly, he was pinned on the ground by heavy hands and sharp knees, the guys on top of him shouting about invasions and tyranny.

Bodies bounced against each other.

Shouting.

Screaming.

A blistering pain that made him blackout.

That's when the panic attacks started in earnest.

The infirmary staff stitched him up to save his life, but the pain of being sliced open and sewn back together blinded his other senses, scattering his memories. Had he been conscious? When he came around, he was in the infirmary for all of an hour or two before they discharged him to sleep on his wooden plank of a cell bed, bandaged and sore.

His fingers followed the line of his scar, still puckered at the top. His journals were filled with triggers and thoughts surrounding the attack but he'd never made sense of it. Why had he been sliced open in broad daylight? Who had stopped them from finishing the job? Why his side and not his vital organs if they wanted to kill him so badly?

"Never take your eye off the ball," Jerry had said in his attempts to relate prison yard politics to a soccer field so Xander would understand.

Jerry would have been able to read the situation like a book, explaining the synchronized movements of the gangs in the yard or deciphering the micrography he'd received on a "kite" from another cell. Xander had received about two years of education from Jerry before losing his information source completely and attempting to survive on his own.

Xander hadn't joined any of the gangs, citing his religion— one of the few exceptions the gangs would make. He didn't hide a mobile phone in his rectum or razors in his upper lips. Perhaps he'd brought the violence on himself, or—the way he saw it—he avoided the trading of his soul and the additional violence that came from a prison gang. In a way, he'd suffered without the protection of others, but he'd survived, though not without scars.

Hauling himself from his bed, he showered and ate again. The house was so quiet without Gia he couldn't stand it. Her presence empowered a room. His chest ached from missing her. When he dialed her number, it went straight to voicemail. The distance felt too great between them.

He grabbed an apple for the road and went back to the office.

Mindlessly, he packed together the kids' kits he'd designed until he ran out of the supplies. His computer sat, taunting him. Surely, there were answers in the depths of the internet for his predicament, but he didn't even know where to start. He was the cartoon staring up at the piano falling on his head. And he hated it.

Chapter 13

It was Saturday, but that did not stop Gia from copying the new plans she'd finished late last night and sending them over to the rest of her team. They wouldn't see them until Monday which gave her too much time to second-guess her decision. Drawing up a completely new revision of the outdoor space was a huge gamble so late in the game, especially since they'd already approved most of the last set she'd had them look at.

She blew out a breath.

Her nerves needed a diversion. Downstairs, her family loudly breakfasted in several different rooms. She parked herself at the breakfast bar next to Uncle Ronaldo, three pages deep into a newspaper.

"What do you hear from that man of yours?" he rumbled.

"He was out with his brother last night. Said he'd call me sometime today to catch up," she said. He'd better block out a chunk of time, because she had things to talk about.

Uncle Ronaldo turned the page. "Are you going to tell him about the dead animals with your name on it?"

Her name on it? That was a tidbit Andy failed to mention yesterday during their escape from the office. Her fingers pressed into her eyes. "I'd be upset if something like that happened to him and he didn't mention it to me. It might have him on the next flight down here to save the day though."

"I thought women loved it when men dropped everything for them." Uncle Ronaldo moved his paper to the side, frowning. "What do women want?"

Her superstar uncle, a professional *futbol* player for Brazil, who'd had countless women vying for his attention over the years was asking her about what women wanted? She burst out laughing.

He scrunched his face. "Were you being facetious?" He turned the page. "I don't get kids' humor these days."

"No." She sighed. "He just has a lot going on and can't get away right now. And, frustratingly, there isn't anything any of us can do to fix this. Andy and Amos are professionals at this and haven't managed to crack it yet."

"Well, he obviously loves you, so keep him updated. Nothing puts the brakes on a long-distance relationship faster than not sharing your day-to-day with each other. Trust him to not overreact."

She didn't know what to believe anymore. It took her a minute to notice the moms huddled in the corner of the kitchen, whispering. Dread sank from her heart all the way through to her stomach.

She called over to them. "What is it, Ma? Bad news?"

Ma glanced at her and offered her a worried smile, then looked behind Gia to the family room where Cara, Breno, and Antia worked on a puzzle. Ma motioned Gia into the group.

"Joey called. He was robbed at knife point in Portugal. They took his credit card, cash, and passport. Thankfully, he's unharmed." Ma leaned in. "Cara doesn't know and I don't think that she should. It'd just make her more depressed."

Neves crossed her arms. "Antia and Sara say she's never around. She says she will meet them, but flakes out."

"I've been thinking about setting up a girls' outing. Sounds like tonight needs to be the night." Gia bit her lip. Wonder how much notice Andy needed to work an evening shift. "She hasn't really seemed to want to let me in on how she's feeling. I'm not sure I can help her."

Judita rubbed Gia's arm, the warm touch a comfort. "She may not need help. She may want you there, sitting with her in her grief and happiness. You can't understand entirely what she's going through having lost both parents too early, but you can listen. Having you be fully present can be the best show of love."

Girls' night, it was. Maybe a few bowls of queso and chips would loosen Cara up.

As Gia walked over to make herself a plate for breakfast, the realization hit her. She'd never truly believed that being there was enough for her family, not deep down. Love had a price tag, a to-do list attached to it.

That was why she'd always lugged around the endlessly heavy guilt, wasn't it?

Something inside pushed her to try to fix the situation. It's all she'd ever done. That wouldn't change overnight.

She yanked out her phone to text Andy about him watchdogging their girls' night. Then she took her plate over to where her cousins hunched over the puzzle table.

"Cara. Antia. Girls' night. Tonight. 6:30."

Breno walked to the top of the basement stairs. "Girls are out. TVs are ours tonight, brothers."

Shouted cheers echoed up the stairwell. Breno smirked. "Have a nice time, ladies."

Antia snorted. "Like you guys haven't been dominating the TVs and game consoles every night."

Cara smiled at Breno's offense. "Too easy a target," she murmured. "I can't come tonight, but you girls have a great time."

"No, no. You can't back out. Antia and Sara leave a few days after the holidays. This is our only chance." Gia wasn't sure that was entirely true, but she was desperate to keep Cara on the hook.

Antia threw a grape from her plate at Cara. "No back outs. Family first."

Cara's argument scrolled across her face. Gia cocked her hip and the protest died on Cara's lips. "Okay. Family first."

"Good. You can wear something from my closet so you don't have to go home." Gia planned on keeping her busy as much of today as possible so Cara's disappearing act didn't get center stage tonight.

When Cara focused on the puzzle again, Gia motioned to Antia and mouthed, "Watch her."

Antia nodded.

A few minutes later, Gia's phone vibrated.

Andy's text read, *Name the time and place.*

Gia replied, *The house at 6:00. We'll leave at 6:30.* She didn't have any good ideas for what they would do yet, but she had the day to think about it.

Roger, was his reply.

She spent the rest of the morning moving from room to room to interact with her family. The moms and cousins especially seemed keen to engage Cara, keeping her nearby so she didn't take off. Their love for her was on full display as they laughed and teased with her.

During their late lunch as Gia sat back soaking in the loud and hilarious conversations around her, she understood what Judita meant. None of these people had to do anything for her to love them. Their presence was a comfort and being themselves was enough for her.

With lunch cleaned up and Cara fully engrossed in trying to beat Silva in interactive tennis, Gia sneaked away to the library to call Xander.

His face popped up on her screen with the biggest smile she'd seen from him in a while. Her doubts about them vanished.

"Hey, baby. It's so good to see your face," Xander said. "How are you? And I want the truth." His tender expression made her heart ache.

His probing opened the dam. The last day and a half of stress and the inspiration that came from it flooded out in one long story. "And tonight, we're taking Cara out to see if that helps her open up. I've been so busy finishing Joey's project that I haven't had as much time with her as I've wanted and I'm trying not to blame myself for her distance, but…"

"You do."

The defeat came out in a huff. "Yeah."

"I do it, too." His voice was soft, his expression vulnerable. "It feels impossible to accept being pushed away by family when you were raised believing family is everything."

This was why she loved this man. No judgment. No lecture. No solution to fix something she barely understood. Just understanding.

"I'll let you know how tonight goes. Now, you tell me what is happening with you."

Xander ran his hand through his hair, creating the disheveled look that had her humming in pleasure. "Well, things have gotten a little…dicey recently."

His tone set off warning bells. "How so?"

Her panic grew as he relayed the alarming train of events.

"Xander, call Daddy. See if he can contact the private detectives from Denver he used to use for you or at least get you some security. What if someone gets pissed enough to pull the trigger?" Her voice pitched higher as she went. Flashbacks to his body in the ER bed earlier in the year had her heart pounding in her ears. She'd barely known him then, but even Joey had seen right through her concern to her growing attraction to Xander.

His lips lifted in a tired smile. "I'll keep it in mind, baby. I have to play this right or I'm going to be inviting more trouble."

"Or dead."

He wiped his hand over his face, his tone resigned. "I can't afford private security or a private detective right now. And I'm not going to ask your parents to foot the bill."

The arguments built in her mind ready to blast him for his stubborn hypocrisy. If she'd done the same thing, he'd lose his mind.

"I thought about not telling you, because I didn't want to worry you. But you deserve to know. You're the love of my life and I want you to share all your news with me, too."

Uncle Ronaldo's words from that morning smacked her in the face. She trusted Xander to not overreact and here she was about to bodyslam him with her frustration. Daddy couldn't be the savior for Xander's every problem or hers.

Her boiling anger reduced to a simmer. "Just don't let your pride keep you from getting help. I'll pay for it or loan you the money for you to pay back, if you think it's taking charity. Whatever keeps you alive so I can love you longer."

He tilted his head. His handsome face lifted in a huge grin. "Babe, that's the sweetest thing anyone has ever said to me."

She huffed at him, not ready to forgive his stubbornness yet. But when he raved about her new design for the hotel's outdoor space, she eased up on him. The long distance was driving her mad, intensifying all her emotions but especially the bad ones.

They were saying their goodbyes when a flash of movement out the window caught her eye.

Cara was sneaking to her car.

"Gotta go." Gia hit End and sprinted outside, barefoot. "Where are you going?"

"Ah!" Cara jerked and whirled around, her eyes big. "Oh, uh. I was going to go home and grab a few things for tonight."

Mm hm. "I'm sure we've got it here. Or Antia and Sara can bring theirs. What do you need?"

"My phone charger, my heels, and my credit card." She fished around through her purse. "Oh, here's my charger."

"I'll pay and you can wear those red heels of mine you love," Gia said. They made her so happy and confident, Gia debated giving them to her. But it kept her coming back to Gia's closet which Gia loved. Cara was the closest thing to a sister Gia had ever had, and Joey her brother. She'd do anything for them.

"I'm not really feeling the red heels today." Cara pushed the hair from her face. Dark circles rimmed her eyes, her skin pale in contrast. She'd lost a lot of weight in the last few months. Gia longed to pull her into her arms as if that'd make all her troubles disappear and soothe her grief.

She held out her hand instead. "Let's go see if I have anything you want. If not, we have Ma and Judita's shoe collections to look through. It could take us a while."

Cara slowly stretched out her hand to take Gia's. For those brief moments while they walked into the house with Cara's hand tucked under her arm, everything felt normal again. Like there wasn't a widening chasm between them that couldn't be bridged. Maybe their sisterhood could survive this overwhelming grief, after all.

"I'm sorry I haven't been home more. This project Joey left me is…" How did she say it without ragging on Joey? "A true challenge. I haven't done anything like it in so many years."

"I understand. He warned me he was going to ask you to finish the project. He's a visionary like that." Cara squeezed her hand. "I miss that giant goon. I should have gone with him. He offered to get us both out of town, but I thought I should be home looking for a job so I don't waste my life being a leech." Her derisive snort shook her body. "No one wants me right now."

Gia paused at the entrance to her closet while Cara flopped onto the bed. "So, join him." Cara waved a hand toward her. "I'm serious. Buy a ticket and meet him over there. Don't have regrets on top of grief, Cara. Life is too short. No one hires around the holidays. Come back refreshed and hit the ads hard in the New Year."

A guttural noise came from the bed which Gia interpreted as conversation over. Buying a ticket herself to join Joey sounded like bliss right now. Escaping this stalker nonsense would be worth every penny.

She made a note to talk to Ma about convincing Cara to meet Joey in Portugal. He'd be there until the embassy could issue him an expedited passport. The more she mulled over the idea, the better she liked it. International travel could be just the thing to help her.

Gia stepped from her closet with two options she thought Cara would like best. Cara stared glassy eyed, then declined them. Eight options later, Gia gave up and fell onto the bed beside Cara. They said nothing as they lay there staring at the ceiling. When she finally thought of something to say, she turned to find Cara asleep.

It lasted only a few minutes until Antia and Sara burst into her room with their arms full of everything they'd need to get ready.

"Look what Tia Judita gave us to wear tonight," Sara squealed, dumping shirts and bottoms on the bed. Antia followed with dresses and shoes.

Cara shifted with a groan. "Can we go somewhere that allows jeans and t-shirts? Getting dressed up is so…" Her nose scrunched. "Much unnecessary work. And I'd argue that we might have a better time because we're comfortable."

Gia, Sara, and Antia stared for a second. "No," they said at the same time.

And for the next two hours, they proved Cara completely right. Getting fancy was a ton of work, but way more fun when done together. Gia straightened her hair for the occasion and Sara did everyone's makeup. By seven, they were finally ready and descended the staircase carefully in their heels.

Daddy stood next to the front door, chatting with Andy who straightened when they came downstairs as if they were his dates for the evening. Gia's heart sank. She'd forgotten about their babysitter. For a brief second, she wanted to shake him into telling her what she needed to know about Cara so they could actually enjoy their evening and be done with the secrets.

The others rounded into the kitchen.

"Mm. He is a beautiful man," Antia said in Portuguese to their group.

A grunt came from Breno, standing in front of the open refrigerator. "Please wait until I leave the room before you lust out loud."

Antia wiggled her fingers at her brother as he disappeared into the other room with a cold drink in hand. The girls said their goodbyes to the rest of the family and piled into a GetThere vehicle with a driver. While they'd gotten ready, they talked about the plan for the evening. Since they wanted to try as many different places as possible, they decided on a progressive dinner.

An appetizer, dinner, and dessert, each at a different restaurant. Live music or a live show would be a bonus.

First up, Sara chose for them to have an appetizer on the roof of a hotel overlooking the Mississippi River. The Christmas lights added an intoxicating sparkle to the old-style buildings. Wreaths, Christmas trees, candles, and garland captivated every window and doorframe. It was the one thing most of the city could agree on.

Cara stayed quiet, letting everyone dominate the conversation, unless asked a pointed question. Her sullen attitude grated on Gia, but the fear of chasing her away had her holding her tongue. She didn't have to pretend to be okay, but she could talk about it and let them in on her feelings.

Andy sat with another guy she'd never seen before. Their backs were to the wall so the whole rooftop was in their field of vision. If she hadn't been looking for him, she wouldn't have noticed him. They blended right in.

Finished and paid, they walked the three blocks to Adolfo's and had a drink at Apple Barrel Bar downstairs while they waited to be seated. Although they'd been to the small restaurant a number of times since arriving, Antia had begged to go again. The steak and special house sauce were an easy choice to agree to.

Cara had racked up four glasses in front of her by the time they were ready to be seated. She told them she'd meet them upstairs at the table and slowly worked her way through the crowd to the bathroom. Gia only needed to glance around to see Andy and his friend already seated at a table with plates of food in front of them. How had they gotten in without standing in line like everyone else? Adolfo's didn't take reservations.

When Cara returned, she forgot about them as Sara and Antia told stories about their failed dating attempts over the last couple of years. The dating scene in Rio was dismal, but the male tourists made going out a cheap, fun event. Her cousins hadn't ever struck her as the freeloading types so picturing them angling for free food and drinks by tossing their long, dark hair and dancing with strangers had her enraptured.

As they paid their bills and waited for Cara's barely touched plate to be boxed up, Gia had an idea. "Hey, how about we grab a few desserts to go and take a nighttime river cruise?"

Cara shrugged, her expression bored though her eyes never stopped roaming around the room. Antia and Sara glanced at each other.

"I thought we were going to that sundae shop," Antia said.

Sara nodded. "Yeah, that sounded really good."

Gia squinted at them. Antia loved the paddleboats on the river and Sara didn't love American ice cream. "What's going on?"

Sara fidgeted with her purse in her lap. "We had a plan, that's all."

"It's called flexibility," Cara said with a smirk, her finger jabbing into Sara's arm. "Live a little. You should be more spontaneous."

"It's not that we can't be spontaneous," Antia said. She glanced at Sara. "We told everyone that we'd be going to the sundae shop, so we want to honor that."

"Aw, it's cute that you two have to check in with your parents on everything." Cara lifted her drink to her lips. "You should try having no parents, like me. Then, you could do whatever you wanted." Her words were a stab to the heart. She muttered something about overprotective watchdogs and leashes.

"It's not our parents that are worried," Sara said, receiving a sharp elbow from Antia.

Gia tapped the table with her finger. "Explain."

Antia offered her an apologetic smile. "Your parents want you to be safe while we're out."

But Sara's expression said there was more.

"Sara?"

Her face crumpled slightly. "Andy gave us an approved list of places to choose from for tonight. We promised to stick to the plan, so you wouldn't be exposed to whoever is out to get you. It's for your safety."

Cara's loud laugh made Gia jump as her hand landed on Gia's shoulder. "It always comes back to Princess Gia needing protection from something. Sheltered and spoiled since day one."

Gia pressed her lips together, fighting to keep her anger in check. "I didn't ask to be targeted by the stalker. Joey didn't tell me what he'd been going through before he left."

"That's because he thought you wouldn't take the project for him if you knew you were going to be targeted, especially after your drama with Bronc." Cara rolled her eyes. "Come on. He knows you better than that."

Heat rose in her cheeks. Cara had gone way too far this time. Shifting in her seat, she faced her full on. The verbal blow she was ready to deliver paused on the tip of her tongue. For the first time, she noticed Cara's bloodshot eyes and dilated pupils.

"What do you have to say, Your Highness? We're all awaiting your treasured words with baited breath," Cara said, clasping her hands to her chest.

Gia grabbed Cara's wrist to look at her arm. "Are you doing drugs?"

Chapter 14

His video call with Gia interrupted the stare down he had been having with his computer. Their conversation was rocky, at best, but it had ended on a tender note. Words didn't soothe like a hug or simple touch could. And they had to spend a lot of words on calming each other down over the past few months.

If he never had to do long distance again, it would be too soon.

His arms ached for Gia to be in them, to soothe the paranoia and fatigue that haunted him at the moment.

After he dropped into bed that night, his phone pinged.

You coming to Mom & Dad's for Christmas brunch in the AM? Avri texted.

Xander muttered a colorful word into the darkness. This weekend kept getting better. Mom had invited him weeks ago to their annual Christmas brunch that they held for their neighbors and coworkers. A twenty-seven-year tradition that—of course—hadn't stopped because he was in prison. Instead of giving gifts to friends, Xander's parents threw a party to feed the families of the people they felt obligated to invite.

To be fair, a small portion of the attendees were obligatory. The rest had been invited because they ranked high on his parents' list of people who mattered. That he had been re-invited this year, his first Christmas outside, had Xander cautiously optimistic that he was no longer a dark stain on his parents' crisp, white reputation.

Yep. See you at 10:30.

The anxiety of showing up at his parents' tomorrow paled in comparison to what it was he was supposed to be handing over to criminal organizations. Still no word from his anonymous note sender. The thought made him very angry.

In the morning after a fitful sleep, he dressed in a collared shirt and his dark wash jeans. As kids, his parents had always insisted they wear khakis and a collared shirt to this occasion, so undoubtedly that would be what his parents still expected. But he wasn't that same kid who complied with ridiculous external rules in order to please his parents.

He wasn't out to smear it in their faces, but their opinions had no bearing in his life anymore. If he was going to be at an uncomfortable party, he was definitely going to be dressed respectably, but how he wanted to be. On his way to their house, Xander stopped by the store to grab gift bags for the gifts he'd made each family member.

Parked on the street, he stuffed things in the bags. It felt strange to be sitting here, in front of his parents' house for the holidays. He had a lifetime of December memories at this house that were nice, that made this "home for the holidays." Yet five years away and relational distance had transformed him into a visitor, lucky to have an invite to the party.

A knock on his window had him scrambling halfway across the car. Avri's laughing face flashed by as she bent in laughter at scaring him.

If she only knew…

"Yeah, yeah. Very funny," he muttered as he opened his door, dragging his gift bags with him.

When she'd wiped away the tears of laughter, she pulled him into a hug. "I thought you might want someone to walk in with, especially since there are probably a ton of people there you don't know."

How'd he get so lucky with a sister like her? He held her gift out to her. "Here. No use in me taking it in. Merry Christmas."

Avri pushed her glasses up her nose as her eyebrows raised. "What's this? Giving gifts out early?" She took her bag and then stopped with a gasp. "Does this mean you aren't coming Christmas Day?"

Well, that came up a lot faster than he'd hoped it would. Hands stuffed in his pockets, he accompanied her to her car which was parked a few cars down from his. "I hadn't decided yet. Thought I'd bring the gifts today to be safe."

Stopping at her driver's side door, her hand dove into the gift bag. His skills with the tissue paper seriously lacked because it took no time for Avri to extract her three custom cutting boards tied together with a shiny ribbon.

The bag dropped to the ground as her fingers ran over the smooth, stained surface. "Wow," she breathed. "Did you make these yourself?" When she flipped them over, his initials were burned into the back. "These are gorgeous. Thank you."

She set them in her car and hugged him again so tightly he couldn't inhale. But it was perfectly Avri. A string of shrug-offs came to mind about how he didn't know what girls her age liked or that it'd been a long time since he knew what to get anyone as a gift.

Her delight silenced his negativity. "You're welcome."

"Let's go get some of Mom's southwest breakfast skillet before the rest of the crowd gets here." She tucked her arm under his and ushered him safely into the dining room where the feast of a hundred colors and as many flavors crowded the table top.

None of the faces he'd spotted were familiar. The din of talking and laughter was still relatively low since they had arrived ten minutes early. Avri left him in charge of getting her a drink while she went to the restroom.

When she returned, they wandered into the kitchen together. Mom glanced up from plating little egg tarts, fresh from the oven. She yanked off her oven mitt and glided toward them with open arms.

"Merry Christmas, Avri and Alex. I mean, Xander." She wrapped Avri in a hug and kissed her cheeks, then did the same with Xander. Her familiar perfume stole the tension from his chest. Her slight frame felt so delicate in his arms.

"Merry Christmas, Mom. It's so good to see you." He inspected her face, graced with a few more fine lines he hadn't noticed last time he saw her a few months ago. "I put gifts under the back of the tree, but they aren't labeled."

Her pencil-darkened eyebrows drew together. "I hope you didn't spend much. You need to save your money for groceries and necessities."

He'd used his office resources to make his family's gifts this year. It didn't seem enough, but with how slow sales were, it was the best he could do. "It's been a few years since I've been able to have a gift for you under that tree, Mom. It's a pleasure."

Her eyes instantly watered in that way only moms' eyes can, then blinked the tears furiously away. "You two get out of here while I finish putting food out. Go eat your fill."

She shooed them out. Maybe Mom had gotten more lowkey over the years, but from the looks of the presentation, she had buckled down to make the appearing feast look effortless. She couldn't fool her kids who'd been forced to help every year to pull it all off.

Dad certainly hadn't ever done more than carry a dish or two when asked by his frantic hostess wife.

Xander sipped his punch. Where was Dad?

Avri politely made introductions as they conversed their way towards the basement stairs where, as kids, they'd hid away from the stuffy adult conversation and the pretentious laughter of their parents.

They'd almost made it when the back door slammed, closing Linc and Dad into the hallway. Dad made a sharp gesture as he whispered into Linc's ear. Neither really seemed happy.

Linc nodded hello to some people nearby as he wiped his boots on the door rug. Dad started into his presidential routine of shaking hands and welcoming the crowd. He could turn it on, on a dime.

Everything inside Xander wanted to slink away lest Dad see him and his smile evaporate.

Linc's eyes scanned the rooms. A huge smile took over his dopey face when his gaze landed on Avri and Xander right outside the basement door. He motioned toward the food and then nodded back at them.

He'd meet them in the basement with his plate of food.

Avri and Xander laughed as they cleared the stairs. In their twenties and still stealing away from the crowd—some things didn't need to change.

"You guys been hiding in the basement every year in my absence?" Xander said, sinking onto the couch.

Avri shook her head. "With just the two of us, it was harder to hide from Mom and Dad. They liked to have us around as buffers to talk about our exciting lives." She rolled her eyes and scrolled through the TV menu in search of a good movie to watch.

His snort shook his chest. "Might have been to avoid the more unpleasant topics like their suffering mental health and the greatest shame of their eldest son in prison." Did other people talk about their family member in prison ever? Probably, if they actually cared about him.

Avri gave a sympathetic hum as she chose one of the new Jumanjis.

"What'd I miss?" Linc stomped down the steps. He had never been the quiet one out of the four of them. Hockey suited his personality beautifully. Falling back onto the sofa, he plopped his socked feet on the coffee table with a loud "Ah."

With his cup raised, he made eye contact with Xander. "To surviving another Christmas party…" His emphasis was not lost on Xander.

Avri lifted her cup higher. "To Xander's presence saving us from forced, awkward conversation with people who have 'heard all about' us and seen so many pictures of us when we can't reciprocate the nicety."

Xander looked back and forth between them. "To your good health…"

They laughed and sipped their drinks.

"If it makes you feel any better, Xander, they never hid your pictures or took you off the Wall of Fame. But you're right. I think Mom and Dad have been avoiding hard topics our entire lives, and we learned that from them," Avri said, glancing at him and then back at the screen.

"I don't think Mom and Dad told anyone I was a hockey player until I'd been featured in a big-name sports magazine for one of my sponsors." Linc shook his head. "Like I was a kid messing around with my life instead of someone who had a legitimate career."

Those family dinners had been so tense when Dad had expressed his concern every chance he had that Lincoln find a career that paid the bills instead of skating around bashing teeth in. Then, he tried to get everyone else to talk to him about it so Linc might start taking life seriously. Dad hadn't ever picked on Xander, because he'd been proud that his son had followed in his coaching footsteps.

Proud, until Xander couldn't be man enough to confess his misdeeds to the court. Who would have thought that pleading "not guilty" would be a reason for your parents to disown you?

"As the youngest, I was lucky enough to get the brunt of the life talks at dinner. 'Avri, choose something you can be proud of.'" She cleared her throat and deepened her voice. "Or 'Choose a career in a respectable field. Don't be like those other airheaded girls who choose the easiest major and then party away their schooling.' Really, it was an honor to listen to all the inspirational speeches."

They laughed, but Xander felt the pain stirring deep down. Pain he'd ignored for most of his life. Had any of them really ever been good enough for their parents? For anyone? Making it to the men's national soccer team coaching staff was confirmation that he was on the right track with his career, his life.

Looking back, it was a crutch.

He was the oldest and supposed to have his life together. It was easy to pin his problems on his past, where the deep-seated doubt and insecurity had developed. It wasn't so easy to root that out and replace his lifelong beliefs with the truth.

If he thought his siblings deserved every happiness in life, then he did, too. A happiness that involved claiming Gia, for richer or poorer.

If he knew she could love him at his lowest, then any high they hit would be a bonus.

Time to go after what he wanted most.

"So Avri," he said. She looked alarmed. "What do you think about solitaire settings for engagement rings?"

A squeal accompanied her bouncing to his side, the movie forgotten. "I've dreamed of this day."

She pulled up a well-known jeweler on her phone so fast it was as if she'd had it bookmarked for the occasion. And, if he wasn't mistaken, Linc moved in a little closer, too.

Interesting. That'd have to be a topic of conversation soon.

By the time they'd surfaced from engagement rings, his earlier confidence was a mere flicker in his mind. He needed to do more research, sell more products, and overall have way more money in his account than he did right now.

"Let's go see if there is any dessert. We should probably show our faces again so they don't think we ate and bailed," Xander said.

Together, they waded into the crowded upstairs

"What are you doing about the thing you are supposed to have?" Linc murmured in his ear amongst the din of the party.

"I told the cops. Now I'm just waiting for a revelation."

Linc shook his head. "Did they agree to protect you?"

"Not even a little bit," Xander said. The subject sent his heart rate into overdrive and he did not need a panic attack in the middle of his parents' party. "What were you and Dad disagreeing about earlier?"

"Money."

Xander motioned for him to continue.

"He's overextended his refinance on the house and wants a loan for some high-risk stocks to invest in that would help pad their retirement. He used a lot of their savings for Mom's mental therapy appointments, but didn't tell her. She's planning on retiring from teaching next year without any knowledge that they are essentially broke. He's trying to make the money back with some high-risk moves that I don't agree with."

Broke.

Dad had been preaching the importance of saving for retirement since he could remember. He'd been diligent to the point of not helping any of his kids pay for university courses because that was money that would be taken from their retirement. The way he presented it was he could pay for college or retirement, and putting his money away for retirement was the only way he could see them not being a burden as they aged.

Xander didn't argue with that. It was their money to do with as they pleased, and he'd earned scholarships to get him through the in-state fees.

Surely, Dad hadn't spent all their money on therapy. He was too conscientious to do that. There had to be more going on.

"So, what are you going to do?"

"I promised him I would talk to my investor guy about the best way to do this. I don't want my parents filing for bankruptcy because of medical costs, but there has to be a better way for them to recoup the losses without such high risk."

"Sounds like Dad might be keeping secrets again," he murmured in Linc's ear.

"My thoughts, exactly."

Chapter 15

Before Cara confirmed it, Gia saw the truth in her eyes, shame and defiance in the same look. The fear slammed into her, knocking the hurtful words from the forefront of her thoughts. Cara was high. There was no other explanation for who this monster inhabiting her mind was.

"Absolutely none of your business." With a hiss, Cara yanked her arm away. "If I were, I'd be justified with the way this past year has been a life from hell."

"Okay. You're right." The ground Gia tread was a thin sheet of ice. If anyone understood the consequences on the body and wouldn't judge, it was her. And Cara knew it. Gia nodded. "It has been one of the worst years."

The pieces fell into place—why Cara had been disappearing, not showing up when she promised to, continuing to lose weight, not having much of an appetite. It wasn't grief alone, as she'd suspected.

Antia recovered admirably. "Let's go get that dessert and go somewhere we can dance. I'm itching to go deaf while I inhale alcohol-tainted body odor and sweat."

As they walked from the restaurant into the cold night air, her mind reeled with one question—how could she be there for Cara best?

When she'd been dating Bronc, under his thumb, she'd dabbled with smoking weed socially and experimented with some pills that scared her so badly she never tried them again. It had given her momentary relief from her harsh reality, made her feel happy before dropping her into the hazy abyss.

The memories couldn't be clearer of stealing away to enjoy it, the anticipation of feeling numb, and the consequences of it all. When she left New Orleans, her new start included going cold turkey on the drugs. Seeing the life drain out of Uncle Angelo in her arms put her whole world and what she wanted into perspective. Cara would have to have that moment, too, or she'd never stop.

The driver took them up and over a few blocks to the sundae shop. No Andy and friend this time, but the shop was small with a few patrons at the tables. They didn't have much to say as they shoveled the ice cream into their mouths. When she finished, she excused herself to the bathroom to text Xander about their night.

At Cara's request, they capped off their girls' night at a jazz club, a fraction classier than the dance club Antia had mentioned. Someone must have texted him the plan, because—like magic— Andy and his friend showed up at the table right next to theirs. They had jackets on over the collared shirts they'd been wearing for the evening. Fit right in to the atmosphere.

Except for exchanging the occasional comment, they had their heads on swivel, nodding to the music. Whenever one of the girls ordered something, one or the other accompanied the waitress to and from the bar with the drinks as if they had a conversation they were desperate to continue.

The music seemed to lift Cara out of the funk she'd been in. Gia watched her hands for shakes or withdrawals of any kind. So far nothing. Her belligerence now gone, the drop would come soon.

How hard would she fall? Would Gia be able to help pick up the pieces?

The music shifted to a slower, more melodic set, propelling Antia and Sara onto the dance floor. Across the table, Cara sat with her eyes closed swaying to the music. Gia moved her chair next to Andy's in the shuffle. His cologne was light but an enticing scent.

"Did you know about the drugs?" she said into his ear.

Andy tilted his head so he looked her straight in the eye. "It's our business to know as much as we can."

The anger swelled in her chest. She hated him a little bit. "So what? You were going to keep it a secret until when? She ended up in a dangerous situation or worse—dead?"

"It isn't a secret we are keeping, Gia. The people who need to know do."

Oh, she loathed his words and everything they implied. Once again, Daddy knew and said nothing. Biting her tongue, Gia stood and weaved her way to the dance floor where she could keep an eye on Cara. The change of location gave her a second of perspective. Maybe they were helping Cara somehow. Maybe they didn't want Gia to be overly stressed on top of the project she'd agreed to.

It wasn't her place to know everything, never had been, but it stuck in her craw that she was exactly what Cara had called her— a naive princess in need of sheltering by everyone from everything. She'd worked so hard at making a way for herself in life, protecting herself, becoming independent and self-sufficient, trying to live up to everything she wanted to be as a woman.

The next morning, the wound was still raw as she pulled on black jeans and a ruffled red blouse to join Ma and Daddy at the charity function they sponsored and served at every year. The door to Cara's guest room was still closed. Would it be too much to hope they'd see her later? Her family had served every year at this event.

Instead of an awkward Christmas party everyone dreaded each year, they served breakfast out of one of their warehouses to the city's homeless and underfed as well as their families, and anyone else they wanted to bring along. At the end, everyone left with a Christmas dinner basket and a bag of necessities. Her parents worked with a half-dozen charities in the city to set this up every year. The charity directors came and enjoyed the meal as well without lifting a finger—something they were not accustomed to.

The cost was astronomical and came mostly out of Ma and Daddy's pocket except for what others pitched in. In addition to food, they gave out grants, scholarships, and paid off medical debt.

Because they'd struggled to make ends meet and having been on the receiving end of a generous hand-up had been a game changer for them.

Both of them.

And that wasn't something they ever wanted to lose sight of.

This year, all of Ma's visiting family wanted in on the event, so a part of them went back to help set up the trays and the others prepped the serving area. Gia nibbled at her lip as she glanced at the door. Cara hadn't showed yet. Her family had done this with them every year since they started, no exceptions. The idea that none of Cara's family would be here this year took some of the wind from her sails.

They had plenty of help, though. The C-level executives of Ma and Daddy's companies, their families, and some of the lower management paraded in to prepare the dinner baskets to give out. A hired company had come in the last night to set up the chairs, tables, and Christmas decorations.

A security team was at the door, and every door, this year, checking people in and looking at IDs. Bright and cheery, Andy appeared at her side after she'd finished shaking hands and wishing everyone a merry Christmas, next to Ma and Daddy. No trace of fatigue from yesterday's late night out showed in his face or general carriage. In his three-quarters-zip green sweater and gray slacks, he fit in perfectly.

"You're going to be serving bacon this morning at the table closest to the kitchen. I'll be serving the sausage on your right side. If people ask, I'm part of your cousin squad. Silva and Breno are the muscle bringing the trays of food to our serving table. You don't go anywhere alone. Okay?" Andy asked, his tone happy.

Fatigue clawed at her chest. She narrowed her eyes. Six a.m. was far too early to be this happy. "You got it, Cousin Andy."

He motioned to the back. "Let's eat before the event starts. I don't want to have to worry about your food or drink being messed with when the crowd arrives."

Typically, once everyone was served, those who were serving plated food for themselves from what was left and had their breakfast scattered amongst everyone. The breakfasters mingled with the executives, talked about the problems they were facing, and sometimes even left with a scheduled interview.

Gia grabbed a plate from the end of the serving table. The serving trays filled fast. Eggs, potatoes, sausage, bacon, grits, pancakes, fruit salad, and cornbread. The whole breakfast lineup made an appearance.

A little something for everyone.

She dished up a small plateful of eggs, bacon, and fruit, enough to jumpstart her energy. Andy took every food she did but in larger portions and a second plate with a couple of the carbs thrown on.

No one would know the kitchen was makeshift, brought in the night before and set up. They sat on a couple of stools pulled up to a prep table near the stoves. A few aproned chefs laughed and traded stories as they prepared the variety of foods. Eating in public had never made her nervous, but eating next to Andy was another stark reminder of the danger awaiting her. Frankly, she was over it. Maybe she didn't want to eat, after all.

She watched as he took the first bite. When he noticed her stare, he stopped chewing. Then with a grin, he stabbed his fork into her eggs and shoved them in his mouth.

"Waiting for me to die?" he said around the food.

What was it with this guy? Such an enigma. He fascinated her. Without blinking, she nodded slowly. "Absolutely, yes."

"We've been watching the whole time." His head tilt had her looking over at a tall, alert man standing off to the side of the stoves. Supervising. "Don't forget to look for the cameras. We beefed up the coverage for today from what is usually in here. We have guys monitoring every angle and people at the door. These guys are hound dogs. We're close to finding the person responsible for this. Then, you can go back to the life you want, instead of worrying about watching your back endlessly," Andy said.

She didn't want to talk about it again, not really. No use in letting her breakfast get cold. She dug in. "Did you run into any trouble last night as you popped in and out of the back doors of places like celebrities?"

"No, everyone cooperated nicely. We had a tiny bit of resistance at the jazz club since we hadn't given any advance notice," he shrugged, but didn't seem annoyed, "but with a little explanation they understood the severity of the need. And they also know how word travels quickly about accommodating security needs. If they want to attract a certain clientele, they need to be flexible with private security being on site."

Gia raised an eyebrow. "You flexed on them by reminding them you could tell other security teams about their compliance or lack of?"

"Professional security is a relatively small world around here. Three, maybe four organizations are actually reputable enough to be used by higher end clients. Most of us run into each other quite a bit around town." Andy smirked. "Would you rather have me slipping dollar bills in their hands, throwing money around like Hollywood half-brain?" He snorted and shook his head. "Now, there's a way to get targeted quick."

"Honestly, I'd never considered it before." She held her hands up to hold back his incredulity. "My parents have kept me out of the limelight. People know who my parents are, but not me and that's how everyone wanted it. It had worked really well for us until recently. In my years living in Golden, I protected myself knowing that my ex-boyfriend might come after me. The danger I feared most wasn't from strangers."

Andy nodded. "It's a new mindset to adjust to, people you don't know wanting you harmed or dead. The stakes are high."

The military had given him a strong dose of that poison to swallow over and over. Not something to dwell on today. She pointed her forked grape in his direction. "What are you doing for Christmas Day? Hopefully not working. We'll be at home all day."

Andy didn't look up from his plate. "I'll see family at some point."

"Good. Because if we have to see you at our place on Christmas Day, you can guarantee you'll be getting beaten in every video game you play with Silva, and Antia is pretty lethal at card games."

"Noted. What about you? What Christmas festivity are you good at?"

She paused. "Skeet shooting." His military training required he be excellent with a gun, but she tossed the challenge out anyway. She hoped she'd get the chance to compete with him in skeet shooting. His type didn't take a day off or prioritize holidays. In her sharpshooting training days as a kid, she'd grown familiar with the way of life. The military guys at the ranges joked and talked like she couldn't understand because she was young, but she heard everything and absorbed their thought processes.

Not everyone valued what she did or prioritized things how her family did. She learned a lot more than sharpshooting in those alleys.

With her plate finished, Gia tossed it into the trash. On her way to the table, she teased Breno and Silva for their aprons and took her place, clicking her tongs in her hand behind the tray of bacon. Everyone took their places as the doors opened and the trickle of hungry people descended on the tables. Christmas wear of every kind passed by. Someone even dressed their baby as a tiny elf.

It wasn't until the line had subsided that she noticed the little elf crying in the corner with her mom pacing and shushing her. The plate at the table nearby sat untouched. Gia wove her way to the mom.

"Hey, I'm Gia."

Up close, the woman's wide eyes and flyaway wisps gave her a desperate look, near tears. "I'm so sorry for the noise. She'll fall asleep soon, I hope. She won't stop crying unless I'm moving."

Gia reached over and patted the tiny baby's back. "The noise isn't a problem. It looks like you haven't eaten. Can I hold her while you finish breakfast?"

A moment of hesitation flickered across her face.

"I won't go far. I just want you to be able to enjoy it while it's hot."

The woman pushed the hair from her tired eyes. "It's not that. There's security everywhere here." She huffed. "I just don't want to inconvenience you or get kicked out."

Gia shook her head. "Neither will happen. You eat your fill and enjoy. I'll keep her on the move to see if she'll sleep. What's your name?"

"Marie. And this is my daughter Audrey," she said as she handed the infant over to Gia.

The tiny body barely had any weight to her, but a warmth and decent lungs.

"Relax, Marie. Please take your time eating. Audrey and I are going to be great," Gia said as the baby cried against her shoulder.

Marie tucked a dirty cloth between the baby and Gia's shirt. "I don't want her getting your clothes messy."

Off Gia walked before Marie could say anything else. She felt so strong under the baby's frailty. Andy broke off his conversation with the security guy near her and walked to her side.

"You stole a baby. Nice." Andy smiled. "And I thought I needed to watch out for others doing the crime."

Audrey wailed.

"Audrey wasn't letting her mom eat, so I took her." Gia lifted Audrey off her shoulder and held her out to Andy. "Here. Can you hold her for a second? Follow me, if you would. I need to talk to someone."

Andy took Audrey without hesitation. "If you're trying to freak me out, it's not going to happen. I've held way more dangerous things than a tiny baby."

Gia tried not to be obvious as she slowly made her way to Charlotte, the director for the at-risk mom and baby charity. When she reached her table, she leaned down to her ear. "Can I see you for a second?"

Charlotte nodded, her straight silver-streaked black hair moving slightly. Gia walked her toward the kitchen. Charlotte fell in step beside her.

"I'm watching a little baby for a mom while she eats. Do you, by chance, have one of those wrap carrier things handy?"

Charlotte's sharp eye picked out the crying Audrey in Andy's arms immediately. Her thin red lips curved into a smile. "You know I drive the best mom-mobile in town. If I can borrow that young man holding the baby, I'll be back in a flash."

They walked over to Andy and he agreed so long as Gia stayed right where he left her, in full view of the other security guards. Gia paced, holding Audrey in different positions to see if she had a preference. Nothing helped.

Poor Marie must have been so frazzled.

Charlotte returned without Andy. With a few flicks of her wrist, the cloth in her hand became a snug cocoon for Audrey, held loosely against Gia's chest.

"Can we make it tighter?" The wrap needed to come with a manual.

Charlotte smiled. "It goes much tighter, but see how Audrey is sucking and gnawing on her fist? She's hungry. I grabbed hypo-allergenic formula from my trunk. Andy is checking with Audrey's mom to make sure it's okay and then we're going to feed her before wrapping her up tight."

Sure enough, Andy came toward them shaking the bottle as he walked. He handed it to Charlotte who propped the baby at an angle by manipulating the wrap in her magic way. The crying stopped the second the bottle nipple touched Audrey's lips. Gia couldn't take her eyes off Audrey's.

"I'll be back in a few minutes," Charlotte whispered in her ear.

There was an intense pride that swelled inside her. She'd managed to help this baby, this mom. This could be her with her baby someday.

The future opened in front of her eyes, shutting the fear and pressure of the present out firmly. She'd get through this all. There was more to live for and to work for than what she had. Her world could change in a moment in the best way.

For the first time, the idea warmed her instead of scaring her. A way forward. Another reason to go there.

Chapter 16

The nerves hit with a full-body current the second Xander pieced together what day it was. Monday morning. Early.

The interview.

Since his heart was already racing, he went out for a run on the same route he'd run one of his first days out of prison. His feet pounded the pavement as if he could punish himself into being someone who never felt the sting of rejection. He couldn't outrun his life then and still wouldn't manage it now.

The guilt washed over him as he reviewed his conversation with Gia last night. She'd been so open and honest about how she felt after finding out Cara's secret drug use. Xander hadn't known Gia had used drugs while she dated Bronc four years ago. It didn't surprise him though. Bronc had a strong, relentless grip on Gia, making her abrupt move to Colorado even less of a spontaneous bolt of fear and more of a desperate plea for a clean start.

They all had a past, didn't they?

So why didn't he feel comfortable telling her about the interview scheduled for today? The job offer wasn't a sure thing. Telling her in words wouldn't get his hopes up any more than they already were, if he were honest with himself. But one negative word from her would bring the whole thing crumbling down around him. His hopes of returning to his career of choice dashed.

He could trust her with his hopes and dreams as concretely as she could trust him. This morning wasn't the time to spring it on her. A cramp in his side drove him to his knees next to a chain-link fence that led to the high school. There on the other side was a track that ovaled a soccer field.

Ironic.

Stretched and still feeling guilty, he picked up where he left off. It wasn't a crime to want a part of his life back and do what he loved. How would his old self have prepared for this interview?

At the house, he grabbed the mail, tossed it on the island counter, and turned on some hype music as he got into the hot shower. It didn't help. It made his nerves worse because he couldn't hear what was going on in the house.

Showered and dressed in his charcoal suit, light blue collared shirt, and dark tie, he sorted through the mail. A plain white envelope with his name on it but no address was in the middle of the junk again.

Finally.

Be something helpful for once.

He ripped the envelope open. To his relief, the writing on the note covered most of the page. He needed answers, now.

They don't care that the cops know about getting your attention. It could get worse. The release date of the information they want is the end of the year. They know that. They'll keep you alive at least until then. No information will be disclosed until closer to that time in order to keep you safe. When they corner you, remind them that they control whether the information gets leaked or not. They simply need to follow my instructions. I will be in touch.

This was madness. Who was setting him up this time? Why was he constantly someone else's fall guy? A Denver gang or two wanted information from him which he wasn't going to get.

Nine days until he was officially on their hit list.

He could run to Gia's and hide under their private security's protection until he thought the storm had passed, but gangs could find him anytime anywhere and he'd always be looking over his shoulder. Gia needed a man who could take care of himself and her, instead of hiding behind her parents. He would be that for her.

His alarm buzzed. Out of time. He grabbed his bag, his lucky one that he took to all his interviews over the years, and drove downtown to the offices. The normalcy of the moment soaked in. The excitement, the fear, the anticipation of if they would like him rushed over him without a hint of anxiety or worry that they'd toss him out because of the scandal he endured. They knew his past already, yet had still contacted him for an interview.

He owed Ronaldo big time. Bringing Xander along to his official *futbol* appointments made him a class act in Xander's book. Ronaldo was a really big deal in Brazil, but he didn't act like he was. The man had character in ways most celebrities would never understand.

Xander double-checked his shirt tail was tucked in as he walked into the lobby. His heart raced in overtime. The building boasted several floors, but his interview was on the second floor in suite B. Glass walls separated him from the receptionist. It wasn't too late to turn around, though.

"I'm here for an interview with Burt Candes," Xander said at the reception desk. His stomach burned with the nerves and for a few seconds thought he might need to excuse himself to the restroom to get control.

The receptionist called to let Candes know and motioned toward the chairs. Xander chose to stand. Frames on the wall told the story of the history of soccer in the United States. Pictures and plaques merged in a timeline leading up to the recent success of the national teams in the under 17 and under 20 teams of the United States Soccer Federation.

"Reinerman, welcome," a low voice called to him.

Turning, he stuck out his hand to greet the short, middle-aged man with white hair walking towards him.

"Burt Candes. Nice to meet you. Come on back." Burt led him through a hallway lined with offices and conference rooms with more plaques, pictures, and framed jerseys hanging on the walls.

He stopped at the entryway to an office with big windows facing the city's interior. "Very cool that you were at the event with Cruz and Cevere in New Orleans recently. How are you connected to them?"

"Cevere is my girlfriend's cousin. He took me to the event where he introduced me to Cruz. They played on the Brazilian national team together. Really nice guys." Sharing his connections felt like name dropping which, for some reason, felt dirty. He was so out of practice with this. How much did he want to reveal about who his girlfriend was if he wanted to get the job based on his own merit? "I didn't know anything about blind soccer before I went. It was truly incredible to learn about."

Burt smiled as he shuffled some papers around on his desk. "Tell me about your coaching experiences and any accomplishments that go with it."

Now this—the facts of the past—he could talk about. "As I listed on my resume, my most recent coaching position was as an assistant coach for the men's team at the University of Colorado. I ran practices, drills, game strategy and logistics, and worked directly with the head coach to oversee weight training and cardio workouts in the off season. The guys and I had a great relationship with mutual respect." Until they found out someone had been pumping them with steroids and all signs pointed to him. "We were top of our division during my years as assistant. Several of my players were recruited to major and minor league teams. I was privileged to receive the 30-Under-30 Coach Award as well as a place on the 50 Impactful D1 Assistants' list. Also, I completed my Masters in Soccer Coaching degree, Master Coach diploma, and Sports Performance diploma. When asked, I made guest appearances at youth soccer camps and spoke at local award ceremonies for volunteer coaches. And I was on the shortlist to be added to the US men's national team as an assistant coach."

Life had been exactly what he wanted back then. He'd set himself up for the success of his dreams.

"Your record certainly speaks for itself. Are you doing anything with coaching at the moment?" Burt asked.

Xander licked his drying lips. "This is my first interview for a coaching position." The anxiety built in his chest. The truth was the best answer, wasn't it? "I thought perhaps once my wrongful imprisonment settlement was over that might help clear my name and allow team leadership to see the truth about me and not the black stain I've been given. I'm eager to get back to coaching. I've really missed it."

Burt's interest shown brightly on his face. Clearly, this was the dirt he really wanted to find out about. "When is the settlement taking place?"

"We're in the process now, but I'm not at liberty to talk any more about it." That killed the fascination sparking in Burt's eyes. "I'm confident that I could really be an asset to a U-19 team as a coach and to help the guys prepare for the big leagues."

Assuming he still had the chops for it.

Burt nodded. "Let me tell you about what we're looking for." For a solid twenty-two minutes, Burt talked about the practices, off-site training, tryouts, policies, sportsmanship, games, rosters, watching tapes, and carried on about what his most successful coaches did.

The more he explained, the more excited Xander felt. He wouldn't be second seat to anyone. This would be his team to guide however he wanted. Some of these men could easily attract the national team's attention which would get him noticed, too.

It was a full-time position with a fair wage, considering he'd be starting fresh after a five-year gap. With bonuses, game-winning incentives, and benefits, he would be close to where he wanted to start back in the industry. Certainly, a steadier income than the sales he had now.

All of that depended, of course, on if they'd actually offered him the job.

And if, when he talked to Gia, she agreed that this job would be the right thing for him, for them.

As they wrapped up the interview, Xander shook Burt's hand and looked him dead in the eye. "Thank you for the invitation to interview. I'm really thrilled about the opportunity to work with these guys. It's been my life goal to be a professional coach. I can't picture myself anywhere else."

He wanted to promise that he'd never give them reason to doubt him or distrust him, but that wasn't something he'd be able to promise anyone ever after what he went through.

Burt held his eye contact. "Your coaching record is impressive. You've shown how you can overcome in difficult circumstances. You've networked quite a bit in the past few months which proves you have drive. You're a solid contender here, Xander. I'll be making the decision in the next couple of days and will contact you regardless of the outcome."

Despite his initial bloodthirst, Xander liked Burt. He ran things according to the books without any tiptoeing around the unpleasant. Straightforward and to the point.

The equal parts hope and fear he carried with him to the car weighed heavily on him. It could work out so well. Or not.

When exactly was the right time to tell Gia about this?

He texted Ronaldo, the man who'd encouraged him to get back into this in the first place. Maybe he'd have something to say. Ronaldo texted back quickly saying that he'd call him later to talk it through. If anyone would have decent insight about the career move and the relationship move, Ronaldo would.

On the way back to his office in Golden, his phone rang. Tucker rarely did more than send him the occasional text. Apparently, Lucy was keen on them all having a double date sometime and Tucker liked the idea of going to a basketball game. Xander shivered. He clicked the button on his wheel to answer the call over the car's Bluetooth system.

"Tucker. Everything okay?"

A heavy sigh filled the car. "Well, I have a bit of a situation that I could use some help with."

"Name it. What can I do for ya?" Anything to help him avoid his current situations which were spiraling ever downward at an increasingly alarming speed.

"Well, I planned on proposing to Lucy tonight at the Denver Nuggets game and had a photographer lined up to be secretly taking pictures of us throughout the night and then capture the moment I popped the question during a commercial break and she hopefully says yes." His awkward snort-laugh made Xander bite the inside of his cheek. What if Lucy said no in front of all those people? "But that photographer caught the influenza and can't do it. I don't know who else in town to ask last minute."

Out of respect for Tucker's predicament, Xander buried his usual snide remarks about basketball games. "So, I come to the game, stay incognito but close enough to get pictures of you two throughout the night, and then video the proposal?"

"Oh, a video of the proposal would be epic," Tucker said with a squeak. "I've got the photographer's ticket that she won't be using. Maybe wear a disguise. I'll pay for your food and drinks as a token of my intense gratitude."

"Does it matter that I only have my phone camera to use?"

"Don't matter much to me, so long as we have the memories for the rest of our days."

He mentally thanked Gia for insisting he upgrade his flip phone to a decently rated smart phone a few months ago. "I'd be happy to, Tucker. I still owe you big time for picking me up on my release day and providentially introducing me to Golden. I will do my best to capture as many moments as I can."

Honestly, it'd be a relief to not have to sit and pretend to care about the basketball game. And being a creeper with a camera could be fun.

When he got to the office, he sent a taunting text to Gia. *Guess what I get to do tonight.*

Then he sent another text asking Avri if he could borrow her nice camera for the evening. His phone would be fine, but they'd be even more over the moon if their big night had quality pictures instead of mobile phone photos. She responded immediately saying she'd bring it by in a couple of hours. Guess she really didn't have much going on during her Christmas break.

For the first time in a long time, the repressive weight against his chest didn't overwhelm him as he opened his email. Being a business owner had taken its toll over the past few months. The constant pushing and hustling, moving money around, watching the books, making decisions, trying to figure out the best way to move forward exhausted him in a way that doing all of the same things as a soccer coach hadn't.

Three new orders had come into his inbox. He packaged up the items that had sold and sent them off. Reggie's work seemed to attract more buyers than anyone else's. He made a note to get permission to feature Reggie on his website as a builder. People loved supporting talented kids.

He sat down amongst his materials and tools and put together four new items to sell, complete with Reggie-style finishes that made them look unique. Sure, plain stuff sold, but that eye for detail seemed to go so much further.

Avri stopped by the office an hour before Xander needed to leave for the stadium. She carried in a medium-sized bag with her.

"What is all of that?" he asked as she set the bag on the floor gingerly.

Her giant grin set him on edge immediately. "Well, as you know, I have done the photographer assistant thing before. You have to look the part." With an unnerving amount of glee, she pulled out a Nuggets t-shirt with a player's name on the back.

No idea who that was.

Next came a Nuggets baseball cap. Then her black padded camera case went onto the table. And finally from her Mary Poppins bag, she pulled a pair of glasses.

She straightened with triumph. "You don't want to be recognized so you need to keep your disguise as legal yet effective as possible."

He wanted to protest the shirt and cap since they'd likely be used this one time only, then stuffed in his closet. But she had a point. With how vocal he'd been about refusing basketball game offers, Lucy wouldn't expect him to be there and dressed out to support the team. It was the perfect disguise. "Not sure I need the glasses, Av. My face will probably be hidden behind the camera most of the time."

"Glasses are for when you're not behind the camera. Like if you have to walk past them to go to the bathroom or get a drink. Or you see them in line for food."

He rubbed his fingers over his forehead. When had his little sister gotten so smart?

That was exactly what he looked like as he took his stadium seat an hour and a half later. Tucker and Lucy had seats on the short side of the court and his seat was diagonal in the section over on the long side of the court. With his disguise, there wouldn't be a good chance that Lucy could recognize him.

As they walked in, he snapped a few photos of them carrying their drinks and food to their seats. He could easily take close-up photos with Avri's camera. He sipped his drink, keeping an eye on Tucker who hadn't stopped smiling yet. Lucy, however, he caught in a variety of poses.

On his mobile phone, he took a selfie with the court and sent it to Gia who had sent a host of heart and laughing emojis at the fact that Tucker had persuaded him to go to a basketball game by himself for an engagement of all things. It wasn't so bad. His seat neighbors didn't attempt small talk while he had the camera to his eye, so he kept it there especially during breaks.

Finally, two-thirds of the way through the game the overhead screen flashed with a "big announcement" while the in-house cameras landed on Lucy and Tucker. He took a series of shots as Tucker got down on one knee and the whole stadium erupted in a deafening roar. Lucy's face was a mixture of embarrassment and shock.

Tucker finished his speech and looked up at Lucy with a hopeful expression. Lucy didn't say anything right away. He snapped away in an attempt to catch her response. But when she started talking, she said…no?

Chapter 17

"I'm sorry. I should have told you earlier. This coaching job isn't a sure thing. I might not get the offer at all, but I should have told you that I was invited to interview and accepted." Xander's expression was remorseful. His handsome face looked tired and pained.

His words punched her in her middle, taking her breath away. Gia rubbed her chest where the ache grew but still ended up grinding her teeth while thoughts and emotions competed in her head. Oh, she had some words for him. "We're in a serious relationship, Xander. You're supposed to be able to trust me with whatever is going on. Taking an interview is a huge deal. One that we should have discussed together."

What would she have said? Don't take the interview? Wait for something in New Orleans? They weren't engaged or married. She didn't really have that right to dictate that part of his life, did she? Telling her she couldn't take a job she wanted was something Bronc would have done while they dated. Once again, Bronc's past abuse proved that he'd ruined her ability to know what a good relationship looked like.

"To be fair, your life hasn't exactly needed any more stress than what you are already going through. I was hoping that we could decide what to do together if I got the offer and after you finished the preliminary prints."

A little bit of her steam disappeared. He'd done everything he could to make this work. Her anger wasn't solely directed at him. This stalker had everything tied in knots. Her family was hurting in so many ways that she felt like she couldn't fix. And long distance? She was over it.

"I am almost done with this project. And I want to see you as soon as I'm done and the stalker finds something better to do. Let's revisit this conversation then. I will think about it some more. If you think we have a future together, Xander, then I have to be a part of the next steps you take."

"I promise you will be. I'm not sure I can handle us being apart for much longer. It's making me crazy. Giving me doubts about us that I never would have had in person." He sighed.

Her lips quirked in a humorless smile. "Yeah, me too."

"My lawyer hasn't heard about when the next date will be for our settlement case. He's getting nervous about the delay when the mediator very clearly wanted to wrap this up quickly."

Another delay in their plans to reunite. She was ready to hit something.

They finished up their conversation as Gia pulled her car into the parking garage at Joey's office again. Andy said he was already waiting for her near her usual parking spot. The dead animals had been cleared and the offices cleaned since they had to bail last week.

Gia had a few final touches to put on the prints before she sent the final preliminary rounds. The double monitor and open drafting table offered her an easier time than her home office. Today was going to be the day she cleared this off her plate.

She swung her car into the spot next to where Andy stood against the bumper of his car, talking on the phone. A warmth spread through her chest. In the desert of long distance, it felt good to have a kind, fearless guy paying attention to her, even if it was his job. She shoved those thoughts down deep.

He offered her a small wave as he followed her to the stairs and up into the building. Not until she swiped her key card and opened the offices' back door did he move the phone from his ear. As was custom, he entered the room first to clear it of any surprises.

But this time he didn't move. He stood in the doorway immobile and muttered a curse. Her heart lurched. She bent her knees to look past his side.

"Oh my gosh." Her breath caught in her chest. The office had been ransacked. Cubicle walls lay on their sides. Papers littered the floors next to open file cabinets. Someone destroyed the place.

Andy brought his phone back to his ear. "Amos, the office has been torn apart." He listened. "Yes. No. Yes." He glanced back at Gia. "We're going to grab a thing or two and head back to the house. Okay. See you there." He took a few photos of the disaster and stuffed his phone into his pocket. He pulled the gun from his ankle holster and slid it in his waistband. "We came for a second monitor. Let's see if we can grab one and head back."

Wading through this mess seemed like asking for more trouble. Gia balked at the door. "I can connect my computer to one of the television screens at home. They won't be side by side but it'll work okay."

He tilted his head to the side. "Aren't you curious about what Joey's personal office looks like?"

She closed her lips and nodded. He chose his steps with painstaking care, picking only hard surfaces not covered in papers. She placed her feet where he did. "Amos is sending over the detective team to investigate before the police get here. He'll contact the office manager to have her run point on this."

"What a nightmare," she mumbled as they passed where Andy had been sitting each day in front of her and Joey's office door. Joey would lose his mind if he knew this was going on in his absence. How serious did it need to get before they tracked him down to ask him to come home?

Knowing her parents, the business would have to be on the verge of folding and they'd never let that happen under their watch for any of their family.

Andy snapped a picture from the doorway of Joey's office and stood back. A tornado had blown through. Shreds of paper and ripped up books topped everything. There on the floor under shattered glass lay the picture of Joey's family on the beach in Rio. She bent to pick it up.

"Don't touch anything." Andy stopped her arm. "We might get some evidence from this room if we're lucky."

"The one thing that isn't a mess is his extra secure file cabinet with all the past plans of every project he and his dad had worked on since beginning the firm." Sure, there were dents in it and probably a load of scratch marks where someone wanted to get it open, but it was still intact. It had done its job.

She made a mental note to buy herself one of those for her firm. Uncle Angelo bragged on it back when he'd upgraded to it years ago. Fire proof. Water proof. Virtually impenetrable. It had seemed excessive at the time, but now the wisdom in his security had paid off in dividends.

"We'll have the team bring the cabinet to the house while this mess gets cleaned up."

A loud bang echoed through the room, interrupting their conversation. Andy whipped his gun into place, his body shielding Gia in the doorway. Nothing but silence greeted them.

"This must have been recent. Let's get out of here," Andy said, motioning to the back door. Gia led the way with Andy at her back, his weapon still drawn. When they reached the back door, he typed out a quick message on his phone, and then exited the office first. "Our guys are already at the front door of the office. I just told them we are cleared. Someone will come this way to make sure if anyone is in there they don't get away now."

Chills prickled her neck. Someone could have been in there watching, listening, the whole time. She glanced above them in the stairwell. Nothing was up there. The building had another five floors above them which hadn't vacated.

Oddly, none of this felt quite as personal as the chaos Bronc had created in her life in Colorado. Perhaps she would be free from personal security after the prints were sent over. But how would the stalker know when she'd sent them?

None of that was announced publicly or within the firm until the end of the quarter when Joey sent out an update on the projects that were live and those they'd finished and how they affected quarterly bonuses.

The end of the quarter was in seven days, but Joey wouldn't likely be sending that email out. Like Uncle Angelo, he took that part of the job on for himself as a way of keeping his finger on the pulse of the firm.

In the parking garage, Gia walked next to Andy with her head up, scanning the cars. "Do you think if we somehow spread the word that the design is finished and out to the engineers that these attacks will stop?"

"You think whoever is doing this is just trying to slow or halt the design progress and not trying to shut the firm down completely as retribution for the design?" Andy asked.

She shrugged. When he put it like that, she felt she wasn't seeing the bigger picture that he was looking at. "Would it be worth a try? Or would that aggravate the situation?"

Andy raised his hands. "I'll bring it up to Amos as a possibility. Everything is getting run through him and the Venha public relations team."

Once again, Gia closed herself into her car with her head reeling. If it were her offices, she'd be in there cleaning every inch of that office by hand, finding the correct folders for each paper and receipt.

Two days before Christmas.

Grabbing her phone, she dialed up Lucy. The morning rush would be over by now. The ringing was replaced by a high-pitched squeal. Laughing, Gia scrambled to turn down the Bluetooth volume.

"I'm engaged," Lucy shouted into the phone.

Gia grinned as she drove home. She'd completely forgotten to drill Xander about last night after he sprung his interview confession on her, first thing. "Congratulations, girl! I'm so happy for you. Tell me the whole story."

"So, I dressed for the game in my Nuggets t-shirt and cut-off jeans with my fancier hen necklace. Thankfully, I did my hair this time instead of my usual baker's bun. Edith convinced me to take the afternoon off to go get my nails done." Lucy gasped. "She must have known. Well, anyway, I was really feeling down about my appearance recently. We've just been so busy at the shop that I haven't had any time for more than a quick shower and falling into bed. Because I got my nails done, I went ahead and did some basic makeup to class myself up a bit. It's been a while since Tuck and I have had a date. We got to the stadium and he bought me nachos, a slice of pizza, a drink, and cotton candy for dinner." Which was pretty much Lucy's love language. "And then, on one of the commercial breaks the whole stadium was looking at us as he got down on one knee and said he'd loved me for a long time and would always love me. Promised to do his best to give me a good, safe life and would I marry him?" She sniffled.

"And what did you say?"

"Well, I said there would be no secrets and absolutely no toleration of abuse and if he could promise me that, then yes I'd marry him. And everyone around us cheered so loudly Tucker dropped the ring under the seats and had to fish it out to put it on my finger."

They laughed.

"His hairline to his collarbone was almost purple with embarrassment. We are thinking maybe a summer wedding here in Colorado. Maybe at sunset." Her voice got all dreamy. "I'll make my own cake, of course."

Gia's heart ached. "That sounds perfect, Luce. Like a fairytale. You deserve it."

"Oops. I just looked out the door and Edith is swamped. I will talk to you later, okay?"

"Send me a picture of the ring." Gia called as Lucy said goodbye once more.

In her driveway, Gia rested her head against her steering wheel. She missed Colorado, but more importantly, she missed her quiet little life and the amazing people she met out there. New Orleans almost had her feeling claustrophobic in a way she'd never felt before when she called it home.

Xander was right. Their life was out in Golden for the next half of a year, at least. She had contracts still open, and commuting to Colorado for meetings really wasn't feasible, not when she could stay there until she'd given them warning that she'd be moving out of state. Her contract with the government that she'd won this past summer had listed her residency in Colorado as a way to show they were keeping the work local.

There really wasn't a good reason for Xander to not take that coaching job if they offered it to him. And being there this summer would give her a chance to wedding plan with Lucy. Tucker had been slowly making his moves for a couple of years, deciding what he wanted. This year, he'd made up his mind.

Bolstered by her new decision to return to Colorado, Gia grabbed her bag and made a beeline for the library. It was time to get these prints off her plate and out of her hands. She dragged the desk closer to the wall to connect her computer to the TV set hanging on the wall. With her things spread out in front of her, she set to work finalizing, checking, rechecking, redrawing, coloring in, and making the final adjustments the engineers had requested. She had to crane her neck to see the TV up on the wall when she dragged something from her computer screen, but it was worth it to see the final in colorful, large dimensions in front of her.

She took a screenshot of the final mock-up to send to Xander. It was a huge miracle this had come together in the past few weeks as it had. She wrote out the email, copied Joey, and attached the plans. This feeling of pride and relief was what she'd chased those long hours—the euphoria of a completed draft.

Nothing could beat it.

With a click of the button, the email disappeared. She sat back in her chair, tempted to call and text everyone she knew to say she'd finished. Instead, she emailed the picture of the final to Xander and opened her text string to Andy.

Prints are officially sent off. Ball's in your court.

He replied immediately. *Roger that. Can you come to the security room?*

The security room was a converted music room on the first floor. The piano Gia had learned on now sat pushed off to the side and a half dozen tables with cords and monitors coming out everywhere took up the center of the room.

Three guys sat at monitors and Andy stood over the shoulder of one. His brow was furrowed and his jaw set. Nothing changed when he saw her and motioned her over.

On the screen, they watched the footage of a black-clothed figure destroying Joey's office space. With each cabinet drawer opened, the person grabbed handfuls and tossed them into the air like confetti at a celebration. A few dance moves in between each cabinet, then more celebratory destruction.

"What is going on?"

The guy at the monitor snorted. "This person has been very odd with behaviors. Nothing has been gender specific yet. It doesn't take a very strong person to tip over an empty file cabinet. I have seen plenty of women strong enough to wipe a desk with a chair."

"Fast forward a bit," Andy said. "There."

The camera stopped as the figure ran his fingers along the wall casually until they stopped at the doorway of Joey's office. He easily picked the lock and stood back as the door opened in front of him. Then, with a stretch and a large step, into Joey's office he went.

"He's putting on a show," Andy murmured. "This is a game to him."

"Sick," the guy at the monitor added.

"So far the detective team hasn't noticed any patterns or personal items taken in the destruction. You can see the person has on gloves and shoe coverlets. There wasn't any attempt at hiding what was happening. The badge scanned to get in was Brady Caveneau's, but when we contacted him, he had no idea it had gone missing. Last time, he had it was at work after the rodent incident. He kept it in his wallet, so someone could have lifted it any time over the weekend." Andy raked a hand over his head.

"No one unusual came in the doors?" Gia asked.

"Everyone that came in through the door from the garage had a badge. None of them Brady," the guy manning the monitor said. "Everyone who came in the front doors landed on a floor different to our offices. Someone came in, went to a different floor, and then made the move to go down and destroy our space."

When the person had downed a particularly troublesome set of cubicle walls, he stood back and did another dance move. One she'd seen before. Gia froze.

"Go back to the dance," her voice trembled.

They watched as the figure pulled a silly butt-out, lasso-twirl move.

"Antia did that a couple of times to make us laugh when we were dancing at the jazz club the other night. It's her way of mocking cowboy Americans who don't know how to dance. Whoever this is had to have been there and seen her do it." Gia covered her mouth with her hand. She felt sick, stunned.

"Good eye, Gia. That's just the kind of break we needed. The jazz club has an eye on everyone all the time. This fool hopefully just made his last mistake." Andy pulled out his phone and stepped away to make a call.

Chapter 18

The glass case Xander stood over beamed like the surface of the sun. Every single item inside glowed and shone in response to the lights on them. They were all nice, fancy in their own right, worthy of a queen.

But they weren't Gia.

Hands stuffed in his pockets, he walked out of the fifth jewelry store in the mall. That was everything this mall had to offer by way of engagement rings and the selection was disappointing.

None of them jumped out at him.

Her admitting to her doubts and using "if" about their future really set him back. He felt like he was losing her. Maybe to distance. Maybe to reality. Maybe to Andy, the newest knight in the duel for her affection.

Buying an engagement ring could be a huge gamble with the way they'd left things at their last conversation.

He hadn't been inside a mall in seven, maybe eight, years that he could remember. His meeting today with a specialty toy maker, David Thalton, ended that streak for him. Xander wanted to get his products placed in David's store of non-plastic, earth friendly, sensory-sensitive toys. The guy had his work cut out for him in a world where lights and buttons and automation reigned.

David was a sixty-something retired Air Force officer that began making toys for his granddaughter who was on the autism spectrum and only wanted toys she could dismantle and each one needed a textured surface to help her identify parts. His work was absolutely incredible and offered a tailor-made option in a huge market void, but where David thrived in the custom-made, he lacked in the ability to move products online.

Email was the extent of his capabilities. His son-in-law insisted on building a one-page website so David could be found, but orders had to be made via phone or email.

He and Xander mutually agreed to help each other.

As he left the mall, Xander dialed his website designer, Cade.

"Hey, Xander. How can I change your world today?" Cade's deep voice gave him the image that he sat at his computer with a fifty-pound dumbbell in his non-dominant hand, flexing.

Xander laughed. "I have a fairly complex problem I'm hoping you can solve."

"Magic is my specialty. Tell me more."

He sat on a bench outside the mall to focus. "I want to post products on my site that will send the product sale information and invoice to a completely different person but keep a small percentage of the commission for hosting them. Is that possible?" The thought had crossed his mind that he could just forward things to David, but then he'd have to constantly be the middle man and monitor his email.

Cade was quiet. "A store within your store?"

"Yes, essentially. But each store can have its unique identity so that people know they aren't buying the products directly from me."

"There is a popular site out there that does this already. It's got a cutesy name. I forgot what it is. Anyway, people can create a store on their website and sell homemade stuff. Is that what you're going for?"

"Yes, except upcycled and specialty market. At least, we know there is a market for this type of thing."

"It might be hard to compete against, but you can certainly try. Send me the information for the first sub-store you want entered. It will take me a couple of hours, but it shouldn't be hard to configure."

Elation flooded his chest. The world needed David's work out there, especially for those whose children liked toys a particular way but mainstream market didn't suit them.

Maybe he shouldn't go back into coaching.

This kind of thing energized him—seeing the good in the world and people's genius in meeting a need being pushed to the forefront. He typed out the email on his phone and sent it to Cade.

At the top of the parking aisle, he could see a car stopped behind the parked cars. Wait, that was his car that it was blocking. He jogged closer. Someone stood next to his driver's side door, hood up over his head, but obviously a white male, younger. It almost looked as if it were a child. Was it someone putting advertising fliers on all the cars? Was he a gang member? The guy turned and jogged back to his car without a glance in either direction.

Not a flier guy.

Xander didn't get a clear look at his face since he hid behind an SUV two spaces away. He typed the license plate number and an exact description of as much as he saw of the guy into his phone notes as the vehicle pulled away. Not until the car got to the end of the aisle did Xander step around the front of the cars to his.

No physical damage to the car, but an envelope tucked in the windshield.

Annoyed, he snatched it from the window, opening it as he ducked inside the car. Some kid was running point on this madness that was putting his life in danger? What did this have to do with him? He hadn't had anything to do with kids besides Reggie for years.

His parents were teachers, but that was an unlikely source since the police said it was gangs that thought he knew something. He almost wished he knew so these fools would leave him alone to live his life without watching his back.

The note was completely blank.

Tossing the paper to the side, he slapped the wheel. He was so sick of this mess, these games. He didn't care anymore. He had a life to live and the confusion and stress wreaked havoc on his nerves.

None of this made sense.

He started the car and reversed. His earlier delight gone in a blink. A simple piece of paper could not ruin his day like this. How had he been so sure that if he caught the messenger that he would know the message sender? On his way back to the office, he glanced at the paper at each stoplight.

A blank page.

It made him furious.

He grabbed the paper, ready to tear it to shreds. But something caught his eye. Words? He righted the page and held it up to his windshield where the sun caught it full length.

Xander,

They've been watching you and hunting for me. They are getting closer to finding me than I ever imagined. I can't risk them finding me before the information is released. You hold my insurance policy. Take this note with you and go to Benny's Veterinarian Hospital in Kittredge. He'll know what to do. Then, you can be free from all this. I'm very sorry you were involved in the first place. I will make it up to you.

Not signed.

Xander pulled his car into a parking lot and searched for Benny's on his maps app. It was a forty-eight-minute drive from his current location, but today seemed like the perfect day to call the head hunters off and get his life back.

Unless the note writer had conveniently left out a step between knowing what to do and being free.

A small vengeful piece of Xander wanted to wait a day to make the note writer sweat, as he had many nights with no information or clues as to what was actually happening. If he was the key to this person's wellbeing, then shouldn't he have been warned that he held a life in his hands?

His finger pressed the "Start Navigation" button. His notifications chimed with an email from Gia saying "Just sent these in! You're the first to know!" There in breathtaking form and color was the mockup of the project she'd slaved over.

This was what he had lost his girlfriend to on those days with no extra time and those nights of exhaustion recovering from going full throttle.

He typed back, "Wow! That is stunning. I'm so proud of you, sweetheart. What an incredible accomplishment. I love you, Xander."

If he'd been the first to see the final mockup, did that mean she wasn't still mad at him and ready to give up on them? His teeth snagged his lip. It was worth the hope.

When he finally pulled into Benny's, it was ten after eleven A.M. He folded the paper into his pocket and walked to the front door feeling every bit as nervous and relieved. There were a lot of things that he anticipated when he pulled at the front door, but it being locked was not one of them. A sign hung in the window stating that the hospital closed at eleven A.M. on Tuesdays.

He muttered an expletive as he kicked the railing nearby. The lights were off inside. No cars besides his were in the parking lot which he had failed to notice in his anticipation. Truthfully, he had expected Benny to be waiting for him at the front door to free him from his tyranny.

Foolish.

His shoes crunched in the gravel as he made his way around the building to the back. A motorcycle sat propped up on an oddly placed concrete pad. Otherwise, no other sign of life. Xander tried the back door.

Locked.

He knocked at first, then banged on the window with his fist. Now that he'd made up his mind to get this over with, he had no patience left to wait. He banged again. "Come on, Benny. Answer the door. Someone's life is in danger and they are depending on you and me, apparently."

His shouts went nowhere. To one side of the building was a deserted gas station. To the other was a small ammo shop with its own gravel parking lot surrounding it.

As he was about to head back to his car, the back door creaked open. A wide-eyed girl's head poked out. Xander would guess early to mid-twenties. "Can I help you?"

"Yeah, I'm looking for Benny."

"Sorry. The hospital is closed for office hours. We'll be open half-day tomorrow since it's Christmas Eve Day," the girl's floating head said, already retreating.

"Please. This is crucial. Can you call Benny and let him know that I'm here on behalf of a friend of his who is in danger?" Where was this urgency coming from?

The girl looked around. Xander had no pet with him. And with no appointment, there was no real reason for him to not be dismissed without a second glance. She really shouldn't entertain the thought. "Fine. Come on in. I'll call the doc."

Xander didn't wait around for her to change her mind. "That your bike?"

"Yes." Her answer was very short.

"Nice ride."

Once the door closed behind him, the girl locked it. "You can hang out in the waiting room for now. I'll call Benny."

With a nod of thanks, Xander walked through the hallway to the sound of dogs barking chaotically. How could anyone stand that noise all day every day? And that smell.

The girl popped her head into the waiting room as if she were always a floating head unattached to a body. Her eyes seemed to assess Xander with suspicion. "What's your name?"

"Xander Reinerman."

"Hm. Benny said you'd say that. He'll be in shortly." Then the head vanished behind the swinging door back to the cacophony of animal noises.

Benny knew who he was. In his smart phone, he searched Benny's name. Nothing besides veterinarian services and degrees came up on the first two pages. By page three there were obituaries and other seemingly unrelated mentions of people with the same name.

Twenty minutes later, a small, gray-haired man walked through the door to the waiting room. "Hi Xander, I'm Benny." His voice was soft-spoken, every word a sort of sigh, and he didn't look at Xander in the eye, but right below on his cheek or nose. "I had just uncorked a '94 merlot to enjoy with my wife, so let's get this over with by the time it is done breathing."

Xander stood and handed him the paper. Benny stared at it. "I know who you are, Xander. If you'll follow me, we can take care of your problem."

Take care of *his* problem?

"What problem are you referring to, exactly?" Xander said as they exited the hallway into an open room with a surgical table in the middle and cages surrounding it. Thankfully, the cages were empty, the room quiet.

Benny didn't respond but continued to work at the side table, his back turned to Xander. No, he didn't come here to get ignored. He came for answers.

Xander huffed. "Can you please explain to me what is going on or I can leave and we can both go back to our happy lives?"

"Was yours happy?" Benny asked as he turned around with a tray full of metal tools and a… needle?

The panic rose unbidden in his chest.

Sharp tools.

His breaths shortened.

Knives.

His vision darkened. Dizzy.

When he came out of it, Benny stood over him, nonplussed, chattering out loud. "The person who sent you here will explain everything in due time, I can assure you. You'll feel a slight pinch here. I'm not at liberty to discuss anything, you understand."

Xander jerked upward as a sharp pain pierced him right under his armpit. "What are you doing?"

His roar echoed in the room as he attempted to sit up.

"Please don't try to move, Xander. You're restrained. Let's just get this over with," Benny said.

Xander checked from side to side. His arms were strapped down straight out from his shoulders making a T. His legs didn't budge in their ties. A weight pressed against his shoulders. "How did I get on this table?" There was no way that mousy man could have lifted his dead weight in the seconds he'd blacked out.

Benny messed with his tray. "Oh, I was warned about your panic attacks. I used your falling momentum to get the table under you. Then it was a matter of lifting your feet. Physics and Tai Chi would do wonders for your understanding of the world."

Who knew about his panic attacks enough to warn the doctor? A numbness crept down Xander's side and across his back. "What did you give me? What are you doing?"

Benny smiled. "We'll be done in a jiffy." He palmed a scalpel and leaned over Xander's left side. Benny chuckled. "I'm not used to my patients being able to talk to me on the table."

Was this it? Had he walked into a trap and was going to die on a vet's table? "Just tell me why you are cutting me open."

Benny hummed. "Well, according to my sources and my scanner," another chuckle, "there's a chip buried inside your scar, an inch from the top."

A chip.

His laugh was a weird, high-pitched squeak. Of course, there would be a chip inside his body. "Let me guess. You can't tell me when this chip was inserted."

"Oh, I could venture an answer for you. Not sure if it's correct. Judging by your skin, I'd say the chip was inserted while your wound was still open. There's no secondary puncture wound which would be obvious on human skin for a chip this size." Benny straightened, holding a plastic-covered chip in the grip of a very long set of tweezers.

Breathe in. Breathe out. Xander dropped his head back against the table. His mind was blank where the questions should have been. Someone in the prison infirmary had put a chip in him after he'd been flayed like a fish in the yard. He'd had that thing inside his body for years without his knowledge.

Waiting for this exact moment.

Whatever sedative and pain blocker Benny had him on was really good because he almost didn't care. Why wouldn't his life on this side of prison be as equally as unpredictable as it was prior?

"A touch of superglue is all you need, then on to your happy life, Xander Reinerman. Won't even have a secondary scar." Benny straightened from his side. "Okay, we'll let that settle for a second. I should have been a plastic surgeon." Benny opened his computer, inserted the chip into an adapter, and, after a few taps, returned to the table beaming. "Your freedom has been secured. Your life no longer in danger. If someone comes after you, you can show them that the information is not in your possession and is in the hands of people they should fear."

In seconds, Benny untied the restraints on his limbs, leaving Xander to lay with his button-down shirt pooling around him. He stared into the bright light hovering overhead.

For the love of Pele, what just happened?

Chapter 19

"The police have someone in custody," Andy said into her ear.

He'd pulled her aside from the dinner preparations that she got to be a part of for the first time in weeks. Avó was making a traditional Brazilian dish for them tonight. Then Christmas Eve Day and Christmas Day would be two days of feasting on both American and Brazilian traditional foods.

Gia wiped her hands on a dish towel. "That's amazing news. They think this person is the one who has been causing the trouble?"

Andy shrugged. "The guy is being interrogated, but lots of things are lining up that make him look like the one."

She pressed a hand to her throat where she could feel her heartbeat. "Dare we hope this is almost over?"

His laugh made her pulse spike. He hadn't laughed more than once or twice in her presence. It was a good sign that he might be relaxing. "It's never a bad time to hope."

With that, he patted her shoulder and left for the security room again. She went back to making dinner with Avó until her phone ringing pulled her away.

"Hey, baby," she said, stepping into the library where it was quiet. He called instead of videoing which was their norm.

"Gia, I promised you no more secrets," Xander said.

Oh, no.

"Remember how I told you that I was receiving weird anonymous notes? Well, I got another one today and I shouldn't be bothered again. I thought that might set your mind at ease." He coughed and then groaned.

"Babe, are you okay?"

"Yeah, yeah. I'm on my way back from a meeting. I'll tell you more details when we're in person. It's a really weird story and I don't have the whole picture yet."

He sounded breathless and off. Like he was lying about where he was. But he sounded like he was in the car so why tell her differently?

"Well, I'll look forward to hearing the whole story. Andy said they might have the stalker person in custody. We're waiting to hear back after the interrogation," Gia said. Repeating the news made it sink in a little further. This whole ordeal could be ending for her. And soon.

It felt so good.

Her phone buzzed.

"I've been thinking about what you said and us a lot recently. But I want to tell you everything in person. Hopefully a few more days," she said. His response was silence. Maybe he didn't want to see her in a few more days? Why did their whole relationship feel like it was on edge right now? She swallowed. "Well, I need to get back to helping Avó. Talk to you later?"

"Definitely. Love you."

"I love you." She pressed the red button. Immediately, her phone buzzed again.

A text from Cara said, *I need you.* And the next text was a pin with her location.

Gia grabbed her keys and ran out the door, yelling out that she'd be back soon. Andy ran out behind her.

"You can't just suddenly leave without me," Andy said getting into the passenger's seat.

She clicked for the directions to the location. "Cara needs me."

Andy nodded without a response as Gia reversed out of the driveway. In the quiet, she drove the thirty-seven minutes to Cara's location. Andy stayed busy on his phone. The anxiety churned at her stomach. What had Cara gotten herself into?

The address was a neighborhood of fairly unkempt residences, but some were festively decorated for Christmas. She parked in the driveway, strode up to the door, and knocked.

A skeleton of a man answered the door. His question turned into a sneer as he looked her up and down. "Hey, Ferra. Is this hot piece of woman standing at the front door the diva you called the family embarrassment?" He looked back at Gia. "She's been here the whole night and day. She needs to leave."

"Shut up, Dean," Cara said swaying as she tried to shove Dean aside. Cara walked out the door without a backward glance.

Or rather, wobbled.

When she got to the dirt patch that may have once had grass on it, Cara fell face first and didn't move. Dean laughed a wheezy hiss and closed the door. Gia clenched her fist ready to take a swing at that snake.

Andy was already at Cara's side, rolling her over and picking her up into his arms. Cara's limp form broke her heart.

As he set her in the front seat, her head lolled toward Andy. "This man smells like a cologne ad. Good enough to eat."

Gia scrunched her face at Andy as an apology. He gave her a half-smirk as if he got compliments like that every day. She got in and made the executive decision that Cara was staying with them tonight.

"You're quiet. Never a good sign," Cara said. She sat up quickly. "Did I just see a man riding a camel? New Orleans these days is getting so weird."

Gia shook her head. "You're higher than Mount Everest, Cara."

Cara snorted. "So what? Are you judging me now? Clean for four whole years and you get to judge me?"

At her words, the tension in Gia's jaw got tighter. "I'm not judging you, Cara. I'm upset that you put yourself in danger. I care about your safety. Not that you do. I sure didn't when I was doing drugs. There are people out there who want to hurt us or ruin us."

"Not me." Cara sang. "No one cares if I die or get ruined."

Gia hit the steering wheel, giving Cara a jolt. "I care. Joey cares. Ma, Daddy, Avó, the whole family cares."

"Well, none of them are my parents, so I don't care that they care that I don't care that they don't care."

It didn't matter nearly as much to Gia that Cara's words weren't making sense as it did that she believed that Cara had just spoken from her heart, the truth of how she felt. And it crushed Gia's soul.

"After Christmas, you need to check into a rehabilitation center. Get clean. Kick this before you succumb and it destroys you."

"Rehab is for people who have been addicted a long time, not me. It's only been a couple months and could quit anytime I wanted." Cara propped her feet on the dash.

"Yeah? Prove it."

Andy shifted in the back seat. She'd forgotten he was there, listening to their family drama.

Cara was quiet for a second. "I don't have anything to prove to anyone. You didn't run away and check into rehab, did you? I shouldn't have to."

"Actually, I did." Her dirty laundry was out there for Andy to see. At least if he read it in a file she could pretend he didn't know. Gia rubbed her neck. "I had such horrible withdrawals that I was afraid I was going to lose control of myself, so I checked into a place in Colorado. Didn't tell anyone but my parents. It probably saved my life."

Maybe that would give Cara something to think about, to bolster her willingness to agree to rehab, but when she glanced over, Cara's eyes were closed and her mouth hung open a fraction.

She blew out a breath. That did not go how she'd hoped.

When they got to the house, Andy jumped out immediately and lifted Cara into his arms again. "Tell me where to lay her."

Gia led him through the garage to the kitchen, in hopes that everyone was eating in the dining room and would miss the show. No luck.

Ma and Avó were in the kitchen and froze when their eyes landed on Andy and Cara. Ma tilted her head in a question. To which Gia half-shrugged and pointed upstairs. She led Andy up the back stairwell to the guest room. As soon as he laid her down, he walked out of the room.

Gia removed Cara's shoes and dusty jeans. A small bag fell out of her pocket as Gia tossed them on the ground. She checked her other pockets, shoes, and tank top. Nothing else dropped out.

The girl hadn't put on anything warmer than a flannel shirt with the sleeves rolled up to her elbows. Easy access to the veins on her arms with needles of who knew what level of cleanliness. Gia shivered as she dropped to her knees beside Cara's bed, smoothing the hair from her face as she slept.

What would it take to get through to her?

As the tears welled, Gia stood. It felt too much like sitting beside Tia Carolena's death bed.

Gia braced herself for the questions from Ma and Avó when she got downstairs, but Ma motioned her into the dining room with the family. They'd get to it later. This wasn't a pass.

As she took her place at the table, she tried to paste on a happy face. Daddy called to her down the table.

Everyone went silent. Her heart stuttered until she saw the sparkle in his expression.

"Avó says you have some good news." He opened his hands. "Share." Her confusion must have been obvious. "About work?"

"Ah, I sent in the draft for the resort that Joey needed me to finish for him. I'm free to enjoy the rest of your visit!" She lifted her glass as everyone cheered and congratulated her.

They had a week left here which wouldn't make up for the time she'd missed, but it was something. Tonight, they were going to the ballet downtown to watch the Nutcracker, a show Gia and her female cousins had talked about seeing together for years.

The boys were a little more difficult to persuade, but Daddy had a box with his name on it because of his donations to the art center which meant they got drinks and snacks with a show. Despite their busy schedules, Ma and Daddy tried to get to as many performances as they could to support the arts. If they couldn't make it, they offered tickets to someone else in their stead, usually to someone who had a child that wanted to be a ballerina or musician or actor that couldn't otherwise afford a ticket.

After dinner, she changed and left Antia and Sara in the bathroom getting ready in favor of meeting Ma on the back patio while they waited for the cars to arrive. Ma, Daddy, and Avó sat on one side near the fireplace with the space heater overhead while Uncle Ronaldo, Breno, and Silva drove glow-in-the-dark golf balls into the yard on the other end.

They waited as she got settled into a seat, then looked at her expectantly. Why did she feel like she was the one in trouble here?

She took a deep breath and set the bag of drugs on the end table next to her. "Cara texted me this afternoon saying she needed me and sent me her location. Andy and I went to pick her up. It was some dirty drug house on the other side of town and she was high. I talked to her about rehab on the way home, but she doesn't seem open to it or the idea of stopping using."

They nodded.

"She thinks she can quit anytime she wants." Gia rubbed her temples. The fatigue hit her like a high-speed train. The worry, stress, and fear dropped her hard. "I don't know if I'm the right person to try to help her or not. When she's high or drunk, she's pretty hostile towards me, calling me a naive princess or a diva or a family embarrassment."

Avó patted her hand. "Sometimes, the toughest love is stepping away to let others take charge instead of you. It might not feel like love, but if she gets the help she needs, then it will be for the best."

"You two have been like sisters your whole lives. She loves you and probably has a host of other emotions entangled in there, too, because real love is never linear," Daddy said.

"That's why I feel like I'm responsible for her choices," Gia said. "I love her so much. I'd never want her to hurt the way I did."

"We'll give it until after Christmas and approach her about it," Ma said. "I hate to see her headed down this path because she thinks she's alone in her grief."

The doorbell chimed and the alarm sounded throughout the house that the cars had arrived. There was a mad scramble as everyone hurried to get out the door. Cara was still sleeping, so Judita agreed to stay back so that someone was there when she came out of her coma.

Judita loved the story of The Nutcracker, but she also loved reality TV shows which she didn't get to see much of while she was in the States. With her hands wrapped around a mug of mulled wine, her posture seemed relaxed as she watched the whole family pack into two GetThere limousines. Maybe she wouldn't feel she was missing out.

The limousines stopped next to a red carpet that led into the side door of the theater. A few photographers stood under the lights. Andy handed Antia and Sara out of the limo and then offered Gia his arm. He was impressively subtle. Being her escort guaranteed he'd be expected to stay by her side the whole night.

He leaned in to talk. "I've avoided the ballet my entire life. I want you to appreciate this is a long-standing streak I'm breaking for you."

Gia laughed. "That's not a bragging right, Andy."

His eyes sparkled in the lights. "It is for my kind."

"Yes, yes. The special forces are far too good for Fine Arts," Gia said.

"We could teach them a thing or two about elegance," he said with a grunt.

Inside, the theater box worked perfectly for the security team. One entrance in and out made life much less complicated for Amos and Andy and one other guy who stood guard. They'd requested pre-packaged drinks and snacks which didn't guarantee something couldn't be tampered with.

Amos and Andy tried to discreetly scan the tray of drinks and food to check for tiny puncture holes. Despite one guy being in custody, they refused to relax regulations. The guy had solid alibis for a few of the events that happened, namely the fires on the front lawn and the drink poisoning at the golf course. The police were positive he was working with someone else.

He had admitted to sending rodents, following the girls on their night out, and trashing the office. He was a staunch preservationist, mid-thirties, intent on showing the world a better way. His explanations for how things happened were accurate, but the detectives weren't convinced that he'd done everything he said he'd done.

They couldn't catch these stalkers soon enough. The lengths her family had to go to right now to feel safe were ridiculous. Everything was a potential hazard. The life of paranoia infuriated her. Her family deserved better, easier.

Once the ballet started, the music and dance enchanted the audience, wrapping them into the story like comfortable blankets. Partway into the second act, Ma stepped into the en suite bathroom to answer her phone.

She came rushing out, not bothering to be quiet. She motioned Amos over. Uncle Roberto leaned in as well as Ma whispered to the men. When she straightened, Daddy grabbed Ma's purse and stood to follow her. Ma's wide-eyed, frantic scan landed on her.

With a quick jerk of her hand, Ma mouthed. "Let's go."

Gia didn't have to be told twice. She grabbed her things and jogged to catch up with Ma and Daddy who were almost to the stairs. Andy's heavier footsteps fell behind her.

What was going on?

A surge of panic coursed through her as she practically ran through the back door of the theater to a waiting car. Inside, they threw their seat belts on.

Worry shone bright on Ma's face in the streetlights. "Judita can't find Cara. She thinks she might have locked herself into the bathroom but she isn't responding. She doesn't know how long she's been in there or missing."

Chapter 20

Xander lay on the couch in Gia's office unmoving, his side aching. He wasn't mad or annoyed. He was absolutely outraged and ready to fight whoever did this with his bare knuckles.

A pawn in someone else's scheme again.

Make it up to him? That was a very unlikely promise to keep.

Every random note had been vague and lacking pertinent details. The puppet master cared for no one but himself which was the opposite of how Xander wanted to live his life.

Spurred by his anger, Xander stood with slow movements. If selfishness didn't take a day off, neither should those working against it. He had a business to run and people like David and Reggie to help make their mark in the world.

His phone rang as he sat up. "Maddox, tell me something good."

"Merry Christmas, Xander. I'm sorry for taking so long in getting back to you with updates. Unfortunately, I don't have great news for you. This is going to take longer than we first thought, but that is business as usual for this type of thing. As you know, Randall refused to sign an affidavit about the confession you got on camera. He told the university that he was under duress from the interviewees and the confession was forced. The university isn't sure it wants to move forward with a settlement at all."

A win for the university that might persuade them to not settle. Xander mouthed an expletive into the silence.

Maddox cleared his throat. "We might not see any movement on this case until the New Year gets underway, so hang in there."

In the workshop upstairs, he grabbed a hammer and some wood. He needed to hit something hard to improve his mood. A loud banging came at the door. Reggie stood on the steps.

Xander mumbled, "Merry Christmas" as amiably as he could muster and went right back to work.

Once or twice Reggie glanced at him, but worked beside him in silence. They didn't have any music on today and Xander respected that Reggie wasn't one of those kids who always had earbuds in, blocking out the world. An hour in, Xander's mood improved enough to pay for Reggie's lunch at Mother Hen's.

In the madness of the morning, he had neglected lunch and his stomach felt the ache as much as his side.

When they walked in, Lucy popped her hand in front of his eyes. He tapped down on his annoyance. Really, he was happy for them both. As she prepared their lunches, she told him the abridged version of the proposal. Tucker must not have let on that Xander was the one who took the pictures for them Monday night.

Xander had sent him the files Tuesday and Tucker had responded with an enthusiastic thanks. One of Lucy's Christmas gifts was going to be a printed album of their engagement night. A "forever keepsake" he'd called it which really ratcheted up the pressure Xander felt, hoping there was something worth keeping.

When they grabbed a table with their food in hand, Xander kept Reggie talking about Christmas with his foster parents and how Christmases had been in the past. Finally, Reggie stopped him.

"Xander, I'd like to eat if you want to take the next shift of storytelling."

Xander had to laugh. "Okay, well. My web designer is working on revamping my website to have the ability to create your own product store within my website. I'm not sure what the legalities would be since you are under eighteen, but when it's time, I want you to be able to have your store where you make your products and upload pictures of them. You keep all the profit and fulfill the orders yourself. You're talented with your designs. You deserve to work for yourself. You would be one step closer to being independent and supporting yourself."

Reggie looked genuinely excited, but his mouth was still full so Xander kept on talking.

"I'll check with the laws to see if we can't get you a store with parental permission now. If that doesn't work, we can keep with the arrangement we have. Your stuff sells like hotcakes."

"Thanks, Xander. My carpentry teacher was surprised that I had 'advanced techniques' for someone so young," Reggie said with a smile.

"Advanced carpentry or beginners?"

"Please, man. I need an easy A. Beginners."

They laughed. He would have done the same thing as a high schooler. "Guess you're not wasting your potential if you're selling your work on the side and what you make for school is just getting a grade."

"That's how I see it."

At three PM, Xander said goodbye to Reggie and closed up the shop. He spent the next hour and a half researching sales laws and minors nationally and statewide without much specific to his question. Finally, he searched for websites like what he wanted to build and read their policies on store owners under eighteen.

Cade had been right. There were other sites out there with big followings that were doing what he wanted to do. He scribbled down a few notes on how to diversify. He'd ask Reggie what he thought, too, since he had some skin in the game.

Then, he turned off his computer. He'd start fresh after Christmas and really hit things hard in the New Year.

Tonight, he was meeting Avri and Lincoln to eat dinner and drive through a Christmas light show. Avri warned them that she'd be bringing her boyfriend, a landscaper who was very sensitive about his title and preferred to be called a "landscape architect."

Guys with his kind of pretentiousness sank quickly in the shark-infested waters of prison. They adopted a meaner nickname really fast. And, of course, he didn't like the guy based on the fact that he was trying to get his sister's romantic attention. The guy had some frat boy name like Tanner or Dylan.

"I'm Chad. Nice to finally meet you." The boy was a head shorter than Xander and stockier than Linc.

Xander shook his hand. Firm grip. Calloused skin. Sturdy like a man who worked with his hands should be. Next to him, Avri looked like a willowy flower and she was no slouch in the athletic department. They stood in the waiting area at an Italian restaurant Linc had picked in downtown Denver.

Avri and Chad offered to grab drinks for them while they waited for a table to open up. As soon as they were two feet away, Linc turned into him.

"Talk fast. What is happening with that thing that occurred in the parking lot?" His eyebrows rose as he spoke.

Linc loved cornering him in a crowd to talk about personal stuff. He needed to find a better way. Xander debated playing dumb just to watch Linc get frustrated, but he would be so annoyed if Linc did that to him.

"Short version." Linc nodded and motioned him to speed it up. Xander rolled his eyes. "Cops never got back to me. I got a note saying that I needed to visit this vet in Kittredge to make this all go away. So, I did."

Linc's jaw dropped progressively as Xander told him the story. With a snap, he closed it. His eyes narrowed. "Stop messing with me. That's not funny. What actually happened?"

Xander blinked. Dang. He should have gone ahead and played dumb in the first place. Brothers.

"You're serious?" he said, far too loudly. He glanced around and moved closer. "Are you for real? Like absolutely no lies?"

Xander nodded.

"Bathroom now. I want to see the wound." Linc pushed him toward the bathrooms right near his wound.

"Ow." He glared back at Linc.

"Wuss."

They passed Avri and Chad coming back with their drinks.

"Bathroom," Linc said, not stopping.

Avri's face scrunched. "Together? Bunch of girls."

He wanted to explain, but Linc nudged him onward. The bathrooms were those individual rooms that anyone could use if they were open. Two guys going into one would certainly draw questions. Linc didn't appear to care. He grabbed the door of an open one and followed Xander in.

Xander removed his jacket and unbuttoned his collared shirt to the middle. "You're going to have to pull it the rest of the way open. I'm still sore."

Linc moved the shirt to expose the bandage. "It's smaller than I expected."

"The chip was barely two millimeters encased in plastic. The vet knew exactly where to find it, too." Xander huffed as he closed the shirt and buttoned back up.

"And suddenly, the gangs will stop trying to assault you in parking lots and destroying homeless shelters to get your attention?"

Xander shrugged. "That's what it sounded like. Benny said that the right people had the information now so coming after me would be useless. Not really how my life has played out the last half decade."

"You could hope." Linc propped his hands on his hips. "How do you feel about this?"

"Livid. Blind with a rage that borders on hate. Played a fool again. I'm tempted to get a full body scan to make sure nothing else is hidden inside me that some secretive lunatic will come for in a few years."

Linc shook his head. "Might be worth the effort if you have a doctor friend that can keep secrets." Then, he unlocked the door and pushed it open.

"I don't have any friends, Linc." Xander followed him out, keeping his eyes trained on Linc's back. There was a line for the bathrooms and everyone saw them exit together. "Merry Christmas. Merry Christmas."

"What did your investor pal say about Dad's plan?" Xander said as they walked back through the throng of people to where Avri and Chad waited for them, staring at their phones.

"He recommended panning for gold in the rivers if it meant avoiding that kind of scam. Get-rich-quick schemes have always been too good to be true. Dad knows it but is getting desperate. It's a pressure play."

"Why can't he be honest with Mom and tell her about their finances? They're married." It was a stupid thing to say. At some point or maybe ever, Mom and Dad's relationship had not been open and honest about money being spent, things the kids did, and what passed for acceptable. The results were painfully obvious to him, even as a kid, that a marriage shouldn't have secrets.

Yet he was headed down the same path as his parents. He'd kept things from Gia, figuring it was best she didn't know the extent of what was going on. That wouldn't magically change if they signed a marriage license. She had every right to be mad at him for withholding the truth about the interview. With her forgiveness and a determination to do better, they'd move past this.

"Stubborn pride, I guess."

"What'd he say when you told him your investor advised against it?"

Linc scrubbed his hand across his neck. "I haven't told him yet. I'm hoping to get through tomorrow without an uproar. And I have a good chance since Dad won't want to make a scene and draw attention to their situation in front of Mom."

"You're banking on his need for secrecy. Clever man."

They stopped next to Avri and Chad and took their drinks.

Avri's suspicious glance darted between them. "Everything okay?"

They nodded.

"To a peaceful Christmas," Xander said, raising his glass.

The others grunted as Chad heartily cheers-ed each of their glasses, oblivious. Xander sat in the tension for a moment, relishing the renewed bond with his siblings. They eyed each other, waiting for someone to crack.

Avri set her hand on Chad's shoulder. "Chad, would you mind running to the car? I forgot to bring in my lipstick." At his confusion, she handed him the keys. "Just bring in the whole makeup bag, if you don't mind. If it's not in the front seat, check on the floors or under the seats. It might have rolled under."

Chad handed her his glass and disappeared out the door.

She leveled her squinted eyes at Xander and Linc. "Spill, you two. We have maybe seven minutes before he realizes I don't have a makeup bag in my car."

The hostess called out "Reinerman, party of four" saving either from having to answer.

As they sat down, Avri waved her phone. "Somebody talk, or I'm texting Mom to tell her what that stain on her carpet she's been trying to hide for years with the coffee table is really from."

Xander really didn't mind if Mom knew they'd had an illegal party at the house back in high school, but he did mind if Linc ratted his business out first. Self-preservation, the sibling code. "Mom and Dad are about to have to declare bankruptcy. They're in deep debt."

Avri gasped. "Because they helped me pay for my tuition?"

Xander and Linc spoke at the same time.

"What? He didn't help me."

"Of course, they helped you."

She looked a little sheepish.

"I doubt it's from helping you pay for your degrees, Av. Dad told me he used their retirement on Mom's therapy," Linc said. "But it couldn't have been that one thing. There has to be more he isn't telling me, not after preaching retirement savings religiously for the last twenty-something years."

Avri raised her hands. "In my defense, Dad told me he had gotten a new tax guy that helped him save on taxes each year, so he had a little extra to put toward my education."

Linc sat forward. "Tax fraud?"

"Wouldn't that be rich? The old man going to prison for something like tax evasion." Xander snorted. He tried to picture his aging dad in the uniform, forced into group showering, eating in the mess hall, working a job that paid pennies to afford another tube of toothpaste, being recruited by prison gangs.

He felt…nothing when he should have felt incredible sadness.

"Prison." Avri blanched. "That would really break Mom. She barely recovered from her endless worry about Xander."

Xander could see Chad walking past the outside windows towards the front door. "Anyone know why Kelsey and Doug aren't coming for Christmas?"

"I think they're having some trouble that they don't want Mom and Dad to know about. Although, this is probably the year they could slide under the radar with Dad being so distracted,"

Linc said. He and Kelsey had always been fairly close since there was only an eleven-month age gap.

Avri sighed. "I can't get her to text me back usually. She's so busy. Maybe she just doesn't want the family drama this year."

Chad returned empty-handed, his expression forlorn. "I'm so sorry, sweetheart. I looked everywhere. Did you drop it somewhere along the way?"

Avri pressed her lips together to keep from smiling as Linc and Xander studied their menus. This guy had to go. Avri needed someone who couldn't be so easily hoodwinked.

Xander exhausted his knowledge of landscaping past his high school days of mowing lawns. So, they listened to Linc tell stories about the crazy stunts he and his hockey teammates pulled and then Avri countered with physical therapy horror stories of people who took years to recover or never did from doing stuff like Linc did. It was a comfortable banter until Chad interjected.

"Xander, Avri said you were in prison for five years. I bet you have some insane stories from that."

He was two breaths shy of dismissing Chad completely. Linc and Avri stared, open-mouthed.

"I do have some interesting stories, because who goes through the most traumatic experience of their life and doesn't have something to say about it, right?" *Be nice, Xander.* "None of my stories are polite dinner conversation, so I'll leave it at that."

Linc appeared ready to physically throw Chad out of the restaurant while Avri barely chewed the food she was scooping into her mouth.

Chad nodded, his expression appropriately chagrined.

They struggled through the dinner conversation, paid the bill, and walked out. Avri said good night to Chad while Xander and Linc waited by her car watching the awkward hug she gave him at his car.

"Fifty bucks says she breaks up with him before the New Year," Linc said.

"I'd give her until right after Christmas, because she's too nice to ruin someone's holiday."

She patted Chad on the shoulder as he got into his car, but didn't stay to watch him drive away.

"Well, I should not have invited him to dinner tonight, guys. I'm really sorry. That was socially horrific, and I just broke up with him," Avri said, digging into her purse. "He asked if it was because he couldn't find my makeup bag."

They laughed in disbelief.

"You broke up with him because of him mentioning my prison time?" Xander asked.

Avri waved him off. "No, I broke up with him because he is a nice guy, but clearly not the right one for me. I knew it needed to happen. Tonight confirmed that to me."

"Single for the holidays." Linc lifted his hand for a high-five which Avri promptly ignored.

Chuckling, Xander pushed off the bumper. "Let me grab your camera equipment, Av." He grabbed the case out of the back and took it back. Avri stared at her phone in horror with Linc looking over her shoulder.

"Chad just changed his status on social media and said he broke up with you first?" Xander smiled.

Avri's brow pinched together as she tucked her phone into her chest. "No, um." She stared at him for a second. "Here. You should see this."

When her phone leveled with his eyes, his smile disappeared. His heart splintered into two. It couldn't be.

Chapter 21

"I told Judita where the key was to unlock the door." Ma paused, gripping Daddy's hand. "I hope Cara didn't overdose."

"I checked her clothes for more drugs. That bag was—" Gia gasped. "She could have hidden them in her underwear." Stupid move. Rookie. She knew how to hide stuff when she really wanted it away from prying eyes. It felt like an invasion of her privacy. Why hadn't she gone there when it could have been the difference between life and death?

Five minutes into the drive home, Ma got another call. Judita yelled into the phone. As she spoke, Ma gasped and covered her mouth with a hand. Tears welled in her eyes.

Daddy searched her face. "What is it?"

"Get to the University Hospital now."

Daddy called out the change in plans to the driver.

Ma continued to listen to Judita, then told her they'd meet her at the hospital. The tears poured down her cheeks. Gia's chest tightened. Ma rarely allowed herself to become so shaken.

"She overdosed? Is she breathing? Unconscious?" *God, please let her be okay.*

Ma gripped Gia's hand and inhaled a shaky breath. "Cara tried to commit suicide with razors to her wrists in the bathroom. She's lost a lot of blood. Judita called from the ambulance. The medics are not sure she's going to make it."

Her words didn't compute. Cara did what?

Then it hit her with enormous force. Willing herself to breathe, she pinched the bridge of her nose.

A warm hand rested on her back.

Her fingers searched for the window controls on the door panel. The cold air hit her face as she gulped for air.

No, she couldn't lose Cara, too.

Not to drugs.

Not to suicide.

Not to anything.

At the Emergency Room entrance, they walked into the waiting area. Their clothes drew half of the rooms' attention, but it didn't matter. Judita sprang to her feet, her clothes covered in blood. Ma threw her arms around Judita's neck, murmuring in Portuguese her apologies for not being there with her tonight.

"She's in critical condition." Judita smoothed her hands over her hair. "They've repaired her arms as best as possible, but they're running out of blood. She's AB positive."

"I'm A positive. I can help," Gia said.

"I'm O negative. I'll donate," Andy said from behind her.

Within minutes, a nurse had them all hooked to bags to take their blood. Daddy's blood type wouldn't work for

Cara, but the donations were their desperate pleas to be doing something to help in a situation that was far beyond their control.

They sat Andy on the other end of the room since he was O negative and they'd be taking his blood directly to processing in case they needed to use it for Cara.

Since Judita was from Brazil, they couldn't accept a donation from her so she stayed in the waiting room to hear from the doctors. When the nurse left them for a minute to grab more supplies, they were left alone in the silence.

The most pressing question burned in Gia's mind was something she wasn't sure she should ask, but these were her parents. Dare she speak out and criticize? Summoning her courage, she turned to Daddy. "Have you known about this since she started? The night I found out, Andy said that the people who needed to know did. He was talking about you, right? I mean, you and Ma keep close tabs on everyone."

Her words sounded harsher than she intended. Their watchful eyes had spared her a lot of grief, but why draw back now with Cara so exposed?

Daddy shifted in his chair. Gia almost apologized for confronting him. She bit her tongue, intent on waiting him out. She wasn't a little girl anymore. They'd shielded her from so much, but she longed for answers, to be allowed in on the dangerous world that was coming after her this year. It was time for her to know.

Daddy's tongue darted out to wet his lips. "Do you remember when Cara was little, she'd have those seizures?"

"Yes, she had to go on medication and then they said she grew out of them."

Daddy nodded. "About three months ago when Carolena started declining quickly, Cara started noticing slight tremors again and periods where she'd black out. Nothing like her seizures returning, but enough that the doctors who had monitored her her whole life took notice. Instead of traditional medication, she opted for medicinal marijuana. It helped tremendously. However, she was still experiencing depression and anxiety with Carolena's illness. Carolena noticed a change and asked us to watch out for her."

"It was the last thing Carolena asked of us before she lost her ability to communicate entirely," Ma said.

"When we dug a little deeper, we found that she'd started using heavier drugs." Daddy rubbed his face with his free hand. His fatigue showed through. "It wasn't a constant use, so it made her feel as if she had power over when she used and didn't. Since Carolena died and Joey left, no one is home to keep her accountable. And drugs have made her dependent. We offered for her to live with us. She declined. She doesn't need a parent and she resented the idea that we would suggest she live somewhere that she would have company. We lost track of her movements and usage when we had to pool the security resources for protecting the rest of the family from these lunatics. This is my fault." Daddy sighed, resting his head against the seat back.

The tears streamed down Gia's cheeks. "I know you were protecting me and trying to keep her confidence, but can you include me in things like this? I'm trying my very best to be here for my family like I wasn't the last few years. I failed in that. I know. It hurts so bad to find out that I'm the last to know anything, even things that directly affect my life. I'm not asking for gossip. I'm asking to be let in on the real day-to-day issues our loved ones are facing. People aren't telling me what is going on. Maybe they don't trust me, because I got Uncle Angelo killed. Or they think I'm too delicate to handle real life. I don't know, but I can't go on living in the dark."

A hiccup stole her breath. "I should have been on the front lines of telling Cara what drugs would do to her, what they did to me. I hid my rehab from her thinking I'd protect her from the ugliness of it. Instead, she missed the danger completely. She thought I had quit without any help."

The sobs came full force. She felt to blame for Cara's drug use. What she thought was shielding her family had made them more vulnerable. It was the exact same thing Daddy and Ma had done to her.

What part had she played in Cara deciding to take her life?

The nurse interrupted their conversation by taking the bags and handing them juice. They stayed in the donation lounge, silently watching a Hallmark Christmas movie with captions on the screens. Ma was on the phone with someone from the family, telling them what happened.

Gia wasn't really taking in what was happening. The endless questions cycled through her mind. The movement was something to stare at while she processed this reality. She couldn't demand that people let her into their lives. She couldn't ask her parents to break the trust of family so she'd feel clued in.

Why didn't Cara trust her with her darkness? She'd been there, but Cara must not have known.

She had failed Cara so miserably. The shame washed over her in waves. Perhaps she should take the first step by letting others know her real feelings about things going on in her life. Somehow, that felt impossible.

Andy called her name softly from his side of the lounge. "You'll want to see this." He motioned her over. His expression was guarded. She stood slowly to her feet and made her way to him.

As she neared his chair, he pointed at the TV on the wall across from him. Entertainment Insights was on.

"I'm sorry," he said.

There in beautiful color were action pictures of her and Andy from the red carpet that evening. She schooled her annoyance. Telling the world about something as trivial as her going to the ballet was what the press did. Everything was a story.

She started to turn away when the headline scrolled onto the screen. "Carter's New Love Interest?"

Then, someone she'd never met spent over ten minutes dissecting the pictures that were making their way across the internet, the body language, the smiles, Andy leaning in to tell her something. Someone had started a hashtag for TeamNewGuy which offended the staunch TeamXander, inciting a verbal duel again between complete strangers who decided they wanted to comment on her life.

The nausea rose from her stomach to her throat, so she dropped into a nearby chair. Her phone had no notifications. What had Xander told her he was doing tonight?

She clicked his speed dial number, willing him to pick up so she could explain. He probably hadn't seen the headlines, right? He didn't watch entertainment nonsense. They'd laugh about how easily a story could be fabricated to fit a narrative and move on.

Straight to voicemail.

That meant he'd seen them, didn't it? Or was he dead in a ditch somewhere with that random person coming after him?

She put her phone down for a few minutes and called him back. This time, she left a message telling him to call her, because Cara was in the hospital, fighting for her life.

In a fog, she followed her parents to the waiting room. Cara had been stabilized. The doctor had reported that the surgery repairing the damage was going well so far despite the hours they had still to go. The medical speak flew over her head, but the doctor was hopeful she'd recover full use of her hands.

Ma would stay the night by her side, and Avó would come early to replace her. While they were making the plans, Uncle Roberto, still in his suit, came in carrying Ma's overnight bag.

Shock and then pained compassion registered on his face as he saw Judita's bloodied clothes. She ran into his open arms. They talked quietly for a bit in the middle of the empty waiting room.

Gia's heart ached. How she wished it were Xander walking in, instead.

"Car's here," Daddy said, pointing to the door.

Gia hugged and kissed Ma goodnight. "When Cara wakes up, tell her I love her and I'm glad she made it."

Ma nodded, disappearing into Daddy's arms. Gia followed Roberto who ushered Judita to the waiting car. Andy got in behind her. The car ride home was silent.

When they finally trudged through the door, the whole family waited for them. Her movements felt as if she were underwater. Everyone got a hug, then Antia led her to her room to change.

Antia unzipped Gia's dress and laid out comfortable clothes. "Want to take a bath?"

Gia sat on her bed, staring at the wall. "This was my fault."

"You can't be responsible for her decisions, like she isn't responsible for yours." The bed sank as Antia sat beside her and rubbed her back.

She nodded, partly because it was the right answer and partly because she had no words left to say. Nothing inside her felt that Antia's words were true at this moment, though someday she knew she would acknowledge the accuracy of it.

"I think I will take that bath, then head to sleep."

Antia started the water while Gia hung her dress in her closet. She'd never be able to wear that again without thinking of tonight's nightmare. As she sank into the hot bath, the tears started afresh.

She longed to have Xander here to put his strong arms around her and reassure her that life gave good with the bad. Though, it certainly didn't feel that way. Would he ever put his arms around her again?

How much damage had those photos of her and Andy done?

Shoving it to the side in order to address the much bigger problem would be justified. Dealing with the fallout when not everything was falling apart at the same time was her preferred method. She'd have to wait for him to call or respond.

When the water got cold, Gia hauled herself from the bath. After dressing in her comfiest pajamas, she stopped in the family room, but mindlessly watching something on TV didn't appeal to her. She walked through to the library.

Amos had Joey's vault-like security cabinet brought to the house while the offices were being redone. The thing was an impenetrable tank taller than she was. Using the code and fingerprint identifiers, Gia popped the door open.

In the main section, the file folders held original prints and copies for every project Uncle Angelo and Joey had worked on. Some of the more recent files were massive, others thin. Uncle Angelo pared his files down to actual design originals and total cost of the project for each one over ten years old. The newer designs had a few more added to it, and then Joey's files were fuller since he didn't have an assistant or want to take the time to only keep the necessities.

At the bottom of the cabinet was decent-sized box labeled Keepsakes. With a smile, Gia slid it from the space. Uncle Angelo had kept a small item of memorabilia from each of his designs, something he found remarkable about the area or materials used or a thank you note or letter of praise from the client. In amongst the rocks and pictures was a booklet.

The cover was worn and tattered. It rankled something in the depths of her memories. The pages were yellowed and covered with Uncle Angelo's writing.

His idea pad.

Quotes, names, important dates, rough sketches, and thoughts in his tiny, meticulous penmanship gave her the most idyllic feeling. Really, it had been a memory log. They'd teased him for carrying a pad of paper with him in the era of digital notes and cloud storage. The aging paper and the small dimensions gave the pad a sort of unearthed treasure feel, as if the answers to life could be found within the scrawled wisdom.

Long ago, she and Joey had asked for a page to color on. Uncle Angelo was horrified. "Never destroy the wholeness. It disrupts the magic."

It always maintained its mystery.

The inside cover listed his name and address. Page after page, his love for others took up every line. A family's need for money. A prayer request for health. An anniversary date of a friend. A silly quote from Joey. A Christmas wish for Cara. A roof design for a library. A wise saying from a book.

Her name made an appearance with her favorite color at the time, lilypad green. Who could forget the time of your childhood when you discovered colors had two or more names which changed the likability of a color completely? The dream house floor plan took on a new depth with a two-name color attached to its walls.

She cringed to think of how she'd pestered her parents to paint the walls of her room electric purple with a cosmic blue accent.

Saints.

On one of the pages, his larger handwriting drew her eye. There was no specific date or quote credit given.

"Hiding from the pain intensifies the suffering when it comes. For pain always will come if you are to experience true and lasting growth."

Gia let her head rest against the wall behind her. She hurt so much in a way she'd never wanted to feel again after Uncle Angelo died in her arms. Life had unraveled in front of her eyes in a similar way. Here once more, she faced a crossroads.

This time she wouldn't run and wouldn't hide her wounds. She would have to learn to deal with the overwhelming grief better, to face the pain with resilience, if she was going to ask not to be shielded from it.

It was an ask she wasn't sure she was prepared for, but she couldn't continue on as she was. Something had to change.

Chapter 22

There on the screen was a picture of Gia, laughing and looking up at Andy with admiration in her eyes. The title on the picture read, "Carter Heiress Steps Out with New Beau for Night at the Ballet."

Surrounding the biggest picture were four other photos of the two, cozy and laughing in each other's company. To add to the smear, the magazine included pictures of people's comments on them. "He's so much better looking" and "Upgrade!"

It was like how she looked at him. Or used to.

His stomach plummeted and his hope went with it.

He cleared his throat as he scrambled for something to say. His siblings didn't bother to hide their worry.

"Well, that doesn't look good" was what he managed to come up with.

"Alex, I'm so sorry." Avri threw her arms around him. He winced. "I shouldn't have shown you that. It took me by surprise to see her with another guy. I have this alert on my phone set so I can see when her name is mentioned to keep tabs on her and you. It's weird. Anyway, you know how those gossip magazines are when they need a story. They make anything up to get people to read their content. It's not even real journalism."

He grunted, unsure of how to respond.

"Who is he?" Linc said, looking ready to bash some heads in. Xander loved him for it.

"Oh, uh, that's her bodyguard, Andy." Xander's voice wavered a bit. "It's probably nothing."

"Bodyguard?" Linc and Avri said at the same time.

Xander checked his watch. He didn't have anywhere to go tonight or tomorrow. "It's a long story, but I have all night if you want to hear it."

"Miss out on my big brother's real-life drama? No way. Come to my place." They followed Avri to her apartment nearby. Her two roommates were out of town for the holidays, so they would have the place to themselves.

In the silence of his car, he absorbed the pain of seeing his girl, the one he loved most, on the arm of another guy. It took his breath away.

It didn't mean she'd fallen for Andy, but he did do the dangerous stuff. He went everywhere with her. He saved her life. He was available and not thousands of miles away fighting secret battles and taking interviews for jobs they'd not discussed.

He was attentive, smart, and a good listener, because he was paid to be. Life had gotten very stressful lately, and, honestly, Xander had not kept up with Gia as he wanted. Now, he was suffering publicly for it.

True, the magazines made stories up, but that smile of Gia's was hard to forge. He wanted to call her up and let his emotions fly. Why was Andy escorting her in the first place? He was security, not a fake boyfriend. It had to be a breach of Andy's contract to be touching the client.

And the cameras. If Andy had done his job, he would have known about the cameras waiting to photograph them. Guess he decided paparazzi needed something to see.

He turned off his phone. He'd deal with this tomorrow. Tonight, he'd only do something he regretted.

At Avri's apartment, they settled into the family room with pillows and blankets Avri brought out in armfuls. It was like she lived in the bedding department of Macy's. Everything smelled flowery, too.

When she finally plopped into the down nest she'd made on her floor, Xander joined her, leaving the couch for Linc. They were missing one sibling, but it was a picture recreated from their childhood except without the overlords being upset about the pillow and blanket forts.

"Start from the beginning with Gia," Avri said, hugging a pillow to her.

So, he did.

From meeting her to the trouble with her ex-boyfriend, Bronc, to trying to keep the love alive long distance, he spilled as much as he remembered. He tried to envision his relationship as they might, though they listened without saying a word.

She could be just another girl.

A girlfriend, not a wife.

Was he sure she was as committed to their relationship as he was?

How much of this was in his head?

They didn't know how much she was his actual lifeline, his anchor in the chaos, his best friend, the embodiment of who he wanted to be.

That sounded like proposal material.

When he got to the part about messing things up with the interview, Linc inserted a cringe and a "bad move, bro." No comment from Avri who was buried under three blankets by the time he finished his long-winded tale.

"So should we break up?"

"Are you kidding? Hard no," Linc said. "She's the best thing that's ever happened to you."

Avri gasped. "Absolutely not. You have to let her explain her feelings first. Yeah, long distance isn't ideal, but when you guys are together, you are like—" Avri flopped over on the pillows. "Magic."

"That was a crazy story, man. Don't do anything until you see her in person." Linc grabbed a blanket and pillow from the floor. "Hey, Av. I'm too tired to drive home. I'm going to sleep on your couch, okay?"

"Yeah, I'm staying, too." Xander covered himself with a blanket.

"Aw. It's a sibling sleepover." Avri grinned. "It's been a decade, at least."

"What are you going to do now that you've ditched frat boy Chad?" The fatigue was starting to steal over him. He still had a hard time believing Benny had pulled a chip from his body earlier today.

Avri sighed, dropping her head to the pillow. "Maybe I'll quit dating for a while. My best friend, Kennedy, told me this wasn't it for me. I tried anyway. He's going to laugh when he hears I dumped another one."

Xander raised his eyebrows. "He? As in Kennedy is a he?"

"Yeah. He said Chad was completely wrong for me. He's predicted the end of every relationship I start. I really want to prove him wrong. Meanwhile, he's not looking for a girl, confident that his true love will just open her eyes and realize he's it for her. Fool." Avri added another blanket to her pile. "Maybe I'm doomed to be single. My taste certainly is questionable."

Why were everyone else's decisions about love more obvious than his own?

Reaching up to turn out the lamp, he grinned. "I think the right one is closer than you know."

"Thanks, Xander. I love you," she mumbled through a yawn.

The next morning, Xander woke up before the other two and sneaked out to grab them breakfast. Never would he have anticipated that dinner and a sibling sleepover would be just what he needed to put life back in his veins.

He turned his phone on and searched for the nearest bakery to grab some sugary carbs after a really late night. He hopped in his car to drive the two miles. The bakery had an airy feel with an enormous amount of seating that Mother Hen didn't have. Call him crazy, but it didn't feel as personal or homemade.

With the box stashed safely on his passenger seat, he pulled into traffic. A gray car moved from where they were parked. Xander accelerated to give him room to get out. Three turns later, the gray car was still behind him at length.

Something struck him as odd.

He was almost to Avri's with breakfast. It was paranoia, right?

To be safe, he switched lanes, made a left turn, and finally parallel parked in front of a shopping strip. The gray car stayed with him, parking when he stopped.

His breaths were coming in short bursts. Keeping his eye on the car, he called Officer Calfi.

"I think I'm being followed by someone. Possibly a gang member," Xander said when he'd explained who he was and what Barley and Calfi had visited him for.

"Drive on over to our headquarters. When you get here, we'll take the description and plates if you have them," Calfi said.

He texted Linc's phone to tell him he was stopping by the police headquarters quickly, but would return with breakfast for them.

Crime didn't stop on Christmas Eve Day.

He zoomed out of his parking space, not bothering to follow the rules of the road too closely. The guy in the gray car behind him was equally as careless. Xander grinned as he turned into the police headquarters parking lot and the gray car drove past slowly as if debating following him in.

He walked in to the headquarters, filed a report, and waited for Calfi at the front desk.

"Come on back, Xander." Calfi led him to an office with a window. Someone in plain clothes sat behind the desk.

"This is Detective Mayfield who is leading the investigation. He is a gang unit specialist. Have a seat, if you will," Calfi said, sitting next to Xander.

Mayfield was thin with thick-framed glasses and a sharp nose. Not the detective show's stereotype of a gang unit specialist.

He nodded to Xander. "Thanks for coming in to answer a few questions for us."

Xander blinked. He hadn't. He'd come to report being followed. "What kind of questions?"

The office was a real office as opposed to an interrogation room, but Calfi sat in the chair closest to the door as if guarding it. Xander couldn't easily walk out of the room if he needed to.

His hair raised a fraction. Panic started at a low simmer in his chest.

"Can I get some water, please?" His voice sounded hoarse. Calfi gave him a strange look as he rose to get the water. Xander took a few steadying breaths.

The path to the doorway was clear. Run now and take his chances with whoever was in that car? Or sit in the police headquarters while they tried to build a case against him and imprison him again?

Maybe they wouldn't. But dare he take that chance? He had no idea what he was involved in. Same problem as before and everyone knows how that ended for him.

"Do you have a room with more windows and more space? I'm claustrophobic and have panic attacks," Xander said. Part of that was true, but most people dismissed his panic attacks as nothing so including a reason for the attacks made it more permissible to some. A reason other than the truth of what happened to him in the prison yard, of course.

Mayfield nodded and walked him to an upstairs lobby area with comfortable seats next to a wall of windows. He pulled three chairs close together.

Better.

If he were a suspect, there wasn't a chance in the world they would have accommodated his request. Calfi followed them from the kitchen area to the seats. As they sank into the chairs, Mayfield extracted a pad of paper from his pocket.

"As Calfi said, I'm the detective in charge of the gang unit division. I see the big picture of gang activities and movement—why they hit certain places, what their long-term goals are, what do their actions mean, and who are they going after. This is to make sure they are staying in their lane, if you will, and not making power plays for the public that we didn't see coming." Mayfield peered over his thick glasses at Xander.

The strategist.

Mayfield was the puppeteer tucked safely away inside the castle, moving pieces of the board game around to understand and predict the future.

"What I didn't understand for a while was what your involvement was." Mayfield tapped his pen against his paper, his head tilted toward the ceiling. "You have no prior gang involvement. And it's well documented that prison gangs do not line up with external gangs and their allegiances. However, you didn't join a gang in prison. You chose to be a free man."

The brown of Mayfield's widened eyes almost sparkled. This was like a game to him. Perhaps he was the one who had been keeping tabs on Xander and sending notes about what was happening.

He opened his mouth to ask but stopped himself. The gamemaster would reveal it all in due time.

"So why are you being singled out and harassed? You're a soccer coach. You don't have ties to any industry that gangs might be interested in," Mayfield said. "Calfi has told me that you were interested in personal protection which means you know just how dangerous a position you are in, being sought out by gangs. Why don't you tell me what you know?"

Xander stared at him. Mayfield wouldn't be asking if he were the one calling the shots. He'd know what Xander knew already. His mind reeled, assessing the angles. How much would he regret revealing what he knew, now or in the future? This guy seemed to hold his cards to his chest. He probably wouldn't expose the big picture to a peon like Xander.

"I was sent anonymous letters explaining that I was being targeted. Something was happening that the gangs didn't like. The person sending the letters said they merely had to do what was advised and all would be well. The latest one that ended up on my car at the mall said they were getting closer than the person had anticipated, so he was pulling the safety cord which would keep me free and clear of the mess happening. No one gave me names. I still don't understand what is going on or the information that is being released that the gangs don't want to be made public."

Calfi didn't say anything as he stared at his hands, but Mayfield nodded as if what Xander said made sense. At least one of them thought so.

"Any ideas of what the safety cord was?" Mayfield said, leaning forward.

"Information on a chip."

Mayfield's eyes narrowed. "A chip?"

"For the computer?"

"How did you come by this chip? Was it given to you in a letter and asked for you to do something with it?"

"It was buried under my skin."

Mayfield hissed. Calfi looked up sharply.

"Let me see," Mayfield said.

Xander glanced around and raised his shirt to expose the bandage under his arm.

Mayfield assessed his side with interest. "Do explain all of this."

Xander repeated a short version of what happened and that someone had said the chip was inserted while he was cut open.

"Who explained this to you recently?" Mayfield scribbled on his notepad, his legs crossed much how the therapist Xander saw one time a few months ago had looked.

"The veterinarian tasked with extracting the chip." At Xander's answer, Mayfield's agitation grew, but still he didn't offer the extra information.

"Give me the whole story, Mr. Reinerman. I don't want to have to keep asking questions to get small pieces to the puzzle. I am a big picture kind of guy."

Xander smiled. He wanted to have the upper hand in this questioning, not be another cog in Mayfield's information wheel. "I received a letter saying that I needed to go see a veterinarian to clear this whole mess up. The vet knew who I was and where the chip was located on my body. He took it out, inserted it into a computer, and told me that the right people had the information now. That is all I know."

"Vet's name?"

"Dr. Ben Kirkles in Kittredge."

Mayfield stared at him. "Give us what the doctor ordered. Could this be what they were referring to?"

"I was hoping you'd be able to tell me, sir," Xander said.

Mayfield narrowed his eyes, startled from his deep focus. "I think that is all the information we can get from today. I'll be in touch, Mr. Reinerman. Please let me know if you get any more of these mysterious letters."

Xander stood, nodded his head, and started towards the stairs. If they kept him any longer, they might find a reason to not let him go at all. As he descended, he looked at the place they'd been sitting.

Calfi was gone, but Mayfield sat there staring at him, an unreadable expression on his face.

How much did Mayfield know that he wasn't sharing? How much of that information would cost Xander his life? An ache grew in the pit of his stomach.

He felt like he was on the edge of a precipice that, once he fell, he'd never come back from.

Chapter 23

Christmas Eve Day Gia awoke early despite the late night. The force of her problems slammed into her, evaporating her chance of going back to sleep.

Cara was in the hospital, fighting for her life.

Xander wasn't answering his phone or calling her back. Their relationship was in serious danger right now.

The churning returned in her stomach. She ran to the bathroom and heaved into the toilet. She didn't want to face today. The cost could be far too great. She didn't want to lose Xander or Cara.

Summoning what little strength she had, she dressed and went downstairs. Her cousins weren't up yet, but her uncles and aunts sat around the table with Daddy and Avó talking quietly.

"What if she came back to Brazil with us? There's a number of great rehabilitation centers in Rio. She'd be around family, have a fresh start, a change of scene without the reminders of what she's lost," Tia Neves said.

"She can get a free education at our college if she lives with us. Might give her a new path to go down if she never regains the use of her hand again," Uncle Roberto said.

If.

Cara had potentially lost the use of her hands? How would she mentally recover from that in addition to everything else she had lost? Gia swallowed hard against the lump swelling in her throat. It would be so hard for Joey if Cara moved to Rio, but if it was the best thing for Cara, no one would argue it.

"She's welcome to work in my shop with me," Tia Judita said.

"That girl is as stubborn as her father. I don't think she's going to move out of the country even if it was the best thing for her," Avó said with a hearty humph.

"We can present the ideas to her once she is off the drugs and has a better idea of what her future physical capabilities will be," Daddy said. "Anyone have any thoughts about when we should tell Joey what is going on?"

Gia couldn't stay. The guilt was overwhelming her. If she had been transparent about her drug recovery years ago, would this have ever happened? Had she been the reason Cara was driven to end her life?

She grabbed a protein bar on her way to her car in case her stomach calmed down enough to be hungry. On her way to the hospital, she dialed Xander's number and this time it rang.

Voicemail.

She left him a message telling him to call her when he got the chance. Short of her flying out and showing up in her own house out there, she wasn't confident she would hear from him.

At the hospital, she stopped at the desk for Cara's room number and made her way up to the third floor. Ma was stepping out of the en suite bathroom when she knocked softly and stole inside.

Ma gave her a tired smile, then glanced at Cara who lay asleep on the bed. Her skin was pale in the window's lighting. Her bound wrists lay elevated on pillows and slings. The machines beeped and whirred as her heart rate and blood pressure monitors measured her vitals.

Gia could hear her own heartbeat in her ears.

"I'm going to grab some breakfast from the cafeteria," Ma said, running her fingertips along Gia's arm. Her expression was soft and pained, as if she wanted to add to her words but didn't know what to say.

With a nod, Gia sat in Ma's chair next to the bed. The quiet breaths didn't soothe her as she thought they would.

"I am so sorry if I had any part in making you feel that this life was not worth living. You are so loved. You are needed." Her voice cracked with her halted speech.

"Gia," Cara breathed.

Gia jerked her head up. "You're awake. I'm so glad. I'm so happy to see you."

Cara took a moment to moisten her lips and clear her throat. The sleep was still thick in her expression. "It's not that I didn't want to live. It's that I didn't want to live *this* life."

Her heavy eyelids closed as her chest rose and fell rhythmically. Back to sleep. She remained that way until Ma came back.

"You need to head home and get ready," Ma said, her tone brooking no argument.

Gia nodded. The tears hadn't come yet, but they would. Cara hadn't seen a way out. Gia had been there almost four years ago. It was why she ran away.

The heavy blanket settled over her.

At home, they ate an early lunch and dressed for the Christmas Eve mass at St. Louis Cathedral at noon. Aside from being a notable icon in the French Quarter, it was the oldest Catholic church still in use in the United States. It was more of a Who's Who event than people wanted to admit since it was church. Ma and Daddy loved the traditional songs and readings from the Catholic church for Christmas Eve whereas normally they preferred their Presbyterian church where Carolena's funeral had been held.

Gia and her cousins piled into one limo and the adults in the other. The mood had lightened considerably since they left the house. She tried so hard to join the conversation about Christmases past and how this year's trip had been one for the books. Her cousins didn't mind that they weren't in Rio for their typical holiday festivities. They'd packed as much as they could into each day and they would have stories to share when they got home.

Her mind kept going back to that dark place of guilt and grief and blame.

If only…

When they got a few blocks from the church, traffic came to a standstill. The traffic cops did their best to unblock the bottleneck but it wasn't working. Andy and Daddy knocked on their limo window.

Silva opened the door.

Daddy popped his head in. "We're going to have to walk the rest of the way if we want to get a seat inside. Stick together. We'll have security in front and behind. Listen for their instructions."

Everyone filed out into a huge huddle on the sidewalk. Andy spoke into his earpiece. When he was satisfied security was in place, he offered his arm to Gia to head up the trip to the church.

It was a gentlemanly gesture—one she didn't care to decline in her current state of mind. She slipped her hand around his bicep and fell into step beside him. "Does this mean they didn't charge the guy they had in custody?"

Andy shook his head, but didn't take his eyes off their surroundings. "They charged him with as much as they could. He didn't admit to much but they found evidence that pins some of it on him like the dead animals and rodents in the office. I'm sure they'll find more as they keep digging."

"Do you guys have a lead on the person doing the big damage like the fires?"

Andy grunted. "We've got our eyes on a few possibilities, but we have to have clear evidence in order for the police to arrest and then have the case stand up in court."

They crossed a street in a tight clump. Happy laughs from people dressed in holiday colors made her smile. The crisp air reminded her of Colorado's autumn which she'd missed out on this year. It was strange to think of her other life, waiting for her halfway across the country.

"I didn't get to thank you properly for your help with Cara at the…house." She smoothed back her hair. She wanted to beg him to forget everything he heard.

"I'm glad I was there. For your safety and hers. I'm so sorry about her attempt last night. It's a really tough spot to be in for everyone." That was an understatement, but she appreciated the sentiment. He squeezed her hand. "None of what happens while I'm working goes anywhere. I've signed a very strict contract that keeps private things private. It protects me and you in different ways. You don't need to worry about stuff getting out. We're here to avoid problems. Not make them."

"I—" The easy dismissal of her feelings was on the tip of her tongue. He'd see right through that. "I trust you. And thank you. We've had a lot of problems keeping our lives private in the past, and the internet hasn't helped."

"The internet always has something to say. Speaking of, there are some paparazzi behind the bushes to right. Everyone, stay close," Andy said over his shoulder.

This heavy weariness wasn't what she wanted to be feeling today. The renewed spark of danger from the unknown relit the suffocating worry that had accompanied her the last couple of weeks.

The sidewalk opened up to a bigger walkway, allowing Gia to reach back and grab Sara's arm so they formed a small chain with their arms looped together. If the cameras were going to see something, it was that, as a family, they were living their lives, not intimidated by the stalkers and haters who were convinced of their evil deeds.

The gray spires with crosses loomed in front of them. Andy turned the group so they walked past the garden to the area where cars weren't allowed. One of the security guys with their group strode up to a cathedral staff member and spoke with her briefly. With a nod, she ushered them to a side door, scanned her badge, and let them inside.

Royal treatment when they had security with them.

They found a hard, wooden pew halfway back that sat them as a group. The daylight filtered in through the windows decorating the painted arched ceiling above, but below the lighting took on a cozier Christmas feel with low lights and candles lit on the sides. She breathed a prayer over the mess of her life.

Here she was again on the verge of the best things in life being taken from her in a heartbeat.

The robed choir started in on a Christmas hymn accompanied by the organ. The familiar readings and the reverent mood soothed her soul. The Baby had been born into a world where nothing was right, yet He brought peace.

That was what she needed. Peace in the midst of the unthinkable.

Last year, she'd been in Colorado hiding, thinking of how her parents would be sitting alone in a pew, listening and praying. This year wasn't in the least how she'd expected it to be.

The last seven months of the year had turned her life into something she didn't recognize. It had brought her Xander and a reconnection with her family she counted as the sweetest gifts amongst the bad. But despite the changes, the Christmas message remained the same, something she could count on. As if it'd heal the gaps the tremors of the rest of the year had created.

When the final amen was said, they moved toward the side door with the heave of the crowd. An excited hum echoed off the high-arched ceilings and stone floors. They were headed to

Brazilian hot chocolate in front of a fireplace as they played games and told stories. A few procrastinators still had presents to wrap in the wrapping room, their storage room off the main basement area. Then they would enjoy a warm dinner and more traditions as a family.

A fantasy life many in this world would never know.

Outside in the alley, she relaxed in the cool city air. Andy again stayed beside her as they moved in a group through the pedestrian zone. The revving of an engine registered faintly in the back of her mind as she and her cousins giggled at something Uncle Roberto said.

As the engine's roar neared them, she glanced over her shoulder. A van was speeding out of an alley toward them. Andy shouted and jumped on top of her, dropping her body to the ground with a jarring pain. A loud whoosh passed her.

Bangs.

Screams.

Fear like she'd never known it crawled over her as she pressed her face into the cobblestone, willing herself to disappear into it before something smashed into her prone body. The weight of Andy's body continued to crush her. Amidst the shouts around them, her shallow breaths were the loudest in her ears.

Screeching replaced the engine noise.

She had to help her family. She squirmed as she took an assessment of her limbs. Nothing hurt. Had she somehow escaped being hit?

With a heave, she pushed the weight off her. A thump followed by a low groan had her sitting up in seconds.

"Andy?"

His answer was a moan. He lay rolled on his back, dazed. Around him, a pool of blood began to take form. Frantically, she searched for the source. She screamed for help as she found a trail of blood from his head.

A couple of people joined her at Andy's side saying something about "pressure" and stemming the blood flow. An officer standing over them called the emergency into his radio.

Sirens wailed through the air. Help was close.

Her family.

Gia stumbled to her feet. Uncle Ronaldo and Daddy stood above Avó, helping her to her feet. Silva and Ze knelt over Uncle Mateus.

His arm was bent at an odd angle. She ran to his side. Silva wrapped his coat around Uncle Mateus's shoulder.

Relief sank into her soul as the paramedics jogged to his side. She spun in a circle counting and naming everyone. Andy and Mateus were the only ones from their group still on the ground that she could see. The crowd started to form in front of the cathedral as the cathedral staff and their security struggled to keep onlookers behind their outstretched arms.

But it wasn't their family that people stared and pointed at.

Further down the pedestrian zone, flashing blue lights drew everyone's attention. A circle of police had a man on his face, his hands cuffed behind his back. Amos was walking toward Daddy from that scene. She made it to Daddy's side at the same time Amos did. Up close, Daddy had a small gash on his forehead and his lip was swelling, but he seemed okay.

She rushed to him, her hands cupping his face. "You're not hurt."

"Did you get hit?" Daddy turned her around, checking her up and down. She shook her head, unable to find her voice. He wrapped his arms around her and kissed her forehead. "Thank you, God."

"Andy has a head wound," she said as they watched him being loaded by the paramedics into the ambulance. Turning, she faced Amos. "That van was inches from me."

Amos gave her a half-smile. "Then, he did his job perfectly. I'll head to the hospital to be with him after we're done here."

Amos shifted his attention to Daddy. "There are a few additional people that were hit that are in critical condition. They're headed to the University Hospital for care. As for the driver, he didn't get away. A traffic officer stood in front of the van and shot out the tires. The driver thought the cop was aiming at him so he stopped accelerating. They have him in custody already." Amos motioned to the police cars.

"He stood in front of a moving vehicle?" Daddy said with surprise.

"She." Amos smirked. "Once the van stopped, she wrestled the driver straight to the ground. She's a little banged up, but she's a national heroine and the press is already all over it." Amos motioned to the vans and cameras lining up to take in the scene. Plenty of phone cameras had already been capturing the aftermath.

"Get that girl a promotion and a raise and maybe a football contract with the Saints," Daddy said with a grunt.

Amos smiled. "I'll look into her record. Maybe she can join our team. Her name will be in the history books, for sure. Once I find out more from the police, I'll let you know our next steps. We're going to need to be here for a while to talk to them. I'll see if they can't release us to the house and interview us there for comfort and privacy. It's hard to believe this is a coincidence and not the guy who has been after Joey and Gia. Here's hoping we got him, Burley."

"We can only hope," Daddy murmured.

As Gia took in the scene from the security of Daddy's arms, the tears fell in rivers down her cheeks. When she thought things couldn't get any worse, life proved her wrong, so very wrong.

Chapter 24

By the time Xander made it back to Avri's place with the breakfast, Linc and Avri were waiting on him to go to Mammie's for lunch and the annual present exchange. Mom's mom, Mammie, was eighty-three but had hosted them every year on Christmas Eve Day as if it were actual Christmas Day, allowing Mom and her sister to have Christmas Day with their kids.

Xander hadn't seen or heard from Mammie for six years which didn't bode too well for her thoughts of him. In his childhood, she'd had a staunch belief that Allens behaved a certain way or the disgrace would affect one's eternal destination. It was why she and Dad got along so well.

The untouched breakfast treats could be his contribution to their gathering, a hostess gift of sorts. Or a buffer to soothe her disapproval of his presence.

They piled into Linc's car to carpool, since Linc didn't trust Avri's driving and Xander didn't want to be tailed again. Avri slid into the back and pushed aside the hockey gear and sports bag.

"Gross, Linc. Wash your sweaty clothes once in a while." Disgust dripped from her voice. "You don't take dates in the car with you when it smells like this, do you?"

Linc froze. "Smells like what?"

She made a gagging noise. "That is why you can't keep a girl. Next time, don't be chivalrous. Just meet her at the restaurant. Your date will last longer."

Linc muttered something about high-maintenance females as he walked around to the other side of the car, grabbed his bag, and shoved it in his trunk. On the way, Xander explained where he'd been and what had happened that morning.

"I got the strangest feeling about Mayfield. Like he was waiting for me to hand him my sources and the keys to the kingdom," Xander said. "I think he knows more than he let on."

Linc snorted. "A cop with a secret? No such thing."

"Listen, guys." Avri leaned forward between the front seats. "When I say I have a paper to write, that means we need to wrap it up at Mammie's and head back, okay? I need to get in the right head space before we spend all day at Mom and Dad's tomorrow."

They parked at Mammie's behind a few other cars. Mom and Dad were already here. As they walked in, Uncle Timothy called his greeting from the overstuffed chair where he sat with his feet up.

"There they are. Trouble's walking in." He laughed at his joke and gave them a wave without getting up. "We were about to start without you."

It was unlikely. Xander walked into the kitchen where Mom, Mammie, and Aunt Tiffany were putting the food on platters.

"Sorry we're late, Mammie. I had car trouble and Linc had to bring me," Xander said as he handed her the box of pastries.

"Alex!" She threw her arms around his waist and pressed her wrinkled face into his chest. "Oh, am I glad to see you. Thank you for being here."

He relaxed in her embrace. He hated that his first thought was to assume his family didn't want to see him, but years of silence didn't usually mean anything good. Mammie brushed at her cheeks as she went back to fixing lunch.

"What can I do to help?" he asked as he hugged Mom and his stiff-armed aunt.

They sent him to the table with two platters of meat—a roasted ham and a crown roast of pork.

"They got you in there doing women's work?" Uncle Timothy called to him as he set the food down.

Disgusted, Xander stared as Uncle Timothy laughed from his recliner. What world did this man live in that saying crap like that was okay—as if he was some royalty to be served? "We all eat, Uncle Timothy. And we'll eat a lot faster if there are more hands helping make it happen."

Linc and Avri were in the kitchen when Xander returned. Mammie was slapping Linc's hands as he popped some fruit in his mouth instead of pouring it into the serving bowl.

"You'll understand some day when your kids start getting serious about someone, Teresa," Tiffany said across the kitchen to Mom as if three of her four kids weren't in the room listening, as if Kelsey weren't already married off.

"Actually, Xander is serious about a beautiful girl from a really fabulous family. She has a heart of gold and she's perfect for him." Mom propped her hands on her hips. "Her race has absolutely no bearing on who she is as a person. I, for one, can't wait to have her around more often."

Aunt Tiffany spluttered a bit and then bustled out of the room. Xander raised his eyebrows. Wow, that felt incredibly good to have Mom stand up for him and Gia.

Mom gave him a big smile and a wink. "I'm sure you're wishing you were with her for the holidays, huh?"

As he opened his mouth to answer, Avri slapped him on the shoulder. "Xander's looking at rings."

Mom gasped, rushing to give him a hug. Over Mom's shoulder, he glared at Avri who smirked like the little rat she was. He didn't have the heart to tell Mom that the whole world saw Gia on the arm of another man, her security detail, yesterday. His heart ached a bit. Amidst the chaos of the morning, Gia'd left him a message to call her back.

He would call this evening after he got through this family function in one piece.

Mom was right, though. Gia did have a heart of gold. A small part of him didn't believe that she was out with Andy, but he'd find out tonight.

As they ate lunch, Uncle Timothy dominated the conversation, spewing so much ignorance and political nonsense in a loud voice that Xander had to mentally block him out.

"You excited about being done with teaching science soon, Mom?" Xander asked quietly so Aunt Tiffany wouldn't hear.

Mom sighed. "I'll miss teaching, but the kids and the administrations are so different these days. I won't miss the attacks from parents, because they want me to pass their failing child. And the administrations that pander to mediocrity, afraid of losing money."

"Imagine living in a world where our doctors and scientists only ever got participation awards instead of an education," Xander said with a laugh. Truly the thought terrified him. Quality educators like Mom were leaving schools in droves because of the lack of people interested in supporting children.

"Education is no longer a partnership between the parent and child. The mindset is that it's an outsourcing. If the child fails, it's the teacher's fault. The teacher failed to accurately meet the child's educational needs and correctly teach in the way the child needed. Never mind that the kid went home and got shoved in front of a screen or didn't do their homework because of their extracurricular schedules." Mom turned her blue eyes toward Xander, her concern evident in her face. "I'm worried about the next generation of kids."

He almost offered for her to join his non-profit in teaching people to make things. Mom was handy and smart. She could make things from trash. She had improvised his whole life.

Games with bean cans, art with nature, stories from nonsensical words, dinners from a hodge-podge of food lingering in the pantry or freezer while still a few days away from pay-day, an adventure out of routine chores were a few of the ways she'd crafted a life from the mundane, ordinary things.

But he held his tongue. Mom always had something up her sleeve. "Do you have a plan of the things you want to do during retirement? Or are you going to take it as it comes?"

She set her hand gently on his arm and leaned in as if she were telling a secret. "You know, I've always told your dad that I don't care if we are rich, but long ago we made a deal that I would continue working so that when it comes time to retire, I could afford to join the Traveling Science Association. They visit groups and schools around the country and abroad and inspire kids to love and try science. So many kids get it in their head that it's difficult, you know? Knowing that is what is waiting for me is what has been fueling me to get through these last few years."

A wave of dread washed over him. "Do you have to pay to be a part?"

"It's a non-profit. They'll pay me to run classes and programs, but I have to pay my way to the other countries and fund some of my lodging. It shouldn't be too big of a deal. We never go anywhere and we've been putting away money for years. You know your dad isn't going to give up coaching any time soon." Mom rolled her eyes.

Xander nearly choked on his food. His eyes darted toward Dad who sat further down the table. It wasn't his business. Dad hadn't asked him for money or advice. But seeing Mom's dreams crushed because Dad had somehow lost their savings made his heart hurt.

He shouldn't get involved.

And that was exactly what he was telling himself after lunch thirty minutes later as he approached Dad, his heart racing.

"Dad, can I talk to you for a second?"

Dad's pleasant expression disappeared as he narrowed his eyes. For a second, it looked as if he was going to say no. "Okay."

Xander moved into the family room where Uncle Timothy had left the TV on, but muted. Dad followed him. He rubbed the sweat from his hands on his pants. He was thirty years old and Dad had no bearing on his life or relationships. He could do this.

With a deep breath, he started in. "I'm concerned for you and Mom. Linc said you were looking to make some high-risk investments to get back some of your retirement. Mom seemed really excited about retirement at lunch. I would hate for her to not get to follow her dreams."

He was fumbling and Dad was a shark who could smell blood.

Dad crossed his arms and stood a little taller. "It's not your business, Alex. Your mom and I are fine. She's going to retire at the end of the school year just as we have always planned."

Stubborn. "Was it gambling? Or tax evasion? Did you do something illegal, Dad?"

"I said, it is none of your business. You think that coming around for six months entitles you to talk about things you know nothing about?"

"I would know about them if you'd let me be a part of your lives. What will it take for you to understand that I'm not guilty? Guess what—the almighty justice system gets it wrong. Once my settlement is over, you'll see. You will have to admit what you refuse to acknowledge. You'd rather hold a grudge."

Dad licked his lips, his agitation growing. "Your conviction hurt our family in a lot of ways."

Of course, Dad would make this about his prison term. Xander took a deep breath to stay the awaiting explosion. This conversation wasn't about him right now and Dad redirecting the attention was a classic diversion tactic.

In a barely controlled hiss, Xander stepped closer. "Whatever you've done, you need to fix, because you do not want to end up in prison." He lifted his shirt, exposing his scar. "There is no guarantee that you will come out alive. I almost didn't. You need to make right, whatever it is that you've done."

Dad's eyes widened at the sight of Xander's long, thin scar. "I, uh—" His shoulders sagged a bit. "We can talk about it after Christmas. Let's just enjoy the day, because we're never guaranteed next year."

Progress. Xander nodded. He gave Dad a small smile. His good feeling dissolved into a heart-stopping panic when he caught sight of the TV over Dad's shoulder.

No. No. It couldn't be true.

There on the news were the professional headshots of Gia and her parents. The subtitle said three dead, six injured. In large letters on the bottom of the screen, the headline read, "Live from the St. Louis Cathedral—Driver Plows into Christmas Mass Crowd."

He couldn't catch his breath.

"Lincoln." Xander spun around. "Lincoln." His shouts echoed through the house. Everyone ran into the room, wide-eyed and alarmed.

"What? What's wrong?" Lincoln looked from him to Dad, worried.

"I need to go to the airport. Now."

Mom gasped. Her hands flew to her face when she saw the pictures. "Unmute it. Someone turn it on. That's Gia. That's Xander's girlfriend."

Xander didn't bother to say goodbye. If Gia had been hit or was dead, he wouldn't be able to live with himself. *Oh, God. Let her be alive and okay. Please.*

"Do you want to stop by your house for a suitcase?" Linc said, pulling the car onto the main road.

"No." Everything inside him felt numb. He checked his phone. Nothing. She was dead, wasn't she? The stalker actually followed through on his threat to kill her, because she didn't stop the project.

It was a horrible nightmare.

"If she's dead, Linc, I swear I—"

"She's going to be okay."

"How can you say that?" He grunted. "You don't know."

Linc cringed. "You want me to come with you? I have to be back for a game on New Year's Day, but I can miss the practices until then."

"No. Yes. I don't know." Xander felt like he was going to suffocate. He opened the window and sucked in the cold air. Couldn't this car go any faster? "Drop me off at Departures, if you would. If you can stay in the area for a bit, I'll call you when I find out about flights."

"Sure. I'll stay nearby." Linc put a hand on his shoulder. "I'm sorry, Xander. I really pray she's okay."

Xander gave him a half-smile. It felt good to have Linc here. He would never take his family's support for granted. "Thank you. Me, too."

Twenty minutes later, he called Linc from the other side of security as he sprinted to his gate to tell him he'd gotten on the 2:45 flight to New Orleans. In that span, he'd gotten texts from Mom and Avri telling him they loved him and they were sending their prayers.

He had nothing with him except his wallet and phone, wearing the clothes he'd put on for yesterday's dinner out. In the security line, he had to explain to several suspicious officers that his fiancée had been in a horrible accident and he was rushing to be with her, because he didn't know if she'd make it. They patted him down thoroughly even if they did believe his story.

The tears welling in his eyes were real. The emotion was something he wasn't used to—feeling this lost. And he had the entire two-and-a-half-hour flight to think since he didn't want to wear down the battery on his phone.

Insanely alone with his thoughts as he had been in prison so many times before.

When he landed, he called the friends-and-family GetThere number for a ride to the house. Or should he go straight to the hospital?

He opted for the house first.

Not until they reached the Carters' street did it hit Xander what a media circus there would be outside the house. They dodged news vans and crew camping out on the sidewalks. Amos's team must have set the perimeter up pretty quickly.

Xander's car was largely ignored until they pulled up to the closed gate. The driver called through the security box and was let in, but not before a few well-placed cameras flashed in his face.

Wouldn't the entertainment news love that headline?

The front door opened as he stepped up to it. A guy with an earpiece and a very accessible firearm greeted him.

"ID, please."

As he handed it back, Xander tried to look around the mountain of a guy. "Is Gia here? I need to see her. I need to know if she's okay."

The guy's expression didn't change, not a hint of an answer. Instead, he motioned to the library. "Wait in here."

Xander paced a foot from the door and back, hands jammed in his pockets. The prayer in his head on repeat as he made every sort of promise to God he could think of.

"Xander!"

He spun around just in time to catch Gia launching herself into his arms.

"You're alive. You're okay. Thank you, God. Thank you." The tears spilled from his eyes as he buried his face in her flowery scented hair. Her arms locked around him in the tightest squeeze. He welcomed the pain in his side.

Drawing back, he took her tear-streaked face in between his hands. "You aren't with him, right? Andy?"

She shook her head, still crying. Her big brown eyes were red and puffy, but he'd never seen anything more beautiful in his life. He pressed his forehead to hers, his lips a breath from hers.

"Be with me. Marry me, Gia. Spend the rest of forever with me doing what I never could do, and I'll spend our forever carrying you when you feel like you can't go on. I don't have as much to offer you as I want, but I will work hard every day to be worthy of your love and your companionship." He smoothed his hands up her back, bringing their bodies as close together as he could get them. "I can't bear the thought of losing you."

She pressed her lips to his. He deepened the kiss as he hitched her legs around his waist and sank onto the nearby couch, making up for lost time. Her touch, her passion, her strength lit a bonfire inside him. She was his woman, and that wasn't something he ever wanted to doubt again.

Gia was first to pull away. Her hot breath raked against his lips. He longed for more to heal the parts of him that still felt broken.

"I don't need you to offer me the world. We'll build and chase that dream together so it's ours," she whispered. Her hand ran over his hair and his stubbled cheek. "I missed this so much. I missed you. I missed us. Let's not ever do long distance again, okay?"

"Agreed."

"Because once we get married, we go everywhere together, got it?"

Xander laughed. "I like the sound of that. So, you'll be my wife?"

"I'll be your everything, Alexander Reinerman."

Chapter 25

Gia stuffed her toiletries into her suitcase and looked around her childhood room. She hadn't expected to come back for as long as she did, but she was glad for the time. She was a different person than the haunted girl who'd come home to fake an engagement to Bronc and grieve her dying aunt.

It was a new year and time to start her future. Her Brazilian family had left yesterday with tearful goodbyes and promises to see her again at her wedding, wherever and whenever she and Xander decided that would be.

But Gia planned to see them before that. The Venha Resort in Rio de Janeiro was set to break ground in March and she wanted to be on the front row of that ceremony with Xander by her side.

With the stalker and the van driver both behind bars awaiting their trials, Gia felt a lot more at ease heading back to Golden where she had started building a life. The stalker would probably get a slap on the wrist and a big fine, but the driver would be tried for manslaughter, attempted manslaughter, and a few other charges lawyers drummed up. If they were lucky, he'd spend several life sentences in prison.

They'd learned from Amos that the guy's name was Tony Barrett Ramos. He was a former corporate elitist who'd lost his job in the economic downturn of 2008. In 2010, he'd applied for a job with one of the Carter companies claiming that he was a perfect fit but hadn't been chosen for the job. In his words, being denied the job led to a series of bankruptcy filings and losing most of what he owned. The Carters were to blame for his losses.

It had been a hard time for everyone, but there were jobs to be had and ways he could have saved himself from financial ruin. He'd had his hopes pinned on getting that one job and couldn't recover from losing it.

Since then, he'd become an activist against everything the Carters did. They were public figures of success and symbols of what Tony had lost. He couldn't mentally cope with believing he was at fault for his failures, so he'd found somewhere else for the hatred and loathing to go.

Fixated, the police psychologist had called it.

At first, it started out small—bitter rants on obscure forums, negative reviews online, false reports to the Better Business Bureau. It escalated when he found a very active conservationist group whom he fed lines to about the Venha Resorts destroying the forests and green spaces around the world with their disgusting greed. While mentally he vilified Ma and Daddy, he found Joey and Gia to be easier targets to eliminate in the process.

In a very small way, Gia had him to thank for pushing her to create a space she'd never envisioned designing in her career. The team of engineers praised it as the most in-keeping with local culture and preservation friendly design that they'd seen.

She already had submitted to be part of a few other non-profit projects there in Rio with hopes that she could start branching out internationally. The school near Avó had told her they wanted her, if she could get the necessary work permits. Xander had agreed that if she needed to be in Rio, that he would be by her side as much as possible.

Her family had been absolutely thrilled when she and Xander had announced their engagement on Christmas Day. She and Xander had stayed up all night on the couch in front of the library's fireplace talking through their hurts and working out the problems they'd allowed to take hold during their stint of long distance.

And there was a lot more than either of them had thought.

In the early hours of the morning, they'd dozed, cuddled together feeling as if the world was theirs for the taking.

Except they still had life to deal with in their reality.

A day after Cara was released from the hospital, she checked in to a rehabilitation center a few minutes away from her house. She'd videoed with Joey to decide what was best of the options presented. As tempting as moving to Brazil was, Cara wanted to do that when she was well, not when her family would have to check on her constantly.

When Joey had heard about her drug use and suicide attempt, he immediately started to look for plane tickets home that day or the next. She'd convinced him to stay abroad by making a deal that she'd stay in rehab if he continued his travel. Cara saw it as his therapy, and how he'd learn to cope with the grief.

They promised to check in more frequently with each other, and Joey already called her every other day.

He'd texted Gia, too, saying he'd bought a cheap phone with unlimited everything so he could keep tabs on home. When he found out what he'd missed, he was so upset that he hadn't sprung for it earlier in his trip. It was an enormous relief that he wasn't radio silent anymore. She immediately emailed him and told him everything about how she'd been in rehab in Colorado years earlier for drug use. He'd accepted her apology and rejected her guilt for not being more transparent with her life.

Cara made her own choices.

Gia was not responsible for them.

She knew it mentally, but her heart was still adjusting to the truth. Perhaps being back in Colorado would help her get her head around it.

At the airport, she waved goodbye to her parents one more time as she left the security area. They'd been surprisingly laidback about the engagement announcement. Ma didn't rush to start planning the wedding. Daddy didn't insist on seeing the ring. They just smiled and welcomed Xander to the family.

There was nothing to prove to her parents. They knew Xander was the one for her. And that was the best feeling in the world for everything to fit together.

As she walked to her gate, she had to stop herself from constantly wondering if everyone was out to harm her. Amos had cleared her for travel by herself as Andy was staying in New Orleans to heal from his head wound. He'd make a full recovery without losing any of his abilities.

He'd saved her life. That wasn't a debt any of them could repay, but they would all try. Ma and Daddy certainly wouldn't let it slide by.

Amos had been looking for a second-in-command for a while and Andy fit the bill. Carter Corporations were holding talks about creating their own private security company for Amos and Andy that took on short-term projects, especially cases that the police didn't see as worth their time and resources.

She was headed to finish her projects in Colorado and start figuring out what the next steps were for her and Xander. For the first time in a very long time, Gia was excited about her future.

Chapter 26

He had done the proposal all wrong. He hadn't asked Burley for permission beforehand. No ring hid in his pocket. He hadn't memorized a perfectly prepared speech to convince her to marry him. No photographer hid to capture the "forever" moments.

It was raw and honest and everything in his heart.

Somehow, she'd still said yes.

To him.

And while it hadn't magically fixed everything in his life, he felt like he was floating. He had virtually nothing to offer her by way of a home, money, security, and she'd still said yes. Dad would absolutely scorn him asking someone to marry him in his current phase of life and brand anyone who said yes as a fool.

But that time of his life was solidly behind him. Dad didn't get a say. He could support Xander or stay out of his life.

His choice.

Life was starting to take a more positive shape for him a few days into the New Year.

Burt Candes had emailed back to offer him the U-19 coaching job, but after his long conversation with Gia, he declined. It wasn't the right thing or the right time, but Xander welcomed the chance to prove himself one day.

Until then, he had growing businesses to run.

His web designer finished rebuilding his site. Already, Xander could see the magic in it. David's catalogue was listed and his inventory being tracked online. By the sounds of his email, the sales of his specialty toys were skyrocketing with the virtual visibility. Edith had become his biggest fan and had spread the word of his specialty to her granddaughter's friends and support network.

Reggie had made a slew of new creations over his Christmas break and was starting to really turn heads with his designs. Xander had secretly sent an article about Reggie to a young entrepreneur's magazine and had just gotten word that they wanted to feature Reggie with pictures, interviews, and the whole set up.

Telling Reggie would have to wait until tomorrow though. Today, he was dressed in his second-best suit and headed for the mediator's office. Maddox hadn't told him much. They weren't sure if they were going to settle today or give the mediator more information.

As he took his seat at the conference table across from the mediator and down the way from the University of Colorado's legal team, his breathing shortened and spots were appearing in his eyes.

Not now.

He put his hands over his face and breathed in, picturing an oceans' rolling waves and Gia there standing with her feet in the sand on their honeymoon. His heartbeat slowed.

Mr. Hudson cleared his throat. "Thank you both for taking the time to join me today. This should be quick. We have come to a point in which my services are no longer necessary. Mr. Callahan, would you like to elaborate?"

Maddox smiled. "Yes. Initially, the university did not seem interested in settling. However, we have now come across very clear evidence that there was a Brady violation in the initial case. We will be officially taking this case to court with both the university and the police officer who withheld evidence in Mr. Reinerman's original case."

Xander stared, slack-jawed at Maddox. They were going to court? Again?

"Maddox," Xander hissed. "Why did you not tell me about this before we came in? Did you not think that maybe I wouldn't want to go to court?"

Maddox tilted his chin up. "You want your name cleared, Xander?"

"Yes." He did, but without the drama.

A twinkle appeared in Maddox's eye. "This is the way. The university was dragging their feet, but now they need to be terrified because we are going to take them and this police officer to the cleaners and win."

"You're sure we can win?"

Maddox nodded. "Positive. I'll explain later."

As they sat down for lunch together at an Italian place tucked away in a very private booth, Maddox dug into the breadsticks and laid out the plan. "Over the holidays, I was out of the office. But when I got back in, I had a confidential package arrive from a private carrier that I needed to sign for myself. I opened the envelope to find a heavy stack of papers which laid out names, dates, timing gaps, and story inconsistencies of your case.

We're not going to settle with the university for maybe three million. We're going to hit this hard and go for fifteen, twenty million. We're suing the university and the police officer. This is going to be very public, exactly what neither the university want for publicity nor the state want for the police force. There needs to be accountability for this type of thing. We're going to hold them to it." Maddox eyed Xander. "I don't believe in luck, but I do believe that you have an angel watching over you that just handed you the keys to your future. Now, Randall will likely have to testify in court under oath which will corroborate your story or have him guilty of perjury. And, with the hard facts we have on the police officer's indiscretions, we will be looking at a big win and an undisputed comeback for you."

More courts. More testifying. More media attention. He wanted his name cleared though. Maybe this would be the ticket. Maddox seemed sure of it.

When he got back to the house, he grabbed the mail and went inside to make sure the place was clean for when Gia came back in two hours. There amongst the bills was another white envelope with his name on it. Inside this one was an old school voice recorder.

Hi Xander,

This recording is a special device that will only allow you to play this once. Please listen carefully to what I'm about to say.

My name is Dr. Colin Morgan. I once was the top neurosurgeon in the US, but was swept into the government's crush when they found out about an exceptionally rare photographic memory trait I possess. I won't bore you with the details, but I did many things for the government whilst still a surgeon and eventually quit to become an informant.

A few years back, I was deeply entrenched in an international real estate scheme run by international crime syndicates and dangerous gangs while living under a cover name. Because of my ability to memorize sensitive details without a paper trail, I became the go-to guy for gangs who were buying up massive amounts of property around big cities to drive real estate prices higher. With rising prices, gangs were able to not only have a higher end clientele but also control the majority of the cities based on the properties they owned and protected. It was a territory war that the government couldn't let pass.

As a good informant, I provided bank account numbers, thousands of addresses, names and fake names of the people I worked with. When it came time to bust the ring, I naturally went down with it in order to protect my cover.

My time in prison was fairly short-lived and when I was released, I took my freedom and disappeared to a private island to live extremely comfortably.

How you ask?

Because I forced my biggest clients to pay for secrecy. My backup was stored on a chip that was placed in your side a few years ago. Governments only know a fraction of what is actually happening and the world would be terrified to know the truth of who runs and owns over seventy-two percent of the populated world.

Recently, hackers managed to partially crack the impenetrable firewalls I had set around my life, specifically where the money was going when they paid for my secrecy. They started not to believe that their information would be released if they didn't pay. And they figured once they found the gatekeeper to the information, they could intimidate him into giving up the files I have on them which is why they tried to shake you down.

A paid informant was the one who stitched you back together in prison and inserted my chip into your skin, but did so for the payday and without knowing who or what it was all about. People can be easily bought and I couldn't risk anyone else knowing. Eventually, I was able to trust Benny with pieces and, being the intelligent man he is, he put the puzzle together when he met you.

I am also the one who hand-delivered the Brady violation information to your lawyer, Maddox Callahan. I won't apologize for my intrusion. The university was going to attempt to screw you over and not give you a dime and try to discredit everything if it went to court. They might have succeeded, too, but that won't happen now, because I told you I would repay you for your trouble and I will.

Why contact you at all?

Detective Mayfield has been trying to crack my cases for over a decade now without knowing that I'm behind it. The gangs' interest in you has had him sniffing around. Now that he knows about a chip, he will spend all his energy trying to find it and attempting to put the pieces together. He will continue to hound you, but he will only ever find out what I want him to know.

See, I have a little problem.

The world believes I'm dead. You believe I'm dead.

They aren't wrong. Jerry Sorentino, my covert operative identity, is dead. But I, Dr. Colin Morgan, am very much alive. I faked my death in prison, so I could get out once and for all.

A real body with my facial likeness was cremated with witnesses.

I've been free to run my empire from the shadows for the last four years. I tell you all of this to establish my credibility in your eyes and come clean about the trouble you've endured on my behalf.

To further my making good on a promise to do right by you, you should know that your father is headed for prison soon when the investigators get hold of the final key evidence they need to nail the whole operation. I don't care a fraction for your father after the way he has treated you, but he's your blood.

You hold the key.

Either we let them go down together, or we try to rescue your father before the ship sinks.

I will do the heavy lifting as you have more than enough on your plate legally and otherwise. But know, you have a formidable ally when it comes to convincing your sheep-like father to do the right thing.

I'll be in touch. Best of luck with Ms. Carter. Her family are some of the good ones."

With that, the recording clicked off leaving Xander in stunned silence. Jerry was alive. Dad was in massive trouble. And Maddox hadn't been selling him a line. They could win this court case.

He really did have an angel watching over him.

The drama in his life was far from over.

His alarm rang on his phone, his reminder that it was time to pick Gia up from the airport. She didn't know it yet, but they were going ring shopping on the way home at one of those fancy jewelry shops in downtown Denver.

The thought had occurred to him one night that, as an architect, she might want to design her own ring.

And he'd do everything in his power to keep his promises and make her dreams come true. He'd never felt a love this powerful, this free, before. Now that he had a taste of it, he wouldn't ever let her go. She was his future, come what may.

Want to read more from Gia's family?

Order Ronaldo Cevere's story, *In the Shadows.*

Get Perfectly Designed: A Prequel Novella free at cdgill.com

Review:

If you enjoyed this book, would you leave a review on your favorite online retailer? It helps others take a chance on my books!

Social Media:

Facebook: www.facebook.com/cdgillauthor

Instagram: www.instagram.com/cd_gill

Goodreads: https://www.goodreads.com/author/15014967.C_D_Gill

Bookbub: https://www.bookbub.com/authors/c-d-gill

Also, signed paperbacks are available directly from my website anytime: cdgill.com

Acknowledgements

As with every book I finish, the list of people who contributed to its development is always longer than I anticipate when first starting to write it. My gratefulness is deep and heartfelt to these kind souls continue to allow me to invade their world with questions and needs or freely offer support when I need it most.

I have a fabulous wealth of friends who are experts in diverse fields. A big thank you to Chuck Hervas, attorney at law, for the legal advising—both in getting fictional characters into trouble and out of it.

To Peter Gill, my father-in-law and very tolerant medical adviser both fictionally and in real life, I am ever so grateful for your willingness to entertain my uneducated questions about what it takes to live and die.

Thank you, Kyle McVey, for always redirecting my sports world knowledge. It's been invaluable in the creation of Xander's world and beyond.

Clara, Isla, and Joan— your eagle eyes, love of story, and grammatical prowess are lifesaving. Thank you for using your talents to benefit my novels.

Sherri, you are a gift in so many ways that I cannot possibly write out here. Your encouragement and support have driven me to keep on.

No thank-you section would be complete without thanking the ones in my life who allow me the space to chase this dream of being an author. My husband and girls are my biggest supporters and a big reason I write. I couldn't be more grateful for who they are and how they show me love every day.

And to my amazingly faithful readers, your encouragement, excitement, and voracious reading push me to continue. Your support is a lighthouse in this dark world we navigate. I will always be grateful for you.

Thank you to God, who led me to writing as a way of healing and being vocal about the world. His guidance and loving hand never fail.

I hope you are loving Gia and Xander as much as I am. Theirs is a story that I will never truly put aside. We will have one more book to finish out their story and, in the meantime, we get to see them with Gia's cousins' stories. Thank you for reading! Please stay in touch!

All the best,
C.D. Gill